W9-DFC-161

*far from the place
we called
home*

Far from the Place

We Called Home

SARAH SCHLEIMER

FELDHEIM PUBLISHERS Jerusalem / New York

Some of the characters portrayed in this historical novel are
composites of genuine individuals who related to the author
their personal experiences during this momentous era.

Library of Congress Cataloging-in-Publication Data
Schleimer, Sarah M.
    Far from the place we called home / by Sarah Schleimer.
    p. cm.
    Summary: Evacuated to England from Nazi Germany during World
War II, several Jewish children struggle to observe Judaism, rebuild their
lives, and search for their parents after the war.
    ISBN 0-87306-667-7
    1. Holocaust, Jewish (1939-1945)—Juvenile Fiction.
[1. Holocaust, Jewish (1933-1945)—Fiction. 2. Jews—Fiction.
3. World War, 1939-1945—Fiction.] I. Title.
PZ7.S34694Far 1994
[Fic.]—dc20   93-48519

First published 1994

FELDHEIM PUBLISHERS
POB 35002 / Jerusalem, Israel

200 Airport Executive Park
Spring Valley, NY 10977

Printed in Israel

This book is dedicated
to my grandfather, Mr. L. Adler (Ope) zt''l,
who believed that nothing was impossible
and who always believed in me.

ACKNOWLEDGMENTS

To my parents, for their never-ending love and constant support, and for having nerves of steel!

To Yanky — I'm the luckiest sister in the world to have a brother like him.

To Ome, and to Opi and Omi, for their advice and information, and for clarifying some extremely important points.

To my family and friends in England, South Africa and Israel, who are all very special to me.

To Rabbi Hammer, Mrs. Hirsch and the Sulzbacher family, a big thank you for telling me their stories and giving me some extremely valuable information.

To Marsi Tabak and all the staff of Feldheim Publishers, for their continued support and hard work in helping to produce this book.

far from the place
we called
home

Vienna, March 1938

KURT WOULD NEVER forget that day. It was to mark the end of his innocent years of play and shatter his childhood dreams. They were gone forever.

Later, he could not remember when the moment of realization had first taken place. Although something had been building up gradually over the past weeks, there had been a sense of shock at the same time. It was as if a bright light had suddenly been switched on in a dark room. He'd had to close his eyes against it and was forced to blink several times until he was fully able to adjust. Or perhaps it was simply that for a while Kurt had hoped that by not acknowledging the situation, he might make it go away. But like an ostrich burying its head in the sand, he could hide, but that would not free him of the problem. It would still be there when he lifted his head again.

The first thing Kurt had noticed was his mother's unusual behavior. A cheerful, outgoing person, she had recently become withdrawn and serious, paying less attention to her family and more to the radio. She seemed to spend every spare moment with her ear next to its speaker, and if Kurt or his little sister dared to talk to her while she was listening, they were brushed away with a brisk "Later!" But later rarely, if ever, came.

Helga, their maid, was also acting strangely. She used to love it when Kurt kept her company, telling her all about school and his friends, keeping up a steady stream of chatter while she worked. She in turn would tell him stories of her own son, Joachim, who was a few years older than Kurt. He too loved reading adventure stories and playing with toy soldiers, and Kurt longed to meet him. Helga had often invited him to their home, but his mother had always forbidden it. Kurt himself regarded Helga almost as one of the family, but he knew there was an invisible barrier between them. He was constantly aware of it, and he respected his mother's wishes.

Now Helga no longer hummed to herself as she worked, or played entertaining games with Kurt. He had never seen her so silent. When he skipped into the kitchen and greeted her with his usual "Hello, Helga!," a nod of the head was the only acknowledgement he got. "And what delicious food are you cooking us?" She answered this, and all his questions, with flat, monosyllabic replies.

At first Kurt wondered if she'd had an argument with his mother, and he asked his mother during one of the rare moments that she was in the kitchen and not immersed in that other world of the radio. "Don't be silly!" she said. "Why should you think that?"

Kurt started to think that maybe they were angry with *him*.

Kurt had always thought that his father was one of the calmest people he knew, but now even *he* seemed preoccupied and nervous — although he tried his best to conceal it. It did not appear that Kurt was the object of his worry, though. One evening, while Kurt was sitting doing his homework at the dining-room table, he could hear the strange, familiar voice ranting and raving on the radio. "It's that man!" Kurt whispered to himself. He rose from his place at the table and walked toward the living room where his parents were sitting. He saw his father suddenly throw his arms up in the air.

"How could any sane person believe this ignorant man?" he cried. "It's beyond me."

"All the same," replied his mother in a peculiar, tight voice,

"I tell you that it is going to happen."

"No, it is unthinkable," his father said. "He will lose the plebiscite."

What were they talking about? "Mutti!" Kurt burst out. "*What* is going to happen?" His parents gave a start. They had forgotten that he had been sitting in the next room. "*What* is going to happen?" Kurt asked again.

"N...nothing, mein Kurt'chen. We...we were just talking about a...an interesting play we heard on the radio," she replied, giving him a quick, too-bright smile. His father studied the floor and sighed.

"Time for children to be in bed, Kurt." He too forced a smile. From the dining room the grandfather clock began to chime.

"Hurry and change into your pajamas," his mother added, "and I will be along in a few minutes to hear you say *Shema*." Kurt reluctantly went off to his room, unconvinced by his mother's weak explanation and troubled by his parents' odd behavior.

As he gazed around his familiar, cheerful bedroom, he felt better. The tidy shelves, all his books arranged neatly, and his teddy bears arranged in a row at the head of his bed comforted him and allayed his fears. His *siddur* lay in the center of his little night table, on an embroidered cloth that his grandmother had made. All was as it should be.

By the time he was in bed, he began to think he'd been imagining things. But when his mother bent her dark head to kiss him good night, a lump rose in his throat. "Mutti, are you angry with me?"

"Certainly not!" she said, smiling tensely. "Whatever gave you that idea?" She kissed his forehead, turned off the light, and left the room.

Kurt could hear his parents' muffled voices from the living room. He was relieved that his mother was not angry, but he knew that something was not right. Determined to find out what it was, he resolved to ask Helga the next day. She too, with her recent silences, must know what it was all about.

The following day, however, was Friday, and Helga never came on Fridays. In any case, by morning "the problem" was practically forgotten. He had probably imagined most of it anyway, he told himself. Things always appeared much worse at night. At breakfast, his mother was cheerful and warm. The smell of her Shabbos yeast cake baking in the oven helped too.

"This morning," she told him, tying on his little sister's woolen hat, "Ilse and I will walk with you to school." This was something she seldom did. Though his school was in the Second District, the same area in which they lived, getting there involved a short walk and a tram ride. Kurt, along with two friends from his neighborhood, always went by themselves. But, even though he thought his mother's offer a little strange, he saw it as her way of trying to make up for paying so little attention to him recently.

He was not sorry that she and Ilse would be coming, though, because for the past few days some older boys whom Kurt and his friends encountered on their way to school had been chanting insulting things to them about being Jewish. In any case, he had not been very disturbed by it, because he had been taught by his parents and teachers to be proud of being Jewish. Nevertheless, it would be nice to have his mother along.

The streets were crowded and busier than usual on that cold and cloudy morning, and all along the route to school they passed groups of people clustered together in deep conversation. Many seemed to be studying newspapers in great earnest. "Mutti," Kurt laughed, "has everyone in Vienna come out into the street this morning?" But his mother didn't share his gaiety. Clutching little Ilse by the hand, she hurried the boys along while she glanced furtively at the gathered crowds.

On Fridays in late winter, the school day was always a short one. When Kurt came out, there was his mother again, with little Ilse in her arms, waiting for him. "I happened to be passing so I thought I might as well pick you up on the way," she explained. Curiously, his best friend Hans' mother had also just "happened to be passing," and she was there waiting too.

Kurt loved Friday night, and he looked forward to it all week.

It was such a peaceful time, when his father was home early and the family could sit down together without having to do anything else at all, and simply be content with each other's company. They would eat the delicious meal his mother had prepared, and sing *zemiros* Kurt loved and knew so well. His father would say some *divrei Torah*, and they would all have a chance to talk to each other about things there was no time for during the week.

On that Friday night, however, a feeling of tension hung heavily over their beautiful Shabbos table, and the glow of the candles could not dispel the gloom and anxiety. The food was abundant, but it lay virtually untouched and barely a word passed between any of them. "What's the matter?" Kurt asked. "It's Shabbos!"

His father looked at him with sad eyes. "Nothing," he murmured unconvincingly. Then he sat up straight in his chair and repeated firmly, and more positively, "Nothing at all is the matter. You are right, Kurt. It is Shabbos and it is a time to rejoice and be happy. Come, let us sing some *zemiros!*"

Kurt's mother managed a weak smile and began to pile food on everyone's plate. Soon the week's strange worries and troubles melted away; at least for the time being. Kurt could not understand what was going on, or what had passed between himself and his father, but he suddenly felt the need to savor everything that evening. He wanted to imprint everything on his memory, before...before what? Before something happened. He studied the faces of his parents and little sister bathed in the golden glow of the flickering candles. The table, with its gleaming glass and china, was reflected in the silver candlesticks. He would always treasure that beautiful evening and its tranquillity, while all around them there was a turmoil brewing.

Kurt could not fall asleep that night. He tossed and turned, adjusting the teddy bears on the pillow over and over. The feeling of uneasiness which had been temporarily masked was there again. When at last he began to drift off, something made him sit bolt upright, wide awake.

Kurt held his breath. He was sure that he had heard the

sounds of people shouting, but perhaps it had been merely part of a vivid dream. The household was silent as he crept out of bed and slowly wandered around the apartment, checking...for what? For an explanation to his fears, that might be lurking in the shadows. In the darkness the living room was a frightening and unrecognizable place. The armchairs appeared to be people crouched down ready to pounce on him, and every floorboard he treaded on gave a resounding and eerie creak.

He was ready to flee back to the safety of his room when the sound of glass shattering rooted him to the spot. Shouts and wild laughter rose up from the street below. Kurt's breath came fast and shallow as he looked about him, trying to decide what to do. More glass broke, and more crazy laughter. The tumult rose to a crescendo and Kurt edged over to the window, peering from behind the heavy velvet drapes, praying that no one would be able to see him.

His eyes widened as he made out hundreds of uniformed men, marching through the streets chanting slogans and leaving a trail of havoc in their wake. Heavy objects were hurled through the windows of Jewish shops, and the contents strewn across the pavement outside, or simply looted. In the dim light of the street lamps he could see no individual faces. Rather, they were an anonymous mass whose anger seemed to penetrate right through him.

From his parents' room he could hear the frightened sobs of his mother, and his father's reassuring voice. They were sure he was sleeping, he knew. Why didn't he go to them? He did not know himself.

He just tiptoed back to his bedroom, where he sat staring into the darkness, listening to the sounds of violence and fear, and wondering what the meaning of all of this was.

2

KURT OPENED HIS EYES to discover that he was still sitting up in bed. He did not even recall falling asleep, but daylight now streamed into his room. The riot had apparently ended and morning had come. Maybe, he hoped, the night before had been just a figment of his imagination. But one glance out the window confirmed that he hadn't been dreaming, for the morning light revealed the results of the night's activities. Broken glass and rocks covered the pavement below, and all that remained of several of the shops he had known so well were empty burned-out shells.

Kurt said *Modeh Ani,* and hoped that at least no one had been harmed. As he crossed his room again, he could hear from his parents' room a heated conversation in progress. "Why can't you *daven* at home this morning?" his mother was asking. "Please, I don't want you to go out."

"I can't stay home, Eva. It is Shabbos morning and I am going to *daven* with a *minyan,*" his father replied firmly. "What if there are only nine men and I don't come?"

"But it's dangerous."

"Are our homes any safer?"

His parents' door opened and Kurt hurried back to his bed, throwing his blanket over his head and pretending to be asleep. His father opened his door a crack. "He's still sleeping," he whispered, and then closed it. Kurt got out of bed again and recognized the sound of the front closet door being opened.

"Be careful," he heard his mother say in a resigned voice. "*Gut Shabbos.*" No argument was going to sway his father. Nothing was going to stop him from going to shul on a Shabbos morning.

Kurt opened his own door and found his mother in the hall, leaning against the wall with her head in her hands.

"*Gut Shabbos,* Mutti," he said quietly. She quickly recovered herself and gave him a bright smile.

"*Gut Shabbos,* Kurt. Did you sleep well?" she asked. "Ilse is still sleeping."

"Yes, thank you," Kurt said off-handedly. He sauntered off into the kitchen in an attempt to end the conversation, for he knew that if he did not, he would ruin the game he was playing with his mother. He understood now that she was trying to protect him from knowing that something terrible for the Jews — for *them* — was going on around them, and he, in turn, was trying to protect her from the knowledge that he knew.

Out of the corner of his eye, he noticed the newspaper from the day before. He looked at the headlines on the front page. There was that strange word again which his father had used: plebiscite. Whatever that word meant, the newspaper said that it had been called off. Kurt decided that this word was the key to understanding the whole situation and answering all his questions.

He went into the living room and took down the heavy dictionary from the bookshelf, flicking through it until he found the word: PLEBISCITE — "a vote by every person in a country on an important public matter." So there was to have been a vote in the country on an important matter. "But what?" Kurt asked himself. Why was it canceled? Why did it make his parents worry? If they had been worried about this vote, shouldn't they be feeling relieved that it was called off? And why did this cause violence on the streets? Kurt sat down to evaluate the situation and piece together all the information he had gleaned. His parents were worried, Helga had been acting strangely, there was to have been a vote about something important which was now canceled, and there had been trouble on the streets the night before. Nothing appeared to add up.

Then he remembered something. That strange, angry man who had been shouting on the radio the other night, who had been on the radio a lot lately. He had had an extremely unsettling effect on his parents and it was after hearing him that they had the discussion about this plebiscite. His father had said that no one would vote for him, and he would lose. He was obviously quite a powerful man.

That man! He was the one, and whatever or whoever he was, he appeared to be having an effect on everyone's lives, including his own family's.

Kurt paced around the apartment. He would have felt proud of himself for analyzing the situation so well, had it not revealed to him some terrifying facts that he almost wished he had remained ignorant of. He knew that his parents had only his best interests at heart, but now that he understood he decided to ask his mother for a full explanation later.

As she was setting the table for their Shabbos lunch, Kurt walked into the dining room. His mother bent down and gave little Ilse two spoons to play with. "Mutti," Kurt said. She looked up and studied his small, serious face, sensing that he knew something was the matter.

"Mutti," he began again, taking a deep breath. "I saw the riot in the streets last night. I watched all the angry men destroying the Jewish shops, and shouting insults about us. I know about the plebiscite and that it was called off, and that the man on the radio is bad, and that something bad is happening."

His mother put her handful of silverware down heavily on the table. "Kurt'chen, when Papa comes back we will sit down and talk," she said gravely.

All the curtains in the apartment remained closed that Sunday morning and an uneasy silence prevailed. When the family did talk, it was brief and whispered, though no words were needed to convey the way they all felt. Kurt understood most of what his parents had gently tried to explain to him the day before. They had lost a battle without even being able to fight it first. They were an invaded country now, part of Germany, and it had all happened without any struggle. No one had tried to stop it, his father had said. The world remained silent. Once the new "President" arrived it would be official and they would be at his mercy. What this meant, Kurt could not imagine, but his dread and anxiety were great. Why did they hate the Jews?

Only Ilse seemed oblivious to all this as she sat on the floor, happily arranging her dolls on the carpet. Her mother reached down and stroked her daughter's curly head, watching her with tears in her eyes.

"Papa," Kurt said softly, "what will happen now?"

His father smiled though his face remained taut. "Whatever Hashem does is for a reason, and we must always remember to have *bitachon* in him. Our People have withstood many hardships and He will help us to withstand this as well." He went back to studying the *sefarim* spread out on the table. They were his only solace.

Kurt went into his room and sat alone. Outside he could hear the rhythmic sound of marching feet. With extreme caution he peeked through the drapes and watched the German soldiers goose-stepping down the street. It was a bright, sunny day outside. Under normal circumstances he might have walked over to his friend Hans' home, or his parents might have taken him for a special treat to the Prata and let him ride on the big ferris wheel which was reputed to be the highest and biggest in the world. Or they might have gone to visit his grandmother, and then gone to a cafe where his grandmother would have let him choose a delicious cake from the display. They might have caught a tram into the First District and taken a stroll around the Ringasse in the center of town, where the fancy shops and the opera house were. A tear rolled down his plump cheek. He was imprisoned in his home, with the forlorn feeling that he might never be able to do any of those things ever again.

Kurt had always admired soldiers; his extensive collection attested to this. But the soldiers who were marching down his street did not look like any he had ever seen before, neither in pictures nor parades. Their fixed, mechanical actions and strange step made them appear machine-like and inhuman. He stared from them to his collection of cheerful, colorfully painted soldiers on his shelf and then back to them. His lead soldiers seemed to have more life in them than the German ones.

Suddenly, Kurt moved a chair over to his bookcase, stood on it, and in a decisive gesture took a box down from the top shelf and quickly scooped up his entire collection of soldiers into it. What use were they to him? Anyway, toy soldiers were for children.

Kurt's father went to work as usual the next day, but decided to keep his son away from school for a few days and "watch the situation," in the hope that things might begin to calm down. Some people said that it would all be over by Purim, which was only a few days away.

On the third day of their isolation, Kurt's mother was surprised when Helga appeared at their door as usual. The two nodded stiffly to each other and then his mother stood aside to admit her into the hallway. Helga unbuttoned her coat, hung it up as usual, slipped her apron over her head, and strode into the kitchen. She was so familiar with the apartment and its routines by now that she almost always knew what needed to be done without having to be told. She covered the kitchen table with newspapers and went into the dining room to get all the silverware from the sideboard, which she then spread across the table.

Kurt followed her into the kitchen and watched her polishing furiously, working with a zeal he had never seen before. Her formerly cheerful face was set in a determined scowl. She completely ignored him, as she had ignored Ilse's greeting earlier, and he wondered if she even realized that he was there. As tears threatened, he retreated back to his room to read a book.

Some time later, he was jolted out of his reading by the sound of a key turning in the lock of the front door. He hurried to see who it was, afraid that it might be some of the thugs trying to break in. He was even more astonished when he heard his father's voice. His father never, ever, came home in the middle of the day.

"Papa! What are you doing home now?" Kurt asked. For some reason, his mother did not seem surprised.

"Kurt, I must speak with Mutti for a while," his father replied quietly. "Will you keep an eye on Ilse and play with her in the meantime?"

Kurt nodded, and went to look for his little sister, whom he found building a tower with her wooden blocks in the living room. "Come, Ilse, let's play in my room. I'll bring all your blocks in there."

Ilse was happy to come, and she was soon singing a little song to herself as she sat on the floor in his room rebuilding her tower. A low hum came from the living room as his parents talked and talked, and the sound of forks and spoons clanking came from the kitchen as Helga vigorously scrubbed. Then the sounds abruptly stopped. Kurt was not sure why he should have been so aware of it, but he found that he was becoming more attentive and observant to everything lately.

He could hear low, quiet footsteps leading from the kitchen to the closed living room door. Kurt silently opened his door a crack and peeked out. What was Helga doing?! Open-mouthed, he stared and watched Helga standing with her ear against the living room door, listening to every word of his parents' conversation. She had always seemed so trustworthy, so kind, a part of the family. Had he not seen it with his own eyes, he might never have believed it.

On hearing the conversation break up, Helga scuttled back to the kitchen to resume her polishing, and a moment later his parents reappeared from their conference. Kurt waited to catch their attention and then silently but urgently gestured to his father, beckoning him into his room, and told him what he had seen. His father raised his eyebrows and looked grave, but not altogether shocked. He nodded, and went into the hall.

"Helga!" he called, summoning her from the kitchen. Politely but firmly he explained to her that they could no longer afford to keep her. He thanked her for her dedicated years of service and wrote her a check. Wordlessly, she removed her apron, put on her coat, picked up her bag and left, not even stopping to say goodbye to Kurt or Ilse whom she had known since they were born.

His father's excuse for dismissing her had not been altogether untrue. He had just lost his job.

3

PURIM CAME and unfortunately proved the optimists wrong. In fact, Purim had been a particularly difficult day, for in the evening just before everyone was about to set out for synagogue to hear the Megillah, the Nazi thugs had gone around raiding and ransacking Jewish homes at random. Fortunately, the Eisigs' home had not been one of them, but many of their friends had suffered the experience. It was the worst Purim Kurt's family had ever known. They and everyone they knew went through all the motions of listening to the Megillah, giving *tzedakah,* and sending *mishlo'ach manos,* but their hearts were heavy and there was very little celebration.

The winter passed, and spring gave way to summer. While the flowers bloomed and the city was bathed in sunshine and beauty, everywhere around Vienna there appeared signs that Jews were "not permitted": they were not allowed to ride on a tram, or even sit on a park bench. It was particularly hard on the children, because in the hot weather, with the parks forbidden to them, they had nowhere to play.

They all knew that sooner or later the violence would catch up with them, and fear was with them constantly. Kurt's mother only occasionally let him out on his own, even though it was usually the adults who were harassed more than the children. Kurt also had what might have been called an advantage: with his blond hair, blue eyes, and fair skin, he could easily pass for an "Aryan" — a gentile. But Kurt was not proud of this and sometimes wished he had dark skin and hair, like his mother's family. He had no desire to look like what was regarded as the "master race" but who were really, his father had explained, more backward than mankind had been in the Dark Ages. It did mean, however, that he could go out and do the shopping for his mother when there were rumors of incidents in the streets, and she with her dark "Jewish coloring" was afraid to leave the apartment.

But it was neither Kurt nor his parents who were to be first in the family to bear the brunt of senseless Nazi violence. It was his grandmother. They might never even have known had they not accidentally stumbled across the incident themselves, for she was too proud a woman to complain to others. She always said that her family and friends had enough things to worry about without having to add another — herself — to their list of problems; and *Omama* hated to be a burden on anyone.

Summer gave way to fall. One October day Kurt and his mother were walking briskly through the streets, hurrying to do a few errands while trying to remain as inconspicuous as possible. His mother had developed almost a sixth sense for detecting if there was any trouble brewing, and with a swift glance she could discern what was happening in all directions. When she suddenly tightened her grasp of Kurt's hand, they quickened their pace.

"What's wrong?" Kurt asked her, his heart starting to pound.

"I think someone's following us," she whispered. His parents were beyond pretenses with Kurt now. He shared their fears. Kurt turned around.

"No! Don't look back!" she whispered sharply.

"But, Mutti, I don't see anyone there."

"He's probably backed against a doorway, but he's still on our trail."

They turned a corner and made their way down a narrower street, turning right, and then left, through a maze of back streets and alleyways. Kurt was sure that they were completely lost, but somehow his mother knew exactly where to go. Kurt marveled at her sense of direction.

Then she stopped and breathed deeply. "I think we've finally given him the slip," she said, her face breaking into a smile of relief as she kissed his hand, still grasping it tightly.

Moments later Kurt found himself in familiar territory. They were near a town square which he knew well. A large crowd had gathered in the square and there seemed to be some kind of spectacle taking place.

They generally avoided such gatherings, for these days large crowds usually spelled trouble. For some inexplicable reason, however, this time Mrs. Eisig felt the need to go and see what was happening. They made their way steadily toward the square. As the audience jeered and laughed as if they were watching a clown or a street entertainer performing, Kurt's feeling of dread grew. Whatever it was, it certainly was not purely an entertaining act.

"Mutti, can you see anything?" Kurt asked, as he alternately stood on his tiptoes craning his neck, and bent down trying to see between the thickly packed crowd of people.

Before he knew what was happening, his mother was dragging him through the mass of people, sudden anger spurring her on. All the sounds were jumbled and emerged as one cruel laugh.

There, in the center of the square, a group of elderly Jewish men and women were being forced to scrub the street with toothbrushes. Kurt's eyes widened and his mouth fell open. The cruel jeers and taunts of the crowd seemed to pierce Kurt's being. "Work faster, Jews!" Kurt stood as still as a statue and stared and stared at all the old people bent over on the ground, their downcast elderly faces filled with shame. His own cheeks burned with shame, his heart felt ready to burst with sorrow and tears streamed down his cheeks.

"*Untermenschen!*" his mother exploded. "How dare they treat *Omama* in that manner!"

"What?" Kurt asked, confused and overwhelmed with the

shock of what he was witnessing.

"Scrub a little harder! That's not good enough, Granny!" one of the uniformed men cried. He turned around to share this joke with the crowd and received the roar of approval he was looking for.

Suddenly everything came into focus. The person in uniform was not a man at all — he was one of the bullies who used to taunt Kurt on his way home from school. And it was his very own beloved grandmother, his *Omama*, whom this bully was humiliating. It was too much to bear. Kurt had to take a few deep breaths to steady himself. A heat had begun to rise in him and he clenched his fists. He was aware of nothing around him but the bully, his grandmother and himself. Even the noise had faded into the background. All he knew was that he could not let his grandmother suffer any longer. Kurt walked up to the teenager and before he realized what he was doing, he had kicked him, hard, in the shin.

Time seemed to stand still. Kurt stood rooted to the spot, the bully was open-mouthed in amazement, too astounded to even shout from the pain of the blow, and the crowd fell silent. But then his grandmother let out a hoarse cry as she recognized her grandson, and the spell was broken. The bully lunged forward to try and grab Kurt but he was too quick for him and raced into the crowd.

"Get him!" the boy shrieked. A loud, angry rumble rose from the crowd, and Kurt's only thoughts were that he had to get away. In each direction Kurt turned, a human barrier closed in on him rapidly. His heart beat wildly as he frantically searched for a path of escape. Was his mother calling his name? He suddenly saw a small gap between two men and forced his way through it. A hand tried to seize him. He changed direction and propelled his way through another group of people.

At last he was out of the great crush but there was still a vast stream of people on his trail. He took a side street and ran down it, not daring to look back. Hundreds of footsteps shook the ground as he made a right turn into another narrow passageway.

He raced blindly through the streets. He could not feel his feet, but they kept on running as if they had a life of their own. By now darkness was approaching and in the narrow, poorly lit alleys, it was difficult to make out where he was going.

Kurt paused to catch his breath in a doorway. His heart pounded so hard he thought it would burst. He could no longer hear footsteps and hoped that they had lost his trail. With great effort, he pulled himself away from the wall he was leaning on and started off down the road again, dragging one foot after the other while his arms hung limply by his side. He could not walk straight and his head was spinning. The only idea in his mind was to reach home safely and go to sleep.

A cry split the darkness and Kurt let out an involuntary shout of fear. He tensed up, not daring to move a muscle, but then a scrawny cat padded past him and he almost laughed with relief.

Wandering the alleys, he began to wonder how far he had come and exactly where he was. He was afraid to ask the few people he saw for directions in case they had been at the square earlier that afternoon and would recognize him.

At last the roads began to grow a little wider. Surely he would soon find himself in more recognizable surroundings and make his way back home. Were his parents fraught with worry for him by now? Then the question dawned on him: What had happened after he'd fled? Had his mother and grandmother made it home safely, or had they — *chas v'shalom* — been arrested? Kurt went cold. He must get home to find out whether everything was all right, and let them see that he too was unharmed.

Suddenly he heard the sound of footsteps behind him, and he turned around slowly as his heart froze. The person stopped too. The dim streetlight behind him outlined his figure but it was too dark for Kurt to see his face. Two more people drew up on either side of him. The boy in the center pointed towards Kurt. "That's the one!" he shouted.

"Get him!" another yelled.

Kurt set off at lightning speed, his running footsteps echoing in the dark, empty streets. He could hear them gaining on him, but he had no more strength to run. He wound in and out of the alleys but they were always only a few steps behind.

There was no escape. The street came to a dead end and in front of him was a high wall. The boys were gaining on him with each passing second. He tried to climb the wall but with nothing to get a grip on, it was virtually impossible. "Please, Hashem!" he cried, the *tefillah* coming from the depths of his heart. "Save me!"

Frantically, he searched for something to hide behind, anything which might give him some little chance. He made out a large garbage can in the blackness, in the corner by the wall, and crouched behind it, concealing himself as best he could.

"Where did the Jew go?" The boys were out of breath.

"He couldn't have climbed over the wall — it's far too high." They began to move toward the corner where the garbage can was. It was now or never, Kurt decided, if he wanted to make his escape. He rose to his feet and got ready to make a fast sprint when he saw yet another figure in the same Nazi uniform that the teenagers were wearing. This one was silently climbing down the wall. As he reached the ground and headed straight toward him, Kurt shrunk back and held his breath. The others had not seen the fourth youth but he had evidently noticed Kurt, for he was only a few feet away and was staring straight at him.

Kurt held his breath. The boy suddenly put his fingers to his lips and was then beside him. He did not say a word, but reached down and gently took hold of Kurt's trembling hand. Kurt stared, speechless and wide-eyed with amazement, as the youth led him back up the road.

"Look over there!" one of the bullies shouted. Kurt found himself suddenly pushed against the wall behind the silent teenager, who had made an about turn, facing the others as if he were walking toward them, and successfully concealing Kurt.

"Get him!" cried the others, only to stop when they realized they were facing a fellow teenager in uniform. They looked confused and peered into his face.

"Is there something the matter?" the boy asked.

"We're looking for a boy, a Jew who attacked my friend here, in public, earlier this afternoon," one explained. "We thought we saw him around here. Have you seen him?"

"No, I can't say I have, but you must surely be mistaken. A Jew would have to be crazy to come around these parts alone after nightfall."

"Well, most of them are," said one, and his companions laughed. "Thanks anyway. *Heil Hitler.*" He made the Nazi salute.

"*Heil Hitler,*" Kurt's rescuer replied enthusiastically.

"He must have somehow climbed over the wall," the boys said as they turned back, assessing the situation. "Let's try to find him."

The boy made sure the group had their backs turned and were on their way before he beckoned for Kurt to come out from behind him and follow him. He led him through the labyrinth of unfamiliar streets without any hesitation, navigating them like a weathered sailor through rough seas. All this time Kurt's savior said not a word, and all Kurt could deduce about him was that he was several years older than himself, and though he was a Viennese non-Jew, he was not much of a Nazi.

They were soon walking among the familiar streets and buildings of Kurt's neighborhood in the Second District. "Do you know your way from here?"

Kurt nodded. "Thank you for helping me," he said, his voice trembling.

The boy held out his hand to Kurt and shook it with great warmth, his concern and sincerity reflected in his deep-blue eyes. Then he was gone.

Kurt rushed up the stairs of his apartment building, not waiting for the ancient elevator, and instead of bursting into the house, cautiously knocked on the door. He was unsure of what to expect. The door was opened slowly by his father, and as soon as he saw Kurt he pulled him in, and enfolded him in his arms, sobbing. "*Baruch Hashem, baruch Hashem.*" Kurt had never seen his father cry before. His mother rushed to him, crying too. "Kurt'chen, are you all right? Are you hurt?"

"No, *I'm* fine!" Kurt replied. "But what about you and *Omama*? What happened when I left?"

"In the commotion, they forgot all about the old people in the square, and I was able to take her away without anyone paying attention," his mother replied. Then she burst into tears again. "But later, I heard that they had rounded up many Jews and...shot them in the square. I was so worried about you...we thought we might...God forbid...never see you again..." Kurt swayed suddenly and let out a cry. His father caught him before he fell. "*Baruch Hashem,* you have returned safely." he said. "But now we must leave quickly."

"Leave? What do you mean?"

"There is every chance that they will come looking for us. We have got to get away from this apartment tonight."

"Tonight? Where will we go?"

"We will stay with the Kleinhoffs until tomorrow. *Omama* is already there. I was a fool to keep our family in Vienna for this long, and now that the borders are closed, our only way out is to try and get a visa for some other country — perhaps America."

"America? Papa, are you saying we are going to leave the country? Forever?"

"Yes, Kurt." His father's brown eyes filled with tears again. "As soon as possible."

It was one o'clock in the morning when they left. Kurt's mother carried the sleeping Ilse in her arms, and turned off the little light in the hallway. His father locked the door and checked that no one was watching. Then he gave a last look to what had been their home, sighed, and walked furtively down the stairs with Kurt and his mother following.

All they had taken with them were three small suitcases.

4

Berlin, November 1938

ERICH STOOD at his music stand in the large dining room, skillfully gliding his bow across the strings of his small violin. His audience consisted solely of his parents, who sat before him enraptured by the particularly difficult piece he was playing. As soon as he came to the end of it he placed his bow on the low coffee table and his parents broke into enthusiastic applause. Mr. Bildmann rose from his seat and put his arm around Erich. "You are coming along superbly," he said proudly to his son. "That was really beautiful."

"Thank you, Papa."

"Let us hope that when we get to Curaçao you will be able to take proper lessons."

"*Ach*, that really would be wonderful," Mrs. Bildmann murmured, casting her eyes around the room. "Only one more day." She sighed. "All these long months of waiting. It is hard to believe that the time has arrived at last."

"Do they have parks in Curaçao?" Erich asked.

"Of course they do," his father replied.

"Will I be allowed to play there?"

His father laughed. "Certainly."

For months Erich had questioned his father about that mysterious island with the funny name, the country in which they were to make their new home. He could not imagine a country which would be friendly toward Jews and let them live in peace, a country where they could live like other people and go anywhere they pleased. Erich's parents told him that once Germany had been like that, but Erich could not remember a time when there were no restrictions or violent acts committed against them.

His parents, however, never dwelt on how bad the situation was. They had always stressed what was good in their lives and how fortunate they were. *Baruch Hashem*, they were healthy and had enough money to weather the financial slumps and inflation and still live quite comfortably, while many other Jewish families they knew were facing severe hardships. So what if they were forbidden to go to certain places? They could make their own entertainment. Erich learned Torah and Jewish history with his father, and his mother taught him how to play the violin. His parents kept him informed of current events, encouraging him to read the newspaper. They regularly had family discussions on the topic and Erich was always invited to express his opinions.

When misfortunes did occur, his father simply said, "*Gam zo l'tovah* — this too is for the good." And when things looked particularly bleak, he would give his family comfort by saying, "Nothing stays bad forever. If we have *bitachon*, Hashem will help us through."

Erich was basically a happy boy, surrounded by a devoted family and many friends to play with, and as he had never experienced life anywhere else, he did not know any different circumstances or realize how deprived they were. But if life in Curaçao was going to be better, as his father assured him it would be, Erich was more than happy to sample the new taste of freedom.

"Would anyone like a hot drink?" his mother asked.

"No thank you, Klara," replied his father. "I had better go to shul for *Minchah* and *Ma'ariv* before it gets too late. Perhaps I'll stop and buy a nice chocolate cake from the bakery on my way back and we can have a kind of farewell party. What do you say to that?''

"I'd love it!'' Erich cried.

Mr. Bildman ruffled Erich's hair. "I thought you might. I'll see you later.''

"Well, let's go on with our packing, Erich,'' Mrs. Bildmann said. "We still have a lot to do.''

"You know, Mutti, packing makes our trip seem even more real. But it still seems like a dream to me although we've known about it for ages.''

"Yes,'' Mrs. Bildmann replied, smiling sadly. "I know what you mean.''

They began to sort out Erich's clothes. "You must grow a centimeter a day, at least!'' his mother laughed. "Well, you won't need many winter clothes, as it's warm practically all year 'round in Curaçao. Here,'' she said, handing him an old shirt. "Try this on.'' His mother could not suppress a laugh as she watched him struggle into the long sleeves which rode up his arm.

There was a knock at the front door and Mrs. Bildmann went to answer it, still chuckling as she went.

"Hello, Greta,'' she greeted her neighbor. Greta was not Jewish but had always been a devoted close friend of the Bildmann family. Even when the anti-Semitism was rife, she remained constant, though now it was becoming increasingly difficult for her to talk openly to the Bildmanns and the other Jewish neighbors.

Greta looked quickly about to ensure that no one had seen her. "May I come in?'' she whispered.

"Of course,'' Erich's mother replied, puzzled.

"I just came to warn you that there is going to be some kind of trouble tonight.''

"What do you mean, Greta?'' Mrs. Bildmann asked anxiously. "What kind of trouble?''

"I'm not sure. There was something about it on the radio a little while ago. You probably heard about the young Polish Jew, Herschel Grynszpan, who shot the German diplomat three days ago in Paris?''

"Yes, of course we heard."

"Well, the German died today. And they're holding all the Jews responsible."

Erich's mother turned pale and put her hands up to her face. "Well they would, wouldn't they?" Greta continued. "Any excuse to start trouble. While I was out shopping this afternoon I heard rumors that there could be riots. I don't know if there's anything to it, but I would advise you to stay in this evening. Once it gets dark, who knows what they have in store?"

"But Max is out! He went to evening prayers in the synagogue, and he won't be home till after dark!"

"You'd better warn him, then. Get him to come home now!"

Mrs. Bildmann hurried to the closet to get her coat, but Greta put a restraining arm on her shoulder. "Is Erich at home?" she asked.

"Yes, yes, he's in his room."

"Send him instead. He'll be quicker and less noticeable. And surely," she added as an afterthought, "they won't bother a child."

Erich buttoned his heavy overcoat up to his chin, pulled the collar up and tugged his cap down until it almost covered his eyes. He walked briskly down the road. There was a sharp wind blowing and the frosty streets were practically deserted. Night was drawing in and Erich would be pleased when they were all safely back home. It occurred to him that this was the first time he had ever been allowed out on his own after dark.

He could see the shul in the distance now and quickened his pace. Squinting and straining his eyes in the dusk, he could discern a small crowd of men walking out of shul. That's strange, Erich thought to himself. The *Ma'ariv* prayers would not be finished yet. He dashed across the road to the last corner before he reached the shul. It was a good vantage point from where he could view the whole scene. What was this? Men in uniforms were prodding the Jewish men into a straight line. He could make out some of his father's friends... Where was Papa? They all had their hands above their heads and were visibly afraid. One of the Germans was shouting orders and directing the others under his command. A few Nazis rushed out of the shul, and as Erich inched nearer he watched with horror as the building burst into flame. The shul was now ablaze, the flames leaping and crackling against the darkening sky. His beloved shul, where he had gone every Shabbos and celebrated every *Yom Tov*. He had even had his *bris* there. He stood rooted to the spot in horror, as he watched that chapter of his life disappear before his very eyes.

Erich caught sight of his father among the men and, taking a chance, darted across and hid behind the truck into which they were being herded. "Go! Go!" shouted a soldier with a menacing dog at his side, as he pushed the Jews into the truck one by one. There were two men in front of his father and then it would be his turn. "Papa," Erich whispered hoarsely, fearing that a scream and not a whisper would come out. His father turned and looked into the darkness in the direction of his son's voice. Erich, crouching beside the back wheel, beckoned to him, hoping that if his father made a quick dash they might still be able to get away without being detected. But the soldier already had his hand on Mr. Bildmann's arm. "*Erich!* Take care of your mother," his father whispered into the darkness before he was thrown in with the others.

As he watched the unthinkable happening before his eyes, Erich imagined pulling him out, rescuing him, or following him and discovering where he was going and when he would be home again. He wanted to shout at the evil men who were taking his father from him, and who had destroyed his beloved shul along with all the *sifrei Torah* in it. He would have been prepared to take on the entire German army in that moment had he thought it would do any good.

With a heavy heart he crept back to the corner and sank to his knees, sobbing, as he watched the truck start up and head off down the street. He brushed away a tear. "Please don't go, Papa," he pleaded. "Please don't go." And then he could hear the truck no more. Erich pulled himself up and walked toward home. He felt numb.

Strange and terrifying sounds reverberated all around him. He could hear screams and heartbreaking cries, glass shattering, crackling flames, barking dogs, shrieks which did not even sound human. Erich flinched as if it were he who was receiving the blows. He saw Jewish people being led out onto the streets, storefronts broken and looted, and other terrible scenes from which he averted his eyes. He concealed himself in the shadows and vainly attempted to block out the sounds that grew louder and more fierce, never abating.

"Get me out of this nightmare!" cried the silent voice pleading inside him. He knew that things had not been good in Germany for as long as he could remember, but he had never witnessed — nor imagined — anything quite as horrific as this.

Erich's only thought was to reach home safely. Even in his dazed and numbed state he was surprised at his lack of feeling toward his fellow Jews and felt guilty for it. But he realized that had he thought more about them on that treacherous walk home, he would have never made it for he would have either tried to help and be arrested himself or broken down then and there, giving himself away. This numbness, this block in his heart, kept him going and gave him strength.

At long last he reached his apartment, and with his last ounce of strength ran up the three flights of stairs. His door was locked as usual. He knocked, but getting no response, he started to bang frantically on it. "Mutti! Mutti!" he cried, hot tears falling from his eyes and sobs threatening to choke him. He slammed his small fists against the wood. "*Mutti!*"

The door to Greta's apartment across the hall flew open and his mother grabbed his arms from behind and pulled him inside, hastily shutting the door behind her. She hugged him tightly and calmed his cries. "Sh-h, we must not make any noise," she warned him.

Erich checked his emotions but could not stifle the tremor

in his voice. "I...I watched them take him away, Mutti. I saw our shul on fire, soldiers, lots of them..." His mother did not interrupt him and she wept silently herself as she held him. "I...I wanted to rescue him, Mutti, but there was no way I could. I don't even know where they have taken him. When do you think he will come home?"

"I don't know," she whispered.

"Before he got into the truck, Mutti, he saw me. He told me — he told me...that I should take care of you."

Mrs. Bildmann struggled to regain her composure. "We will take care of each other, my son."

Greta brought them each a hot cup of tea, with plenty of sugar in each cup. "Stay here tonight," she told them. "It will be safer for you."

"No, Greta, you have done enough already. If we are found here, you will also be in trouble. We will go back to our apartment tonight."

Greta was reluctant to let them leave. "Are you sure?" she asked, her kindly face lined with concern.

"Yes, absolutely. I do not want to put you in any more danger. Thank you for all you have done for us."

"I have done nothing. I will come in and see you tomorrow."

Erich looked around his living room. How strange and unfamiliar all his things looked. His small violin, its red wood shining in the lamplight, meant nothing to him. His father's *sefarim* sat on the shelves like mute accusers: Where is he?

"Go and get ready for bed now, Erich," his mother told him. "Tomorrow is another day, and hopefully Papa will be back." Erich went into his room, leaving the door slightly ajar behind him. Mrs. Bildmann tidied a few things in the kitchen and then went into Erich's room to check on him.

The room was pitch black and she found her son huddled beneath his window.

"Erich, what is it?"

"I am so frightened." Erich's teeth chattered as he shivered uncontrollably. The windows in his room were closed, but it was not enough to shut out the tumult from outside.

"You have been through a terrible shock. I am very proud of you, of how bravely you behaved. Would you like me to sit with you until you go to sleep?" Erich nodded.

His mother tucked him in the way she used to when he was a baby, wrapping the thick quilt cozily around his feet and his shoulders. Then she sat on the carved wooden chair beside him and stroked his hair. "I am sure things will be better in the morning," she said soothingly. "Papa will probably be home by then. Let's say some *Tehillim* together. '...*lo ira ra, ki attah immadi* — I will fear no evil, for You are with me...'" Erich murmured the *Shema*, and, overcome with exhaustion, soon succumbed to sleep.

The next day, however, brought no return of his father, and only dreadful news of the destruction and arrests of the night before. The smell of smoke permeated the air over the whole of Berlin, and the city resounded with the noise of shattered glass being swept and shoveled. Both his mother and Greta went to see if they could find out anything about his father, but they could learn nothing other than that he had been arrested by the Gestapo.

That evening Erich and his mother sat in the silent living room, staring at their half-packed trunks. By now we should have been on our way to safe, sunny Curaçao, Erich thought. Instead he and his mother sat in their lonely apartment with reminders of what might have been, filled with anxiety about Mr. Bildmann and the family's future.

5

July 1939

DOWN A NARROW PATH overshadowed by leafy, overhanging branches, two boys pedaled furiously on their bicycles. The older of the two had a slight lead but the younger, who was a smaller copy of the older with his thick brown curls and dancing eyes, was slowly catching up with him. "I'll beat you yet, Karl!" he cried breathlessly.

"Don't count on it, Otto!" his brother shouted over his shoulder. The path widened. It was flanked on the left by a grassy hill at the bottom of which flowed a shallow river. Karl turned off the track and raced down with Otto hot on his trail, almost overtaking him. With a screech of brakes they halted by the banks of the river. "You were getting too close for comfort, little brother!" Karl teased him. "Let's dangle our feet awhile to cool off."

They rested their bikes against a willow tree, and pulled off their high shoes and socks. As they sat on the edge of the bank splashing their feet in the clear, cool water, Otto remarked pensively, "I wonder if there are any fish in here. We could take them home to help feed all our house guests. I am sure that Mutti would be pleased." Karl said nothing, but continued to make ripples in the water with his feet. Otto understood little of the situation but occasionally surprised Karl with his perceptive comments. There was not exactly a shortage of food at home, for their family grew most of their own fruits, vegetables and grain on their extensive farmland, but they rarely ate fish or meat these days. Those commodities were virtually impossible to come by and there were only certain times at which Jews were allowed to shop in the market. Besides, it was becoming precarious to go into the center of Berlin, so they only went if necessary — for example, to pick up "house guests." That was how the family referred to the people who were trying to flee the country and used the Alexanders' home as a short stopover. Although they were only a few miles away from Berlin, their small rural Jewish community had been left in relative peace, and Karl's father had chosen to take advantage of this by helping as many Jews as possible to escape from Germany while they could. He himself was optimistic, and hoped that things would improve or that they would simply be left alone indefinitely. But he was also realistic and deep down acknowledged to himself that in all likelihood they too might be forced to escape at the last minute.

"Hey!" a hoarse voice called out, shattering the tranquillity of the afternoon. Karl turned his head to see where the voice was coming from. At the top of the hill five teenaged boys stood defiantly in their Hitler Youth uniforms, their legs slightly apart as if to emphasize their strong physiques, their heads held high and proud. All had cropped blond hair atop of which the diamond-shaped Hitler Youth cap was perched. The tallest, and evidently the ringleader, must have been about eighteen and stood in the center. His followers — who were not more than fourteen or fifteen, the same age as Karl — stood on either side of him. Karl stared at them coldly.

"Jews are not allowed to foul our rivers," the ringleader shouted.

"Yeah, that's right!" his cohorts echoed.

"Oh, is that so?" Karl asked coolly.

"Yes, that is so!" he replied. His fellow Hitler Youth members nodded in agreement.

"Come on, Otto. Let's go," Karl whispered to his brother. "Put on your shoes." As a parting shot, Karl looked up at the boys and made a sweeping gesture with his hand. "Come on down — it's all yours," he said. "We'll leave the river to the animals it belongs to."

The shortest of the Hitler Youth, a stocky boy with a small upturned nose and a receding chin, made a movement as if to come down to them. "Let's get him!" he said, but the ringleader placed a restraining hand on him.

The two brothers mounted their bicycles and pedaled swiftly along the dirt path by the side of the river until it met up with the main path further along. Karl checked to make sure that they were not being followed and then breathed a sigh of relief. "*Baruch Hashem* for that," he whispered.

"What did they want with us anyway?" Otto asked.

"Nothing. They were just being stupid."

Karl slowed his pace to enjoy the beauty of the woods glowing in the afternoon sunlight. Even in the country which was becoming more of an enemy to them day by day, one could still find the beauty of Hashem if one only looked for it. Suddenly Otto let out a cry, and without warning was sent flying across the handlebars as the five young Nazis bolted out from behind the trees and tipped his bicycle forward. "*So* sorry," the ringleader said sarcastically, and they disappeared into the woods from where they had come.

"Otto, are you all right?" Karl asked, jumping off his bicycle and rushing to his younger brother.

"I think so," Otto whimpered, picking himself up and brushing dirt and pebbles from his clothes.

"Does anything hurt you?" Otto shook his head. Karl looked his younger brother over with a sharp eye, and helped him back onto his bike. "Do you think you can go home from here on your own?" he asked Otto. "It's not far."

"Of course I can," Otto nodded.

"Good. Then pedal home as fast as you can."

"But why? Where are you going?"

"I'm going after those boys. But not a word to anyone. Do you hear?"

Otto nodded. "Wait," he shouted, but Karl was already out of earshot. Otto headed for home. His brother was such a hero, Otto thought proudly. He wanted to be just like him one day.

Night was falling when at last Karl found them. They were sitting in a circle around a campfire, roasting potatoes on long sticks, laughing and boasting of their brave exploits against the Jews earlier that afternoon. Karl crouched low in the grass, picked up a small stone and aimed in squarely at the ringleader. It got him right on the side of his head, next to his ear. "Ouch! What was that?" he yelled, and then yelled again and held his jaw in agony as Karl's foot came crashing down on it.

Mr. Alexander was picking ripe plums in the orchard, when he saw his younger son wheeling his bike into the shed. He waved to the boy and smiled warmly, and Otto guiltily waved back. Mrs. Alexander was busy chopping up fresh carrots in the kitchen, with the door flung open wide to let in the summer sun. "Did you have a good ride?" she called out as she saw Otto walking past. He had been hoping to enter the house unnoticed so as to avoid questioning, but it was not going to be that easy.

"Yes, Mutti," Otto replied, nodding, and he walked slowly on, trying not to appear rude.

"Dinner will be ready shortly," she told him. "Where is Karl?"

"He's not here yet. He ran into someone." Otto tried to sound casual and matter-of-fact. Seeing that his mother was quite satisfied with that answer, he flew through the dining room and up to the sanctuary of his bedroom, where he stayed until his mother called him down for supper.

Otto greeted the fifteen or so other people around the table and sat down beside Karl's laid but empty place, to a bowl of delicious homemade vegetable soup.

"Karl is still not back?" his mother asked. Otto shrugged his shoulders. "Maybe he stopped to eat at Uncle Ernst's house," she said in answer to her own question.

Karl cautiously walked down the path and edged past the dining room undetected, where he was happy to note everyone seated around the table. He rubbed his own empty stomach, wondering how he was going to get himself something to eat. Hoisting himself up the drainpipe, he landed with a thud on the veranda above. "What was that?" Mr. Alexander asked, stopping to listen.

"What was what?" Mrs. Alexander asked.

"Didn't you hear a noise just now?"

"No."

"Must have been a field mouse."

Karl carefully slid open his window and clambered in. Then he tiptoed across to his door and locked it firmly.

"Karl, wake up! Time to *daven*! Breakfast's almost ready," Mrs. Alexander said, knocking on his door. "And what time did you get in last night? Where were you?" she shouted through the closed door.

"I got in quite early but I went straight to bed," came the reply.

"Aren't you feeling well?"

"No, not too well, Mutti."

"Would you like me to bring you up something to eat?"

"Yes, please," Karl replied.

Several minutes later there was a short rap on his door. "Karl, here's your breakfast," his mother said.

"Thanks," Karl replied. "Just leave it outside the door, please. I'll bring it in after I *daven*."

"Karl!" his mother raised her voice. "What do you think this is? A hotel? Now kindly open the door and let me in."

Karl reluctantly unlocked the door and, while his mother turned the handle, he made a move toward the open window, where he pretended to be looking at something outside. "If you are sick, why are you dressed already?" Mrs. Alexander asked suspiciously. Something was not quite right and she was determined to find out what it was. "I, um..." he replied, fumbling for something to say.

"Karl, what's the matter?"

"N...nothing."

"Karl, look at me." He stiffened but did not move. "Karl!"

Very slowly he turned around to face his mother. A look of horror crossed her face and she dropped the tray of food she had been holding, sending it crashing to the floor and its contents splashing and rolling around the room. She winced as Karl took a couple of steps toward her and she got a closer look at his bruised and swollen face, blood-encrusted hair, black eye and split lip.

"What happened to you?" she cried, unable to hide the anguish in her voice but trying not to panic. She grabbed a clean towel and dipped it into the basin on Karl's washstand, and began to bathe his wounds.

"Some Hitler Youth boys...*ouch!*"

"*Ach*...so it has started here as well," she said sadly, but not sounding all that surprised.

"Mutti, it was not quite like that, and really, it's not as bad as it looks."

"How did it happen then?"

"A few boys started with us. Teasing, that sort of thing. I answered them back. Later they caught up with us and tipped Otto off his bike, so I went after them."

"Oh, Karl, why did you do such a dangerous thing? You not only put yourself in danger, but all the other Jewish families around here as well."

Karl hung his head. His mother was right, of course. They needed only the slightest pretext to cause the maximum trouble. *Kristallnacht*, which was still too fresh in his mind, had been sparked by one single incident.

"Do you know who they are? Have you ever seen them

before?'' She was noticeably worried by now.

"No, never.'' Karl replied.

"Do you think they know you?''

"No, I don't think so.''

"But how easy it would be for them to find out!'' Mrs. Alexander sighed. Let's finish getting you cleaned up and then I will have to discuss this with Papa.''

While Karl repaired a damaged fence in one of the fields, he tried to picture the conversation his parents were having; but never in his wildest dreams could he have imagined what they were deciding. His rolled-up shirtsleeves revealed his dark tanned skin, the result of a hot summer spent mostly out of doors. As he hammered away, he smiled to himself — even though it was intensely painful — picturing his father telling his mother, ''That boy acts first and thinks later.'' But Karl knew this was not the case. He had known what he was doing. He may have gotten a terrible beating, but one look at his younger brother who sat under a tree a few meters away from him, innocently reading, told him that he could have done nothing else but defend him. He would do the same thing were it to happen all over again.

Perhaps his parents might not let him go out alone anymore, Karl thought. That would be awful. No more solitary walks in the woods, when he could simply contemplate things; no more bicycle rides down country lanes, or visits to his friends nearby... He did not think it would come to that, but if it did, he would have to cope with it. It was probably the worst his parents could do. He was sure they would not punish him for trying to look after his brother.

He could see his father coming toward him. ''Karl!'' Mr. Alexander called. ''Your mother and I would like to see you in the house.'' Karl laid down his tools, and went to join his parents.

The kitchen was their favorite place for family conferences. When the three of them had taken their seats around the table, his father took a deep breath. ''Your mother and I have been talking," he began. "She told me about the incident yesterday. This sort of thing was bound to happen eventually, and the situation is sure to get worse in the future." His father took another deep breath, the lines in his tanned face deepening. "That is why we have decided..." Karl held his breath. "...that it would be best if you and Otto go to England."

"*To England!*" Karl echoed. He was flabbergasted, speechless.

"It would be only for a little while, until the situation improves here," his mother added.

"Why England? When? I don't understand."

"I have some contacts. I didn't tell you, Karl, but I already looked into this a few weeks ago. Several trains have been allowed to leave the country with Jewish children, bound for England. I wrote to someone in London, a fellow I met a couple of years ago in Berlin when he was here on business, and asked him whether he might be able to put you up for a while if need be. His positive reply arrived last week. You both have a place booked on the next transport leaving Berlin, just as a precaution. But now, under the circumstances, I think it would be advisable if you and Otto went."

"When does it leave?" Karl asked, his voice cracking.

"The day after tomorrow," his father replied, his own voice choked with sorrow.

6

IT WAS HIS final night in Germany and with Otto sound asleep, Karl and his mother set about packing their bags. As his mother explained to him, they were each allowed to take only one suitcase with them filled with clothing and a few personal belongings, but no valuables — items of gold and silver, or money, except for ten marks each. Karl was still dazed and confused and mechanically followed his mother's orders, taking down the two medium-sized leather suitcases, sorting through clothes and books, choosing food for packed lunches. There was so much he wanted to tell his mother and to ask her about, but he did not know where to begin. He had hardly said a word to anyone during the last day and a half, and the little he did say was in reply to others — unless the subject was the upcoming trip, in which case he clammed up and said nothing at all.

It was his mother who eventually broke the strained silence. "Believe me, Karl, we do not want to send you away. Please," she begged, "don't be angry or upset with us." Karl noticed that his mother's eyes were red and puffy and he realized that she was taking it no more easily than he was, despite what her outwardly calm demeanor might suggest.

"How long have you known about this?" Karl asked her.

"About two weeks now," she admitted.

"Mutti, I need to ask you something...if I had not gotten into that fight, would you still have sent us?"

"Probably," she reluctantly replied.

"Then why didn't you tell me earlier?"

"We thought it would be better this way."

"When would you have told me, then?"

"We had planned to tell you tonight."

"*Tonight!*" Karl raged. "Why? Didn't you think I was old enough to understand? I'm not a child anymore. I'm fifteen!"

"Then stop acting like one!" his mother cried, her voice breaking in mid-sentence. "Do you think I have enjoyed keeping it from you all this time?" she wept. "Do you think I will relish telling Otto tomorrow that he is simply going on holiday for a little while, and not being able to give him a proper goodbye? You may be right. Perhaps we should have told you earlier. Sometimes I forget that you are no longer a little boy. But it is not only that. There were so many other reasons. It was never one hundred percent certain that you would go. That incident was what finally sealed the decision."

She sat down on Karl's bed, suddenly drained of all strength. "Perhaps it was also that we did not really want to admit it to ourselves," she whispered. "To have actually told you would have made it real. It always seemed way off in the future. We always hoped, prayed, that something might change — as unlikely as that was. I never really imagined tonight, or thought that it would come."

"Mutti, I'm sorry. Forgive me."

"No, Karl, you have nothing to apologize for. I should be the one saying 'I'm sorry'."

"Mutti, you are doing what is best for Otto and me. Really, I think I do understand. You have always been so good and fair with us. We could not have asked for a better mother. I only wish we didn't have to go." Karl could not remember the last time he had cried, but now he let the tears flow unchecked from his eyes.

His mother ruffled his dark curly hair the way she used to do when he was younger. "Yes, yes, sometimes it is good to cry, my Karl. We cannot bear the thought either." She lay his head on her shoulder. "You can still be my little boy tonight. But tomorrow you must be strong. We all must, for Otto's sake. He has never been away from home before. Not even to stay at a friend's house for a few nights, like you have."

"I promise I will take good care of him, Mutti."

"I know you will, Karl."

"When do you think we will be able to return?"

His mother shook her head. "Who knows?"

"Why don't you come to England with us?" Karl said suddenly and wondered why he had not thought of it sooner. He would still be leaving his beloved home, but at least they would be going as a family. And who knows? It might be quite an adventure going to London. He spoke a little English, from what he had learned in school, but everything else he knew about London was from books. He had never even been out of Germany before, except for a short visit to Switzerland once.

But his mother shook her head sadly. "Not at the moment, I'm afraid. Too many people depend on us right now."

"Mutti, there is talk that war is likely to break out between England and Germany in the near future, and the way things are going, this may happen very soon," Karl said gravely.

For an instant her face revealed her despair but then she quickly brushed aside her fears and said a little too casually, "It might still be averted. Hitler marched into the Rhineland, annexed Austria and occupied part of Czechoslovakia and the world took no action."

"No," said Karl, his voice rising, "and they did nothing when the Jews of Austria and Czechoslovakia were victimized and started disappearing. Like Lottie."

His mother looked as if she had been physically slapped. His elder sister Charlotte, who had been married for less than a year, had gone with her husband to live in Czechoslovakia and had disappeared without a trace the previous November, shortly after the invasion. All attempts at finding out what had happened to them proved fruitless and they feared the worst for her and her husband. They rarely mentioned Charlotte's name, acting as if it were just a temporary, political inconvenience that they had not heard from her. At the back of their minds, though, the pain and fear were very much alive.

"You are right, Mutti," Karl went on, speaking gently. "It would be best if Otto and I left the country. But what about you? Without meaning to be disrespectful, you and Papa should not deny that war is coming. You know that if Germany tries to invade Poland, England says that they will declare war. Then what? The borders will be closed and everyone will be trapped."

None of this was new to Mrs. Alexander. She had been through it all in her mind countless times before, but she had never expressed her fears to Karl openly, nor had he to his mother. They had only spoken in passing about the terrible things which were happening, but never about their feelings. In a sense she was quite surprised that Karl understood so much about the state of affairs. Had she treated him too much like a child? It was true that he had the freedom to wander off on his own, camping and bicycling with friends, but that was the independence that came with living in the country.

Now she was overcome with self-recrimination and doubt. Had she spent so much time with all the people who passed through their home, that she had neglected to share things with Karl and Otto? Perhaps she should have persuaded her husband earlier, when there was still time, that they all should leave. Karl was mature for his age, but he was still young, and he had a lot to learn. Was it fair to send him off on his own, and with the added responsibility of Otto? Would it be better to keep them both at home? This had been her argument when she had discussed it with her husband, but eventually they concluded that it would be safest away from Germany. But Mrs. Alexander could not deny that she still had her moments of doubt.

She could stay in the room no longer, and she excused herself, telling Karl that she would be back in a little while. She went to her own room, and sat in front of the antique dresser which had belonged to her grandmother. She began to feel a little easier in her private haven. But she had tried to suppress her thoughts and problems for too long, and now they threatened to overwhelm her.

If only she could turn back the clock and do things a little differently! She should have listened more to Karl. She should have listened more to her own heart, which told her long ago that they should have left the country when they still had the chance. Her husband had answered her that things would be fine. He had connections, and they would be able to leave at the last minute if necessary, whereas there were others who were more needy and could not.

What had happened to their contacts? Where were they now? But it was too late for regrets.

She stood up and went into Otto's room down the hall. He lay under his quilt, sleeping like a baby — which, in some ways, he still was. He understood little about the reality of what was happening in Germany. His world was one of story books. Being the youngest, he had been protected and sheltered. She sat on the edge of his bed watching him. A small night light shone on his face — he was still afraid of the dark. She knew she ought to tell him the truth about why he was going away. But how could she frighten him?

Maybe, just maybe, things would somehow improve and they would not have to stay away too long. She remembered her own father telling her many years ago that one must always hope. Our Sages said, he had reassured her, that even if one has a sword at one's neck, it is not too late to pray.

Nevertheless, if Hashem had made a decree she must accept it. Having *bitachon* gave her great comfort. It was true she could do nothing about the past, and neither, for that matter, about the future. She *could* do something about the present, however. She kissed her small son and went back into her own room.

Karl grew increasingly concerned. But when his mother returned at last, there was renewed courage in her face, which gave him courage too. She took the chair at his desk and turned it so that she was facing him. Karl noticed that she held a small cloth pouch in her hands. "Karl, I do not know how to say this..." she began with difficulty, "but I think it is time I was a little more frank with you." She stared earnestly into his green eyes and said slowly, "It may be a very long time until you are able to return home. And it may be never. Under the circumstances, there is virtually no chance of our leaving at the moment, and if war breaks out..."

"I know," Karl whispered.

"That's why I want to give you this." Mrs. Alexander slowly opened the drawstring of the pouch and carefully withdrew a sparkling diamond ring. Karl recognized it as her engagement ring. "I want you to have this for safekeeping...or for emergencies."

Karl could not take his eyes off the ring. "But what if I am found with it?" he asked.

"That is why we must find a place to conceal it."

"Where?"

"I have an idea," she said conspiratorially.

For the next ten minutes Karl watched with fascination as his mother sliced a bar of soap in half, cut out a hollow large enough for the ring to fit inside, and then carefully molded the two halves back together using hot water. Karl placed the bar in a soap box and closed up his suitcase. "That is the last of my things," he murmured.

"No, wait," his mother said. "There is still something I want to give you."

Karl followed his mother downstairs into the dining room, where his father sat immersed in Torah study. He glanced up as they came into the room and then resumed his studying. His mother pulled down a black leather-bound photograph album from the bookshelf, which contained all the family photographs. "I want you to have this," she said simply. Karl took it from her without comment. "Well," she said awkwardly, "I'm going upstairs. It's late already. You should go to bed too. It's going to be a long day tomorrow."

"I'll go in a little while, Mutti," Karl replied.

"All right." She looked away. "Goodnight, then."

*   *   *

Karl drew up a chair and sat opposite his father at the table. The polished wood showed through the pattern in the lace tablecloth. The silence hung heavy as he waited for his father to finish the page he was studying.

With his eyes still downcast, Mr. Alexander closed his *sefer*, kissed it, and laid it aside. Only then did he face his son. Still he said nothing, but just nodded slowly.

"I'm sorry for the way I have been acting the past couple of days," Karl apologized. "Please forgive me, Papa."

"My son, there is nothing to forgive," his father replied emotionally. "You have always been a good boy. You have never given us any trouble, and I am sure you are going to...to grow up to be a very fine man." His father stood up and Karl fell into his open arms. "Just promise me one thing, my son: never forget who you are and where you have come from."

His father held him at arms' length, placed his hands on Karl's head, and gave him a *berachah*. "May Hashem bless you and safeguard you. May Hashem illuminate His countenance for you and be gracious to you. May Hashem turn His countenance to you and establish for you peace."

7

"WAKE UP," Mrs. Bildmann whispered. Erich unwillingly opened his eyes and rubbed them, quite surprised to find that his mother was waking him so early in the morning. "Mutti, what time is it? Is something wrong?"

"It's almost five in the morning, and the reason I'm waking you so early is because we have got to get you on that train today."

"But you already tried, and you said there were no places left."

"I know, and that's why I'm going to try and smuggle you on."

Erich reluctantly got out of bed. He washed his hands and face, using the jug and bowl on a low table in the cramped room he shared with his mother in the apartment which belonged to Greta's sister. They had moved there several months earlier, days after Mr. Bildmann's arrest, on the advice of Greta, who still came regularly to see them. Since their departure, their own apartment had been visited several times by the Gestapo and had recently been taken over by a Nazi officer and his wife. They had hardly been troubled since moving in with Greta's sister Gertrude, as they seldom left the flat.

Beside the door stood a small suitcase, and his old winter coat — which had become a little tight for him — was slung across it. "I have heard that it can be quite cold in England," his mother explained, trying to sound matter-of-fact.

After his morning prayers, he ate a small roll and drank a glass of water. Gertrude dutifully bade him goodbye and wished him good luck for the future. Erich could not help feeling that she would be glad to see him gone. When they were out of the apartment, Erich was suddenly aware that it was the first time he had been out in the open air, and alone with his mother, for months. He held his hand out in front of him savoring the feel of the fresh, cool morning air. His mother carried his suitcase for him as they walked briskly, trying not to attract too much attention from the few people who were already on the streets. It was only a short distance to Greta's apartment and their former home, and Greta had kindly offered to take them to the train station.

"Gertrude looked as if she were glad to be rid of me," Erich confided to his mother.

"I think she will be quite happy to see both of us gone," she agreed.

"Why 'both of us'? Where are you going?"

"I'm going to be moving back with Greta. Last night the two of them had another argument. Gertrude consented to take us in only as a favor to her sister, but she's fed up with having us. She feels we are putting her in danger, and personally, I do not think she is too enamored of Jews. So I am moving out. I do not wish to be where I am not wanted."

"But isn't it a little dangerous living with Greta?"

"I have no choice. Gertrude threatened that if I was not out tonight she would turn me in to the authorities." Mrs. Bildmann returned the alarmed look on Erich's face with a smile. "But don't worry — she wouldn't dare. Anyway, I hope it won't be too long until Papa is released and then we can all go to Curaçao together and leave people like Gertrude far behind us."

Erich smiled up at her and squeezed her hand in reply.

Karl strolled slowly through the garden, fields, and orchards of his home for the last time. The dew-covered grass glistened in the early morning sunlight and the birds chirped in the trees. Karl sighed as he climbed to the top of the hill. He leaned against one of the tall pines and surveyed his beloved home below. In the center stood his house, surrounded by fragrant orchards and lush fields. It was so much a part of his life that he could not imagine living anywhere else. Physical pain gripped him as he let himself think that he might never see any of this again. His father had brought their old Opel around to the front of the house, and Karl could just make him out placing two suitcases into the trunk. Knowing he could not put off the terrible moment any longer, he hurried back down the hill to join the rest of the family.

Everything happened so quickly after that. Before he knew it, they were all in the car — his parents in the front, he and Otto in the back. Mr. Alexander started up the engine, and the car began to move. Karl stared out the back window until his home disappeared from view.

Kurt woke up with a jolt and it took him a few moments to remember where he was and why he was feeling so cramped. Since they had left their home and gone into hiding, his family had been constantly on the move, rarely staying in the same place for longer than two or three days at a time. They could never relax. They slept lightly, sensitive to any irregular sounds, and it was not unusual for his parents to wake Kurt in the middle of the night to move on to a new safe-house. Every day brought with it new uncertainties. The only thing that had remained constant in their routine over the past few months was his father's daily trip to the American embassy, where he stood in line from six o'clock in the morning to six o'clock in the evening trying to obtain a visa which would enable them to leave the country. Four weeks previously, his father had finally managed to acquire one, but it was for January 1940 — seven months away.

In the meantime Kurt was living the life of a fugitive, missing out on his schooling and the pleasure of mixing with other children his own age. His parents had discussed this with him, and his father explained that he had heard about some train transports of Jewish children who were being allowed to leave for England. Together they came to the conclusion that it would be a good idea for Kurt to go to England and remain there until they could all go to America. A week before the next train was due to leave, Mr. Eisig was able to secure a place for Kurt.

The night of his departure, Kurt's parents and his little sister Ilse had accompanied him to Vienna's Westbahnoff station. A strained atmosphere pervaded the crowd as the children boarded the train. People hardly spoke, and when they did, it was in voices barely above a whisper. There were tears in the mothers' eyes as they bade farewell to their children. "Look after *Omama* for me," Kurt told his parents. His mother nodded.

"We'll keep you informed about everything," his father assured him, "and if we can think of a way that you can send letters back to us, we will let you know immediately. Until then, we'll try and write at least once a week."

"I'm going to miss you!" Kurt blurted out as the time for boarding drew near.

"We will miss you too, darling, but you won't be gone for long, and just think how much fun it will be living in London. Buckingham Palace and Big Ben will be practically on your doorstep," his mother said, forcing herself to sound light-hearted. "And who knows? You might even catch a glimpse of the King!"

"Be a good boy now," Kurt's father added.

"I will be," Kurt replied. "See you soon. 'Bye, Ilse!" His little sister blew kisses at him.

Kurt boarded the train and it began to move. He waved to his parents through the open carriage window until they were completely out of sight. Then he found himself a vacant seat and fell asleep immediately.

Kurt awoke with a start and soon discovered what had roused him: the train had drawn to a sudden halt inside a station. That could only mean one thing — they had arrived in Berlin. Kurt looked up, noticing his young travel companions for the first time, and turned to the window to observe what was happening outside. He shivered inwardly at the sight of the uniformed guards and the thought that he was in the heart of Germany, the source which had brought him here in the first place. He was also beginning to miss his parents. He was all alone, journeying to a country whose people and language were foreign to him, and all that he knew was that a family by the name of Kilern would be there to meet him when he arrived in London. It would be with the Kilerns that Kurt would live for the duration of his stay in London, but he knew nothing of them apart from their name. He sat back in his seat, and tried to console himself: Things could only improve from here on, and, God willing, he would soon be together with his parents again.

Mrs. Bildmann knocked on the door of Greta's apartment and it was opened immediately. "Are you ready?" she whispered. Greta nodded. "And did you manage to get it?"

"Yes, I did. I'll just go and get it. You should go downstairs and keep walking. I'll pick you up on Bauer Strasse."

"Keep calm," Erich's mother instructed him. "Look straight ahead and don't turn right or left." A car drew up beside them and Greta leaned over to the passenger seat to open the door. Erich got in first and sat in the back seat and his mother beside Greta. Erich could detect a note of apprehension in his mother's voice. There was an unnatural stiffness in her tone. Erich himself was in two minds about this. He did not even know whether he would be able to get on the train. He could not believe that he might actually be about to leave the country.

"Here we are," Greta announced. "I'll be waiting out here for you, Klara."

"Where's the—?" his mother began.

"In the trunk."

"Thanks, Greta," she said sincerely, stepping out of the car and pulling the front seat forward to allow Erich out.

Greta leaned out to him. "Good luck, Erich. I hope everything works out for you. I'm very sorry things turned out the way they did. It is really a sordid business.''

Erich shrugged, embarrassed, confused. "Please look after my mother for me," he said.

Mother and son stood outside the station together looking earnestly into each other's eyes. "In case you do manage to get a place, I want to say goodbye to you now, as I may not get another chance," Mrs. Bildmann said. "And I also wanted to give you this..." She handed him a curved leather case, so shaped that it could only be one thing — a violin. But it was much larger than his child's violin. Erich opened the case with great care and his eyes widened as he saw its gleaming body. "It is beautiful," he whispered. "It must be a very special one."

"It is. It's a Stradivarius."

Erich gasped. "Why are you giving this to me?"

"As a parting gift, and...if times get hard...you can always sell it. A Stradivarius would fetch a good price."

"Oh, no, I'll never want to sell it, Mutti! And Mutti, I want you to know that I love you and will never forget anything you and Papa have taught me. Whatever these Nazis do, they will never be able to stop me from feeling proud that I am Jewish. In the end they will get their punishment, '*Middah k'neged middah,* measure for measure' just like all our Peoples' other enemies before them. No one has ever been able to destroy us, and all those great nations have always fallen in the end. Herr Guttman taught us that in Hebrew class."

"You are a very special boy, Erich. I am very...very proud of you." She drew a shaky breath. "Come, we'd better go in."

The platform was crowded with people. Jewish families stood in groups, small children clinging to their parents, and parents trying to keep back tears; soldiers in gray uniforms and guns strapped to their backs marched up and down in their heavy boots glaring menacingly, like birds of prey, at the unusual groups of passengers and their miserable parents. Some jeered at those tearful mothers who were unable to contain their emotions. Erich's mother held him firmly by the hand as she strode through the throng with a purposeful step. Unexpectedly, an official holding a clipboard stepped out of the mass and blocked her path.

"Is your son registered to board this train?"

"Please," Mrs. Bildmann pleaded, "my son *must* get on this train."

"Is his name on the list?"

"No, but—"

"Then I am afraid you must turn back. You cannot come any farther."

"Can't you make one exception? I am begging you," she cried in desperation.

"No, that is not possible. Only those whose names are on the list can board the train. Now, if you will excuse me..." he gave a slight nod and walked off.

"What are we going to do now?" Mrs. Bildmann whispered as the tears fell. Erich felt numb. He just stood silently, not moving.

"May I have your attention," said the voice over the loudspeaker. "I will be calling out a list of the passengers in alphabetical order. When your names are called, your children are to board the train." A tense silence ensued as everyone froze in their places and listened attentively to the names being announced. "Abert, Adler, Alexander..."

"That's us!" Mr. Alexander said. Mrs. Alexander smiled at her young son, but her moist eyes and pale face betrayed her real feelings. "You're going to have a wonderful time, Otto," she said.

"But when will we be coming home?" he asked.

"Soon." There was a distant look in her eyes. "Very soon." Mr. Alexander hugged Karl, who stood stiffly.

"Goodbye, my son," he said emotionally, "and don't forget, if you keep your *bitachon* you will be strong and able to overcome anything."

Karl grasped his father's hand before turning to his brother. "Come on, Otto," he said in a reassuring voice. "We don't want to miss the train, do we?"

Mrs. Bildmann stood behind Erich, her hands on his shoulders, listening to the names being called out. Perhaps, she thought, in the commotion, she might be able to slip Erich onto the train without anyone noticing. Or he could jump on just as the train was leaving. Mrs. Bildmann refused to believe that she stood no chance.

A young woman next to her wiped her eyes and glanced up as her name was called. She took her little daughter's hand, about to proceed toward the train, but suddenly stood rooted to the spot. "I can't do it!" she whispered, and then in a louder voice cried, "I can't let her go!" Mrs. Bildmann hardly dared to believe what she was hearing, and stared at the woman who had bent down and was holding her young daughter in her arms. She could not have been more than about four years old and she looked back at her weeping, anguished mother with a frightened, puzzled expression on her face. "I can't let you go," cried the woman again.

Seizing the opportunity, Mrs. Bildmann tapped her on the shoulder. "Excuse me, but are you certain you do not want to send her?"

The mother nodded, tears rolling down her face. "I know I should, but I cannot bear it."

"Then please, let my son have your daughter's place."

The woman hurriedly removed the identity tag from her daughter and gave it to Mrs. Bildmann. "Here. The Firestone family, that is who she was supposed to stay with in London." And with that she rushed away in the crowd with her little daughter grasped firmly in her arms.

Mrs. Bildmann grabbed Erich's hand and ran toward the train with him. She attached the tag to him and handed him his suitcase and violin. Standing not far from them she noticed an older boy who was about to board the train with his brother, a boy about Erich's age. "Excuse me," she cried. "This...this is my son Erich...please look after him on the journey!"

"Of course," he replied, turning and smiling at Erich.

"Oh, thank you!" Then Mrs. Bildmann bent down to Erich. "Don't forget — the Firestone family in London. And write us your address as soon as you arrive."

"I will, Mutti."

The older boy held out a hand to Erich. "Come along, Erich. My name is Karl and this is Otto, my brother. Let's try to find seats at one of the windows so that we can wave to our parents."

The train chugged out of the station and the children watched from the windows as the forlorn group of parents left behind on the platform grew smaller and smaller. The smoke from the funnel enveloped them, making the scene appear unreal and dreamlike. This was how their childhoods would forever remain in their memories.

8

THE TRAIN DREW to a halt again, and in his half-sleeping state Kurt was sure he could hear someone saying "the border." Had they already reached Holland? Kurt had been oblivious to the entire journey across Germany. Lazily, he opened his eyes and instantly shrunk back into the corner of his seat — now fully awake — as a Nazi guard strode through the carriage in his direction. But he began by singling out a small, frail-looking boy wearing a pair of round steel-framed glasses. "Open your suitcase!" he barked. The frightened boy automatically began to do as instructed. He quickly stood on his seat and pulled down his suitcase from the luggage rack above his head.

"Hurry up!" the Nazi shouted, ignoring the difficulty the boy was having. He was trying to open the lock, but his small, trembling fingers would not do as commanded. Kurt saw the boy's fear and panic and went across the aisle to help him. But before he could offer his help, the guard gave him a rough push which sent him reeling and almost knocked him over. "Get back to your seat. Your turn will come in a moment!" he growled.

With a defiant look in his eyes, Kurt regained his balance and returned to his seat with dignity. He was from a great Nation, while this guard was descended only from a tribe of barbarians. He would get his just reward in the end.

One by one, suitcases were roughly opened and searched. When the guard came to Karl's seat, his suitcase was opened for inspection, and he tried to fight mounting fear: If his mother's ring were discovered, then not only he, but the whole trainload of Jewish children would be in danger of being sent back. He watched as the guard rummaged in his blue velvet *tefillin* bag and then tossed it over to one side like a sack of potatoes. The Nazi slid his rough hands beneath the folded layers of clothing. Karl shifted his head slightly and looked from the corner of his eyes, forcing himself to breathe evenly as his washing bag was opened. The Nazi seemed to be studying every item with great deliberation. Then he came to the soap box.

He carefully opened it and stared at the underside of the lid. Next, he lifted the bar of soap and looked underneath it, before turning the soap over a couple of times. Karl felt an immense surge of relief when the soap was put back and his belongings were handed back to him, all intact except for nine of his ten marks which were confiscated, as was every other child's on the train.

"You!" The guard snapped at Erich, pointing at his violin. "Can you play that thing?" Erich gave a fearful nod. "Then play for us. We've been working hard and could do with some entertainment." He chuckled at his own pathetic joke. All eyes were on Erich as he took the beautiful Stradivarius out of its case for the first time and placed it under his chin. He glanced across to Karl who, in the short time he had known him, had come to be his friend and protector, treating Erich with the same concern he gave his own brother Otto.

Karl gave him a look of encouragement and Erich lifted his bow and offered a silent *tefillah.* He glided his bow across the strings and immediately a hauntingly beautiful melody burst forth. For the duration of his piece, Erich was totally absorbed in his music, oblivious to everything and everyone around him. In his mind's eye he was back home with his parents, playing for them the way he used to do. It had been months since he had touched a violin, since the evening his father had been arrested. And now he was being forced to play for the very people who had taken his father away, burned his shul, and uprooted his life.

Erich was jolted back to the present and simultaneously ended his piece. His audience was silent as they stared at him for what seemed like eternity, until the guard broke out into applause. "Bravo! Bravo!" he cheered and gestured with his hands for everyone to follow suit. There was a hollow ring to their clapping and it came to an end almost before it began. The guard picked up the violin, which Erich had placed on the seat beside him, and examined it, making exclamations of approval as he did so.

Then something happened. Even years later, Erich would never understand whether or not it was done on purpose. The guard began to put the violin down again, but missed, hitting it on the top of the seat. There was a sickening crack as the neck splintered and broke away from the body of the instrument. Erich watched with a mixture of disbelief and horror as it fell to the floor and cracked further. He could not restrain the whimper which came unwillingly to his throat. "Sorry," the guard said without much sympathy. "But never mind, you can buy another when you get to England." And with that he did an about turn and left the train.

Erich crouched on the floor and cradled the remainder of his precious violin in his arms. His mother's special gift to him, and possibly his future...all that had been destroyed in a few callous moments.

Karl rose and put his arm around Erich, seeming to understand instinctively how the boy was feeling, without his having to say a word. Erich was too choked up to speak. He buried his head on the older boy's shoulder as the tears streamed down his face.

A whistle blew and in a cloud of smoke the train rushed across the border and into Holland. Cheers reverberated throughout the train. "We're free! We're free!" the children shouted. The tense atmosphere evaporated as the children began to jump up and down, climb over the seats, and crowd around the windows straining to catch their first glimpse of Holland.

Erich stood beside Karl and Otto and could not help but be

uplifted by everyone else's spirits. "Erich, we are free," Karl said with great feeling. "They will never be able to harm us again." Erich realized how fortunate he was to have had the opportunity to leave. He wiped his eyes. When it came down to it, what was the security of an expensive violin in comparison with the security of Hashem's protection? And no one could destroy that.

9

ENGLAND. The children began to stream toward the doors even before the train had drawn to a complete halt at the train station in London. The noise level was tremendous, with everyone trying to talk at once. Some were excited at the prospect of a new life in a new country, while others acted nonchalantly, trying to hide their fears.

Karl pulled his and Otto's suitcases off the overhead luggage rack, only to turn around and find Otto already at the other end of the carriage rushing toward the door. "Otto!" he gestured frantically and shouted above the din. "Come back! Wait for me!" Karl unlocked his suitcase. "Let me just check that we have everything and then we can go," he explained to his impatient brother.

"But why do you keep checking to make sure that your soap is still there? If your suitcase is closed, it can't get out!"

"You're right. I'm just being silly, I guess," Karl replied.

"In any case, I'm sure we can buy soap in England!"

"Yes," said Karl, smiling, "but not soap like this."

Karl and Otto stepped onto the platform of Liverpool Street Station. "So this is London," Karl murmured. And it was not cold or raining. In fact, it was a warm and rather humid day, and Karl felt a little conspicuous and self-conscious in his heavy woolen sweater with his winter coat over his arm. He consoled himself by imagining the beginnings of a humorous letter to his parents.

Studying his younger brother's face for signs of his reactions, he could not fathom his expression. He wondered what he was thinking, and whether or not to ask him. Otto had been unusually silent since they had left the Hook of Holland, the outer port of Rotterdam, and made their brief voyage on the SS *Aardoen* across the North Sea to Harwich, England. Afterwards, on the train to London, he had said not a word. Karl decided that Otto must simply be overwhelmed by all the new sights he had seen.

"Can you see Erich anywhere?" Karl asked him. They had somehow lost sight of him in the crowds.

"No, I can't."

"We must try to find him then. He can hardly speak a word of English. Come on, Otto." Karl picked up the two suitcases and Otto held his arm as they pushed through the throngs of children. "*Enschuldigen Sie bitte* — excuse us, please," he murmured, apologizing to them as they swept past. "Erich!" he called. "Erich!"

"Karl! Otto!" They heard someone shouting and turned around to find an excited Erich, hot, perspiring and out of breath. "I saw you in the distance, but couldn't catch your attention," he panted.

"We were looking for you, too, Erich, so that we could stay together until you meet your hosts."

"Thank you so much. You've been wonderful to me throughout the journey. I hope we keep in touch. You're the only people I know in London."

"We're all in the same boat! Let me just write down our new address for you, and we'll take yours as soon as you have it."

As Kurt stepped off the train he scrutinized the English families — called guarantors — who had gathered on the platform to catch the first glimpse of their new charges. He tried to imagine who was to be his. Not that he was too concerned. All he really wanted to do was go to bed and sleep. He had found the night crossing to Harwich difficult and had been very seasick. He still felt quite nauseated and his head spun as he tried to keep his balance.

The children were ushered into a dingy and lifeless room and told to sit down. Chairs had been set out and arranged in rows behind a rope barrier. On the other side of the room stood their prospective hosts, and between them was a long table where the *Kindertransporte* organizers sat. One of the organizers, a straight-backed woman in a woolen suit, was trying to get everyone's attention. She waved her hands in the air and asked for silence, telling the guarantors something in English which most of the new arrivals could not understand. Other organizers began handing out sandwiches, chocolate, and oranges to each of the children.

Otto watched the other children eagerly taking a bite of their food and started to unwrap his sandwiches, about to do the same, when he noticed that Karl had not touched his yet. "Why aren't you eating?" he asked.

"Sh-h," Karl said quietly, and put his finger to his lips indicating that Otto should whisper. "I'm not sure whether the sandwiches are kosher or not," he explained.

"Oh," Otto replied, crestfallen.

"Never mind. Let's eat our oranges in the meantime."

"Karl, what is the lady saying?" Erich asked.

"I think she was explaining that the guarantors must remain where they are until their names are called. Then they must go to the table where they will sign some papers, and then take their child."

Erich listened intently as the woman started to read what sounded to him like a babble of names. He repeated the name "Firestone" over and over in his mind so that he would recognize it when it was called. When he finally heard it, he was seized by a gripping fear. He rose, went up to the table, and watched the animated exchange which passed between Mr. and Mrs.

Firestone and the *Transporte* organizers.

In a single moment his hopes soared and then were dashed. The moment he saw Mr. and Mrs. Firestone, not only did he feel relieved, but decided that they were the most suitable couple in the entire room. Mrs. Firestone looked like a kind and gentle woman, and her eyes were full of compassion as she glanced at all the children around her. Mr. Firestone had a twinkle in his eyes, and Erich could imagine that he was a cheerful, easygoing person. From their gray hair, both must have been in their fifties — somewhat older than his own parents. They looked decent and kind and seemed filled with a zest for life.

Then Mrs. Firestone caught sight of Erich standing there, and she began to shake her head. The organizer asked her something to which she replied, but Erich could not understand a word of it. If the Firestones did not want him, what would become of him? Would they send him back to Germany? Erich felt his cheeks starting to burn and his heart beat wildly as he tried to catch his breath. The organizer indicated for Erich to return to his place.

He was engulfed in panic. "Karl!" he wailed.

Karl bolted from his chair and hurried to Erich's side. The lady appeared upset and said something sharply to Karl.

"What's happening?" Erich asked him. "Tell me!"

But Karl was listening to Mrs. Firestone, nodding as she spoke. "She says that they are supposed to be getting a little girl," Karl told him.

"Explain to her that the girl's mother backed out at the last minute and that I replaced her," Erich said breathlessly.

Mrs. Firestone nodded to Karl and showed signs of understanding. She relaxed and smiled again.

"What did she say?" Erich gasped.

"She says that she had no idea, but that it does not matter at all. You look like a very sweet boy, she says, and they would be happy to have you."

Erich bowed his head, trying to hide the tears that had suddenly filled his eyes. "Thank you," he said in English. They were about the only words he knew.

Mr. Firestone removed the tag from around Erich's neck. "You won't be needing that silly thing anymore," he said in a broken mixture of German and Yiddish, and Erich understood what he was trying to say.

"Mr. Firestone," Karl said, "could I please have your address? My brother and I would like to keep in touch with Erich."

"Certainly. It is good to have friends and familiar faces around when you come to a new country. Do come and visit us as soon as you have settled in."

"Now, please do go and sit down," the woman in charge insisted. "There has been enough disruption already." While walking back to his seat, Karl could not help thinking how fortunate Erich was with his new family. He was glad for him. At last Karl and Otto had each other; Erich had no one.

Mrs. Kilern smiled down sweetly at Kurt as she finished signing the papers. Kurt returned her smile tentatively. He was not sure what to make of her. She seemed a pleasant enough woman and had been delighted when she first caught sight of Kurt. Her constant exclamations in English could only have been positive. Yet there was something about her which troubled him, something which was not quite right. She was wearing a pretty dress and a wide-brimmed hat, not unlike one his mother sometimes wore. At first glance she appeared quite presentable, but when Kurt studied her more closely he noticed several things: straggly wisps of greasy hair were starting to fall down from where she had tucked them under her hat; the big gold brooch which she wore on her collar was badly chipped in several places; she was wearing bright rouge and it looked rather silly; and perhaps most important of all, her eyes did not change their expression when she smiled. Then again, Kurt was exhausted and not feeling too well either. Anyway, he reminded himself, this was England, not Austria. He could stop being so suspicious all the time.

Mrs. Kilern picked up Kurt's suitcase and made a comment at which both she and the organizer laughed. Then she beckoned for Kurt to follow as she breezed out of the reception area, still tittering at her own joke. Once outside, Kurt looked about for a car but Mrs. Kilern appeared to have every intention of walking. He hoped that it would not be too far, as his fatigue was about to overtake him. Kurt surveyed his new surroundings — the cars driving on the opposite side of the road, all the signs and posters in English, the unfamiliar-looking buildings. Yet at the same time he watched the route they took carefully. They had been walking for approximately five minutes when Mrs. Kilern stopped. Had they finally arrived at what was to be his home? But no. She put his suitcase down on the ground and held her hand on her lower back, letting out a slight moan before shrugging in a gesture of apology. Kurt now understood that she was trying to show him that she had a sore back from carrying his suitcase. He quickly picked it up, and, although it felt like a lead weight to his tired arms, he tried hard not to let it show and smiled faintly as she patted him on the head.

"Wake up," Mr. Firestone whispered gently. "We're here." Erich opened his eyes and looked around. He had been so tired that he had fallen asleep in the back of the car. "What you could do with is a good dinner followed by a warm bath and bed. Then, tomorrow, we could start showing you a bit of London if you feel up to it. Would you like that?" Mr. Firestone asked him, smiling.
"*Ya!*" Erich replied eagerly.
"Good!" Mr. Firestone beamed at him.

Karl and Otto looked at each other from opposite sides of the large oak table in the dining room. The usual sparkle in their eyes had turned to a penetrating somber gaze. A servant had taken their suitcases up to their room — which they had not yet seen — and a maid had set the table and brought them soup and a plate of chicken and hot vegetables to eat. It had been a long time since either of them had eaten chicken.
Mrs. Samson entered the room just as they were finishing. She didn't look as friendly as she had appeared to them earlier.

This time there were no smiles on her full face, and her ample cheeks seemed to droop with disapproval. "I am glad to see that you are both sitting up straight," she began. "One should never slouch at the table, sit with elbows perched, or touch the hair — very bad manners. A knife and fork should be held in the correct manner, food is to be chewed properly, and one must never speak with the mouth full or chew with the mouth open. Proper table manners are of the utmost importance, you know, and we expect you to observe them while you are here." Karl politely agreed, although he had not understood every word she said. "Now," she pronounced decisively, "if you are finished, Lillian will take you to your room where it will be straight to bed for both of you."

"Mrs. Samson," said Karl hesitantly, "I am really not that tired yet. It is still quite early."

"Young man! I think we should get one thing straight from the beginning," she replied firmly. "You are *my* responsibility while you are here, and as such, must abide by my — and my husband's — rules. Good night, Karl. Good night, Otto."

They followed Lillian, in her starched and pressed uniform, up to the second floor and down the hallway to the small, pastel-colored bedroom which they were to share. She drew the heavy drapes and bade them good night.

As soon as she had gone, Karl pulled back the drapes and looked down at the busy street below, the cars going past, and the people hurrying home from work. His heart ached for the peace and tranquillity he had known at his own home. The countryside, the slow pace of life, and most of all, his loving and easygoing parents. How far away they were!

"Karl, I don't like that lady very much." Otto was sitting on the edge of the bed nearest the window, his legs tucked up to his chin, and his arms wrapped around them.

"Why not?" Karl asked.

"She's mean."

"How do you know? You didn't even understand a single word she was saying."

"It was the way she said it."

"She's not mean. She's just proper."

"I don't think this is a very nice vacation. I don't like it here. I want to go home."

Karl sat himself down beside his brother. "We can't," he said softly.

"Why not?"

"Because...because we have only just come, and it...well, it wouldn't be polite to leave so soon after arriving." Karl mentally kicked himself for giving Otto such a weak excuse. But he could not bear to tell him the truth. Not now, not yet.

"When can we go home then?"

"Soon."

It was another fifteen minutes' walk until Kurt and Mrs. Kilern had reached her home. The streets gradually grew more narrow and crowded, and, in Kurt's mind, more threatening. A couple of drunks argued on a street corner, a scrawny dog went trotting by, raggedy children played ball in the street while a few others sat in a circle on the dirty sidewalk playing "jacks."

Mrs. Kilern yelled sharply at one of the children, and Kurt suddenly realized that the boy must be her son. She smiled at Kurt and pointed to a shabby building. This could not really be where they lived! Where he would live! But it was. Kurt was dumbstruck as he mechanically followed her up the iron staircase at the back of the tenement block.

Laundry hung on narrow balconies, and the sounds of raised voices and babies crying rose up to Kurt's ears. A sour smell penetrated the air.

Kurt automatically reached up to kiss the *mezuzah* on the door to the apartment before he entered — but there was no *mezuzah*. He did not have time to ponder, though, for as soon as the door was opened he was surrounded by children. There could not have been more than five or six of them, but in that first instant and with all that noise, it sounded like far more.

Kurt felt the suitcase being wrenched from his hands and

before he could do anything to prevent it, it was gone. He managed to force himself out of the circle and saw that his suitcase was now with Mrs. Kilern, who had placed it on a rickety table — the only table — in their three-room apartment, where she then proceeded to open it. Kurt's heart pounded as he watched her tip all his belongings onto the table and rummage through them, glancing at a photograph in his small family album and flicking through his *siddur,* which she held upside down. When she had finished, the swarm of children headed straight for the table. His possessions were scattered everywhere, as the children grabbed for various objects and fought with each other over the right of possession. Kurt felt powerless, and frozen to the spot. Besides, he did not know English. He tried telling them in German to stop, but no one paid any attention to him over the din. They may not even have heard him.

At last they were satisfied and ran off, leaving him to gather up what was left and put it back in his suitcase. Mrs. Kilern left the room and returned a few minutes later with a chipped cup filled with water and a plate with a few scraps of meat and three pieces of potato on it. Kurt downed the lukewarm water gratefully and sat down on a wobbly half-broken chair, utterly exhausted. He stared down at the unappetizing meal which had been placed before him. The meat looked a little strange and he wondered what type it was. It smelled a little peculiar too — perhaps it was not fresh? His mother had been very particular about such things.

He smelled it again, and did not want to believe the thought that suddenly occurred to him. It could not be! Wasn't this a Jewish family? But there was no doubt whatsoever. He had seen it in pictures, too — it had to be bacon. Kurt was filled with horror as he looked at his plate, and then around the room at the peeling gray walls, broken furniture, torn net curtains, and small window overlooking yet more tenement blocks. Making sure that no one was looking, he opened the window a crack and tipped the contents of his plate out of it.

What kind of place had he come to?

10

THE FLAT WAS mercifully quiet now except for the loud snoring of Mr. Kilern. He had stormed in earlier that evening, ranting and raving in a drunken stupor, and had headed straight for the kitchen where Kurt had been set to work washing the dishes which had piled high in the sink. From the state of the hardened food on the plates, Kurt could only wonder for how many days they had been left lying there.

When Mr. Kilern had caught sight of Kurt in the kitchen, he started saying something to him, but since Kurt had no idea what he was saying or what to say in return, he decided it was best to keep silent. The man said something again. Again, Kurt remained silent and continued to wash the dishes. A fist came down hard on the sink counter, causing Kurt to jump. Mr. Kilern, his red face turning a shade of purple, bellowed at him.

At that moment, Mrs. Kilern ran into the kitchen and began to yell at her husband. He shouted back, and then, grabbing the cup Kurt was washing, hurled it at her. It hit the wall and fell to the floor with a loud smash. Mrs. Kilern picked up a plate, her eyes flashing with anger. Kurt fled from the kitchen, not wanting to see the outcome.

In the dining room (which was also the living room and bedroom) the baby sat on the floor under the table screaming, his face smeared with the food he had eaten at supper. His little blue suit looked almost black with dirt, but no one paid any attention to him. The toddler — a little girl — and her two older brothers, who were about four and six, cowered in the corner behind the threadbare couch, the only piece of living-room furniture there was. A girl of about nine sat on the couch with a boy around Kurt's age, having their own private quarrel, while the oldest, a boy of about twelve, with greasy fair hair and menacingly bloodshot pale eyes, sat on a chair with his feet propped up on the rickety table, carving a piece of wood with his penknife. He was clearly unmoved by all the tumult. He gave Kurt a passing glance as he ran in from the kitchen, and eyed Kurt's well-made trousers, smart white shirt and firm brown closed sandals, no doubt comparing them to his own ragged pair of shorts and grubby shirt. Kurt did his best to ignore the boy, whom he had noticed several times that day staring at him menacingly.

It was several more hours until things quieted down and Kurt was given a bed of sorts to sleep in: a couple of blankets covered by a holy, faded sheet to serve as a mattress, and an itchy blanket to cover himself with. His one consolation, he thought to himself as he lay awake and alone in the kitchen, was that he did not have to share a bed, like almost all the other children who were bedded down in the next room.

Kurt sighed and propped himself up on one elbow. How had all this happened? he wondered. Perhaps it was simply a terrible mistake. Maybe things would be better in the morning, when he would not feel so tired. He lay down and closed his eyes, still feeling as if he were in motion on the boat. He murmured the *Shema* and fell asleep.

Karl reached out and rang the doorbell under the name "Firestone." Then he and Otto saw the *mezuzah* above the doorbell and hastily kissed it. The front door was opened, and the boys were greeted with a beaming smile, dissolving all Karl's fears and Mrs. Samson's disapproval of turning up at someone's house — especially someone whom he hardly knew — without a prior invitation.

"What a lovely surprise!" exclaimed Mr. Firestone. "Please come in. Erich will be so happy to see you. Erich! Visitors!" he called. Then, turning to Karl and Otto once more, he asked, "How are you settling down here in London?"

Karl made a face and shrugged. Otto looked down at the floor and said nothing.

"It is only natural to find matters difficult in the beginning," Mr. Firestone said soothingly. "These things take time. Are you familiar with our Sages' saying: 'All beginnings are difficult'?"

"*Kol haschalos kashos*," replied the boys in unison, repeating the statement in Hebrew.

"Karl! Otto!" Erich shouted as he bounced down the stairs. Mr. Firestone patted him on the head. "Go on into the living room, Erich. I'm sure you and your friends have a great deal to talk about. Mrs. Firestone will be along in a minute with some tea for you all."

The living room was small but neat and homey, furnished with a blue sofa and two matching armchairs which faced the fireplace. In the center of the room was a faded carpet, on which stood a low wooden table which held a bowl of fruit. A bookshelf filled with *sefarim* stretched the length of one wall, and another shelf held silver objects that reminded the boys of home: Shabbos candlesticks, a *Kiddush* cup, and a spice box for *Havdalah*. A lace curtain hung over the French doors which opened out onto the tiny garden of the small terraced house.

The Firestones' home radiated a warmth which was clearly lacking in the clinical atmosphere of the Samsons' antique, painting-filled, museum-like townhouse just a few stops away on the bus.

"Isn't the garden pretty?" Erich asked Karl, as he noticed him staring out of the window. "I think it's lovely to live in a house with a garden. Before this I only lived in an apartment. How about you?"

"We lived in a house," Karl replied quietly.

"With a garden?"

Karl nodded, and suddenly before his eyes swam the memory

of their own garden, of the large stretches of land surrounding his house, of the fields and the orchards...

"Oh!" Erich interrupted his reverie. "My father told me that in Curaçao we would have a house and a garden with tropical plants and palm trees. I wonder if I will ever get there now..."

"Why shouldn't you?" Otto asked.

"My father was taken away." The words hung in the air, threatening and strange in the cozy English living room.

"Taken away?" Otto gasped. "How? Why?"

"He..." Erich was having difficulty trying to find the words to explain what had happened that night. He still found it hard to talk about, and occasionally suffered from nightmares.

Karl put his hand on Otto's arm. "We shouldn't ask about such things," he said gently. "Erich, don't worry. I understand."

Otto looked from one to the other, feeling confused. What had he said that was so wrong? Ever since they had left Germany, Karl had been acting strangely. He had become so serious. It was not that he never smiled or laughed, but he no longer participated in his games or had play-fights with him. Then again, Mrs. Samson would not have stood for it. If they so much as raised their voices they were subjected to a raised eyebrow and comment such as: "There is no need to shout. One can be heard just as well in a lower tone of voice." And then she would walk away without giving them a chance to reply.

Otto disliked her more every day. She had not actually been unkind to him, but had never shown him any sympathy or understanding either. The night before, he had been feeling homesick and did not want to eat dinner.

"Why haven't you eaten anything?" Mrs. Samson had asked, seeing his untouched plate when she came in to tell them that it was time for bed. Karl acted as translator. Otto simply shrugged his shoulders. "When I ask you a question, I expect an answer," she said.

"I miss Papa and Mutti," Otto whispered to Karl, on the verge of tears.

"Pull yourself together! Most Jewish children in Europe

would love to be in your position.''

Otto felt himself to be anything but fortunate, especially listening to Erich tell them how, for the past two days, Mr. and Mrs. Firestone had taken him on trips to see Buckingham Palace and the tower of London, and had taken him on a boat ride on the Thames. Karl and Otto, in those first two days, were forced to spend the morning studying English, and in the afternoon they were taken for a brisk walk, by Lillian, through the local park, which might have been fun except that she said they were not to play on the swings. Upon their return they were allowed to play quietly until six o'clock, when they ate dinner and were sent to bed. And this was supposed to be a vacation.

"Well, Erich, we must be going now," Karl said regretfully.

"Already?" Erich asked. "Why so soon?"

"Mrs. Samson told us to be home by five-thirty."

"She sounds like a witch."

Otto smiled, but Karl replied, "She isn't really. She is firm, but fair."

"What's Mr. Samson like?"

"We've only met him once. He leaves early for work and usually returns late at night. He seems pleasant enough, though."

Kurt weakly lifted another plate and gave it a half-hearted wipe before stacking it in the cupboard above the sink. He looked at the blackened walls, thinking of his own spotless kitchen back home. How long ago had that been? Kurt found that he began to lose track of time. He had not been with the Kilerns more than a few days but it felt like forever. He felt that he was surviving, not living, each day, and began to imagine how the slaves must have felt serving under Pharaoh in Egypt. He still had pain and swelling in his right arm, where Mr. Kilern had struck him the night before.

It had not been Kurt's fault. He had had another tough day of working for Mrs. Kilern, scrubbing the laundry over the bathtub and wringing it out. While waiting for it to dry on the line strung across the tiny balcony, he had swept the floor of the apartment and peeled a bucket of half-rotten potatoes. By that time, the laundry was ready to be ironed and examined by Mrs. Kilern, who pointed with her stubby forefinger at any stains and indicated with sign language what would have to be done over again.

Kurt had hardly stopped for a moment, not even for lunch. Not that he could have eaten much anyway. For the three days he had been there, he had subsisted on water and a few raw vegetables from the kitchen, which he ate at night.

Finally, Kurt was mercifully allowed to take to his bed on the kitchen floor. His aching bones practically collapsed onto it, and immediately he whispered the *Shema* and was asleep. Not long afterwards, however, Mr. Kilern announced his arrival with a heavy slam of the front door which awakened Kurt with a start.

"Why ain't there nothin' on the table to eat when I come in?" he bellowed at anyone who would care to listen. Mrs. Kilern bustled into the kitchen to heat up Mr. Kilern's supper for the third time that evening. Then she hurried into the living room with it.

"I'm not eatin' that!" Mr. Kilern roared, and smashed his plate down hard on the already-rickety table. Kurt buried himself even deeper under the rough blanket in an attempt to block out the sounds from the other room and the pervasive smell of beer, but for the next hour he was forced to listen to the ensuing shouting match.

When the apartment was at last silent, Kurt was unable to fall asleep again. He tossed and turned, though he found even that an effort. He was weak from lack of food, lack of sleep, and physical strain. He lay on his side, his head resting on the hook of his arm, trying to cheer himself up by thinking of happy memories such as the Mozart concert in the Wiener Statdsoper that his grandmother had taken him to for his sixth birthday...when suddenly he heard the sound of scraping not far from his blanket. He lifted his head to see where it was coming from, and stared with horror as a large gray rat went scuttering by, right beside him. Kurt involuntarily let out a cry and the rat disappeared behind a cupboard.

Mr. Kilern suddenly burst into the kitchen, and started to shake Kurt with a vehemence. "What's got into you? What d'ya mean by disturbin' my sleep?" he yelled. Kurt stared at him, wide-eyed with terror and shock. Mr. Kilern sent his fist flying against Kurt's upper arm, and knocked him back onto his makeshift bed. Kurt was crying in agony. "I don't like the way you look at me," Mr. Kilern said hoarsely, and stormed out of the room.

The next afternoon Kurt began to wonder how much more he could take. Thankfully, Mrs. Kilern had retired to her room for a while while the baby was napping and all the other children except for the oldest boy were out playing. Kurt thought that he might actually have an opportunity to rest himself. If only his parents would write and give him a contact address. Then someone could come and rescue him.

Kurt wandered into the living room, ready to collapse onto the sofa and possibly flip through his little photograph album, which always gave him a feeling of comfort. He was thus surprised and taken aback to find Mrs. Kilern's son crouching beside his now open suitcase and rummaging through his things. Kurt stood staring down at him until the boy looked up.

If he had been startled, he did not show it, but gave Kurt a cold look and continued to go through his belongings. He picked up Kurt's *siddur*, and Kurt felt rising panic. He held his arm out to the boy to indicate that he wanted it back. The boy looked at him and then back at the *siddur*, which he pulled closer toward himself, pretending great interest in the pages. Kurt tried to pull it out of his hands, but he was too quick for Kurt and snatched it away.

"*Bitte*," Kurt said. He could not remember the word "please."

"*Bitter, bitter!*" the boy mimicked, laughing at him. Prancing around the room, he waved the precious *siddur* high above his head in an attempt to tease and provoke, chanting, "*Bitter!* *bitter!*" Kurt lunged at him. The boy dodged and changed direction.

Kurt felt dizzy and light-headed and he tripped over the chair. The boy howled with laughter and dangled the *siddur* under his nose. Kurt reached out for it and managed to grab the boy's arm. While he tried to retrieve the *siddur* the boy wrenched his arm free and tossed the *siddur* across the room. Kurt gave a cry of rage, picked himself up and darted over to where it lay. The boy grabbed his foot, sending him flying to the floor. Then he pinned him down so that Kurt could not move. Kurt struggled and kicked, trying to break free of his grasp.

"What's goin' on in 'ere?" Mrs. Kilern shouted as she entered the room.

"'E started it, Mum," the boy whined and quickly stood up. Kurt also rose to his feet and darted across the room. He gently picked up the *siddur* and kissed it lovingly, glaring hatefully at the boy.

"Did 'e now?" Mrs. Kilern glared angrily at Kurt, "'E's a right vicious one, ain't 'e? Think I ought to teach 'im a lesson or two. Go on, get out to play."

The boy smirked at Kurt and then ran out the door without waiting to see his reaction.

Mrs. Kilern grabbed Kurt by the waist and hauled him across the room. "There'll be no supper for you for a start." Kurt cowered in the corner, trembling with fear. A terrible thought crossed his mind: If Mrs. Kilern was so angry with him, what would happen when Mr. Kilern arrived home?

Kurt was hard at work scrubbing the kitchen floor when he returned. He no longer knew where his energy was coming from. Mr. Kilern kicked him aside when he entered the kitchen, but then walked out again. Kurt could have almost let out a sigh of relief.

Fortunately, the nightly argument did not last too long and they were soon all asleep. If he wanted to act, now was his chance.

The idea had been at the back of his mind since his arrival at the Kilerns'. Now he was determined to carry it out.

Carefully, he picked up his way between the sleeping children and found his suitcase. He checked to make sure that his *siddur* was back inside, and quietly locked it up, fastening the catches. The eldest boy turned around and muttered something. Kurt remained motionless and hardly dared to breathe until he was satisfied that he had not awakened.

Cautiously, Kurt opened the door, turned around to ensure that no one had seen him, and closed it slowly behind him, trying not to let it creak or bang shut.

He held onto the railing and began to make his way down the staircase. Then his sandal slipped and he missed a step and almost lost his footing. The iron railing seemed to vibrate as he grabbed it to keep himself from falling, and Kurt was sure he had disturbed the whole tenement block. He steadied himself and continued down the stairs into the blackened streets. He had not been out of the Kilerns' apartment once since he first came, and had barely had any fresh air.

As lonely and afraid as Kurt was, he knew that he was not turning back. He could not stay with the Kilerns any longer. He came to the corner and wondered which way to turn. No direction seemed better than any other. He turned right. "Please Hashem, protect me," he silently prayed. His footsteps echoed on the deserted pavements, and his mind went back to that evening many months ago when he had been chased through the back streets and alleyways of Vienna. Then he'd known where he wanted to get to: home. Now he was on the run with no destination at all.

It was starting to get light when Kurt saw funnels of boats or ships in the distance, shrouded in the early dawn's mist.

He quickened his pace. If there were boats, there must be water, he thought. A crazy idea began to form in his mind. He would smuggle himself onto one of them and somehow make his way back to Vienna and find his parents.

Kurt's legs buckled beneath him and he blacked out.

11

"CAN YOU BELIEVE, Josh, that there's only one more week of summer vacation, and then it's back to school?" Miles asked his friend Joshua, who was gentiy rowing their small boat around the lake at Regent's Park on a perfect sunny afternoon.

"It always goes by too quickly," Joshua replied. "But there may not be any school — I heard someone talking to my dad and saying that war was going to break out very soon."

"Well, that's okay if it means they'll slosh that Hitler. He's a terrible fellow. I've heard talk, too — and I suppose that means that we'll be evacuated from London."

Joshua nodded. "My mum's terrified at the thought. She's heard it's estimated that a quarter of a million people could be killed in bombings, in London alone, in the first few weeks of war. It is a very frightening prospect. And then there's Daniel, who's almost eighteen. He could be called up."

"Your brother a soldier? I can't imagine that...say, did you hear that Marcus and his family may be going to stay with his grandparents in Canada for the duration?"

"No, but I met Saul yesterday, and he told me his mum doesn't want him to be evacuated." Miles brushed his sandy hair away from his face. "Do you know what that means?" he asked Joshua, looking at him seriously with his sky-blue eyes.

Joshua stopped rowing for a minute and the rowboat floated on the calm lake. "No — what?"

"We'll be the only two Jewish children going from our class."

"Hey, I hadn't thought of that. Well, if we're evacuated we'll just have to stay together and stick it out. They say it'll be over by the end of 1939, anyway, and that's not too far away. Speaking of which, tell me about that German boy who's staying with you."

Miles' face grew serious. "Actually, we think he might be Austrian. The labels in his clothes are...the whole business is very curious. We haven't been able to find out anything about him yet. Not even his name! A dock worker simply found him lying unconscious near the docks, and carried him to my father's clinic. My dad said he was in a state of extreme malnutrition and had a fractured arm too. He's slowly improving, but he's still very weak."

"Can't you ask him about himself?"

"Well, that's the problem. All he does is sit and stare into space all day long. He won't say a word."

"But if he's Austrian, he probably doesn't understand any English."

"Yes, we know that, but there's more to it than that. You see, a boy his age — our age — would have learned a little English in school. My father spoke to him very slowly and explained that his name was Doctor Benjamin. 'What is your name?' he asked, but the boy didn't reply. 'This is my son, Miles,' my dad said. 'Miles Benjamin.' Then my father told me to repeat who I was, so I said, 'My name is Miles Benjamin. What's your name?' He knew we were talking to him, but all he did was stare at us. That's basically all he does when we come into his room. And now that he's able to feed himself, he won't even eat until we've left him alone. One day last week when my mother took some of his clothes to wash she found potatoes and bread in the pockets. And whenever I go into his room, he suspiciously watches everything I do. I get the strangest feeling that for some reason he doesn't trust me."

"That is weird."

"Yes. And we think he's Jewish. There was a *siddur* among his things. My father thinks he might be one of those Jewish children who came on the trains from Germany and Austria, like the one my cousins had staying with them until a couple of days ago. The one whose parents were lucky enough to be able to follow him shortly afterwards."

"Yes, I remember him. But he wasn't strange at all. He was very friendly."

"Well, we don't know what's made this one like this. Anyway, that's what my father thinks. But of course he can't find out for certain, because he doesn't even have a name to ask about. The one thing none of us understands, though, is that if he was one of those transport children, how come he was found down near the docks, and why was he so ill?"

"Time for bed, Otto," Mrs. Samson said in English. Otto had heard that phrase so often that by now he knew exactly what it meant. Karl stood up, ready to leave the table and follow him, but Mrs. Samson motioned for him to sit down again. "Karl, I would like to have a word with you before you go to bed," she said. Karl racked his brains trying to think what he might have done wrong that day: "I made my bed, cleaned my shoes, studied English, went for a walk..." he mentally ticked off on an imaginary checklist.

A few minutes later, Mrs. Samson sat down at the table across from Karl. "Karl, as you know, I have enrolled Otto in the local primary school which resumes again this Friday."

"Yes," Karl replied.

"But we have still not fixed anything up for you. Have you thought about it at all?"

"I assumed I would also be going to school."

"No, I'm afraid not. Most children finish their schooling here at fourteen or fifteen."

"Oh, I see," Karl said dejectedly. He hadn't thought of that.

"A few do stay on to take their matriculation examinations, but as you can imagine, the expenses are quite high and our resources at present..." She looked away.

"I understand," Karl replied quietly.

"Had you thought at all about looking for work?"

"No — I didn't expect..."

"I understand. Well, Mr. Samson says that he could offer you a job as a filing clerk in his company. How does that sound to you?"

"It...sounds fine," Karl replied slowly. What else could he say? He did not really have a choice.

"Good," Mrs. Samson said, clapping her manicured hands together. "Then that's settled. When Mr. Samson comes home tonight, he can discuss the conditions and wages with you and then we can set about finding you a room."

"A room?" Karl echoed, puzzled.

"Certainly," she replied matter-of-factly. "You need to have a roof over your head."

"But...I thought I was living here."

Mrs. Samson smiled patronizingly at him. "Yes, but as you know, there is probably soon going to be war between England and Germany."

"Yes," Karl replied, frowning, not understanding the connection.

"If and when war is declared, my husband and I are going to leave London for the duration to live with my sister in the country. Since we will be shutting our home, and our servants will be leaving, there would not be anyone left to look after you."

"What about Otto?" Karl felt a tightness in his chest.

"Otto, of course, will be evacuated with the school."

"What do you mean 'evacuated with the school'?" Karl asked, rising from his seat, unable to control his worry.

"Exactly what I said," Mrs. Samson replied. "The whole school will be evacuated to the countryside."

"But where will they be?"

"The location will be kept a secret, for security reasons, until they arrive."

"Don't *you* know?"

"No — I told you, no one does."

"But he'll be all alone!"

"No, he'll be with the whole school."

"But he doesn't know anyone there!"

"I believe your friend Erich is starting there too, and will in fact be in your brother's class."

"But neither of them speaks a word of English!"

"They will learn."

"They won't understand anything that is going on, and Otto has already found it very harrowing and frightening leaving our parents and home in the first place." Karl's usual facade of self-control was shattering. "I can't let him be separated from me now!"

"He will be just fine," Mrs. Samson said. "In fact, if you don't mind my saying so, he would probably cope a lot better with the new situation if you did not molly-coddle him so much anyway. Don't treat him so softly. He needs a little toughening up."

"But he's my brother, and he's only a child. I...I promised my parents I'd take care of him. Of course I am going to 'treat him softly.' He needs it more than ever right now." Karl looked at Mrs. Samson with firm resolve on his young face. "I am sorry, but I cannot let him go."

"You have no choice in the matter, Karl. You were sent to me by your parents, and now you are my responsibility. I am dealing with the situation in the manner which I believe is best for you and your brother."

"But I promised my parents I would take care of him!" Karl cried.

"How dare you raise your voice when you speak to me! And please sit down!"

"I will not sit down until we have sorted this out," Karl said in a steadier voice. His father had always warned him about his quick temper. He could suddenly hear his father's voice teaching him *Mishlei*: "One who controls his anger is better than a strong man..." Now Karl had let his anxiety turn to anger and get the better of him.

Mrs. Samson was taken aback by his words and his tone. "I beg your pardon?" she said, a flush appearing on her round cheeks. "If that is the thanks I get for all I have done for you, then you can forget about your job, or any help in finding new accommodations."

"I must go with Otto, Mrs. Samson."

"You can't."

"Why not?"

"They are only evacuating children up to the age of fifteen. You are sixteen. You are too old."

"I will take Otto to the school on Friday and speak to the headmaster about it myself."

"Speak to whomever you like, but when Otto is evacuated, you will no longer be welcome here."

Kurt put on the gray shorts and freshly ironed white shirt which had been laid at the foot of his bed. He was picking up his gas mask in its little box in order to examine it, when there was a knock at the door. Miles was most surprised when Kurt came to the door to open it himself.

"Good morning — I am glad to see that you are ready," Miles said to him slowly, pronouncing each word carefully so that Kurt might understand him more easily. "Today school resumes after the summer holidays and you are to come with me. To school," Miles repeated, and then added, "I do wish you would tell me your name, you know. I won't know what to tell the teachers to call you."

"Kurt."

"Come down and have something to eat," Miles went on, miming the actions to reinforce what he meant. "And when Joshua arrives we can all walk together." Miles beckoned for Kurt to follow him down the stairs, and midway down, he suddenly paused and turned around. "You just spoke to me! You told me your name," Miles said, the awareness suddenly hitting him. "Your name is Kurt?"

Kurt nodded vigorously.

"That's great!" Miles exclaimed.

It was the first word Kurt had spoken.

"This must be the school," Karl said to Otto and Erich as they approached a two-storey red bricked building surrounded by a high wall. However, no one was in the playground, and there were no sounds coming from the building at all, which was rather peculiar. Karl checked his watch and discovered they were almost ten minutes late. "That's why no one's out here," he said. "Come on, hurry up. I'll take you to your classroom and then I'll go and speak to the principal."

Karl and the two younger boys wandered up and down the silent, polished corridors and poked their heads around a few of the classroom doors — all of which seemed deserted. Finally, an elderly lady in a dark suit, her gray hair drawn back in a bun at the back of her head, caught sight of them and immediately made her way over to them. She stared down at Otto and Erich through her half-moon glasses.

"You two should be in assembly," she informed them. Then she glanced at Karl with a questioning look on her face.

"I am accompanying them," he explained, "This is their first day here and they do not speak English."

"Oh yes, the two German boys. There's another one from your part of the world in the same class, who is also starting today," she said, "and you may be interested—"

But Karl was impatient. "Where should I take them?"

"Into the main hall. The headmaster has already begun the assembly. It is a very important one, so perhaps you should go in with them if they do not understand English. You can translate for them. I will just show you where it is." Then she smiled. "They may not speak English, but they look like proper English schoolboys with their schoolbags...and their gas masks," she added. "Let's hope they'll never need to use them."

The three boys slipped in unnoticed to the back of the auditorium in time to hear the headmaster — who was dressed in a long black gown and what Karl called 'a professor's cap' — greet the children, who were all standing in his honor. He told them to take their seats, and then he held up his hand and indicated that they should stop talking, for they had begun to chat with each other as soon as they sat down.

"I trust you have all had a good summer holiday?" he asked, not really expecting a reply. The headmaster strolled across the stage in front of the table at which the other heads of staff were seated. They all wore gowns like the headmaster, and they all, Karl noted, wore the same grave expression. "Children, this is not a normal opening-year assembly," he announced somewhat dramatically. "What I have to say is extremely important and I want you all to listen very carefully. I am sure that some of you have heard that it is probable that war will be declared in the next few days. For this reason we are going to be evacuating London *today* for the countryside. There you shall be safe and away from the threat of bombings." The children began to cheer loudly. "Now, your parents have all received letters regarding the evacuation — although we didn't know exactly when it would place — and you should each have your suitcase packed and ready. Please go home to fetch them immediately and we will meet back here one hour from now. We will not wait for anyone who is late, so please make sure that you are back on time. This is very urgent. You are dismissed." The children charged out of the hall, still cheering and excited. "We're going to the countryside! We're going to the countryside!"

Karl stood up slowly, in partial shock. He was emotionally unprepared for this announcement to come so soon. "What's going on?" Otto asked him, perplexed. Karl raised his finger to show he needed a minute to think. He would have to act quickly. "Otto," he said, "I have to go and see the headmaster. Erich, do you think you could take Otto home for me?"

"Yes, of course," Erich agreed eagerly.

"Otto, I want you to listen carefully: when you get back to the Samsons' house, I want you to say the word *evacuation* to Mrs. Samson. Will you remember that word?" Otto nodded. "Good boy. Then you must take our two suitcases and pack all our belongings into them."

"Even our clothes?"

"Yes, everything."

"Are we going home?" Otto asked hopefully, beginning to jump with excitement.

"No, not exactly. But we are going away. Go as quickly as you can and I will meet you back there. And thank you, Erich."

Karl approached the nearest boy and tapped him on the shoulder. "Could you please direct me to the headmaster's office?"

"What can I do for you?" The headmaster asked, leaning forward in his chair, his hands clasped together in front of him. Without the black cap and gown, the headmaster looked like a kindly gray-haired grandfather.

"My name is Karl Alexander. I am the brother of Otto Alexander, who began at your school today."

"Ah, yes, one of the German Jewish boys," he murmured. "Terrible things are happening over there...terrible things..." Karl was afraid the headmaster would become lost in his own musings, but he merely sat up straighter in his chair and sighed. "Is he ready for the evacuation?"

Karl took a deep breath. "Yes, he is ready. I have come to ask your permission to be evacuated with my brother."

The headmaster raised his bushy eyebrows. "And how old are you, Karl?"

"I recently turned sixteen."

"I'm afraid we are only evacuating up until the age of fifteen."

"I know, but my circumstances are somewhat different. You see, neither my brother nor our friend Erich Bildmann, who also joined today, speak any English. Furthermore, my brother has found the experience of leaving our parents behind in Germany quite unsettling, and I don't want him to be parted from his family — from me, that is — again. My request is irregular, but please — say that you will make an exception and agree."

The headmaster removed his glasses and rubbed his eyes. He

withdrew a handkerchief from his pocket and blew his nose. He nodded at Karl, and then turned to his secretary. "Mrs. Hulbert, please fill out the appropriate evacuation papers for this young man. He will be joining us."

Kurt glared at his suitcase which Mrs. Benjamin had handed to him, gesturing that she wanted him to pack. As soon as she left the room he began angrily throwing everything into his suitcase. He had begun to believe that perhaps, with this family, things were finally going to be all right. Well, how wrong he had been. Now he was being told to pack! He slammed down the lid.

"Now, Erich, do you have everything? Your *siddur*? Your sandwiches?" Mr. Firestone asked sadly.

"Yes, I think so," Erich replied.

"We are going to miss you, you know. We want that to be clear to you. Hopefully, this move will not be for long, but I don't think it would be fair — or safe — to keep you in London if there is going to be bombing, God forbid. As soon as it's all over, we will be more than delighted to have you back."

Mrs. Firestone appeared from the kitchen and handed Erich a paper bag filled with freshly baked cookies. "I made these especially for you to have on the journey, Erich. Share them with your friends. I hope to see you back very soon." Her eyes began to water. "Oh dear," she said, sniffing, "I must have gotten some flour in my eyes. Have a good trip, and let us know as soon as you can what your new address is."

"Yes, I will. Thank you both so much for having me and for taking care of me so well. When I see my parents again I'll tell them how good you've been to me."

"It's been our pleasure. Are you all set then?" Mr. Firestone asked.

"Yes."

"All right, let's go. I'll drive you back to the school."

Karl raced up the three steps and rang the bell. Out of breath, he leaned against the door, perspiration pouring down his face. He had run all the way back to the Samsons. To his surprise, it was Mrs. Samson herself who opened the door. "Did you get permission?" she asked.

"Yes," he panted, surprised at her personal interest.

"I am glad."

"Where's Otto?"

"He is upstairs."

Karl flew up the stairs two at a time, and entered their room to find Otto sitting on his bed, head bent down, engrossed in a picture book.

"Otto!" he shouted. "What about the packing?"

"Oh, it's all done. Mrs. Samson helped me."

"What? Mrs. Samson? I don't believe it." Karl shook his head in amazement.

"It's true," Otto said. "She did."

"Is the book yours?" Karl asked.

"No."

"Then leave it. We must rush. We have to be back at school in fifteen minutes."

When they came down the stairs, Mrs. Samson was waiting by the door for them, holding two small packages in her hands.

Karl cleared his throat. "Otto told me you helped him with the packing, Mrs. Samson. I very much appreciate it."

Mrs. Samson nodded her head in acknowledgment. "I've packed you some lunch. You will find some sandwiches, cake and an apple for each of you."

"Thank you very much," Karl said. "We...we had better be off now. We're running a little late. Thank you very much for everything."

"We are happy to have been able to help."

Karl hesitated for a moment. "Yes, well...uh...goodbye." He picked up the two suitcases and started off down the front steps with Otto.

"Karl!" Mrs. Samson called after him. Karl turned around. "Good luck to you two!"

12

ONCE AGAIN all the children were assembled in the large hall, where the headmaster gave last-minute instructions, and checked to make sure that all the children had remembered to bring their gas masks. Two teachers handed out numbered tags attached to a piece of string, which each child was told to put around his neck. Heads were counted, and recounted, and they were all told to line up with their classes. While this was taking place, the children grew restless and became extremely noisy; this caused the already nervous teachers to become even more agitated, and the noise level rose considerably. Karl, Otto and Erich stood apart from the noisy crowd, speaking German, the two younger boys asking questions, and Karl answering and explaining as well as he could.

"Silence, please!" the headmaster shouted over the din. "Two chartered buses are now parked outside the school waiting to take you to Liverpool Street Station, from where you will all board trains which will take you to your destination. Make sure you look after your property at all times, and do not leave anything behind. Hold on to your gas mask boxes tightly. Listen to the teachers in charge of you, and — above all — behave properly. Especially on the train, and when you get to your new quarters, you must set a good example for the school. Hopefully, the next time we meet, we shall have won the war and defeated Hitler. You are all to leave the hall in an orderly fashion, and in a straight single file line.''

The children cheered as they raced out of the hall in an effort to be the first to board the buses.

Liverpool Street Station was teeming with hundreds of children from countless other schools, all of whom were going through the same routine. The pupils of each school followed the teacher in charge, who held a banner proclaiming the name of the school. Officials organizing the evacuation made their way through the crowds of people, directing each school to the correct platform, where parents were lined up waiting to say their last good-byes to their children, and anxiously wondering when they would next meet.

Some parents decided at the last moment not to send their children out of London. Many of the children were crying, frightened and overwhelmed by what was happening. There was a lot of laughter and high spirits as well, for a great many of the children saw it as an adventure, and a novel way to disrupt school. The harried teachers urged the children to keep together and follow all instructions.

Karl stood watching the crowd: the crying parents and the trains waiting to take the children away were a painful echo of how they had left Berlin, and he bit his lip trying to remain strong and keep up appearances for his brother.

As the train chugged out of the station, leaving behind the parents to fight a non-combatant war in their homes, Karl felt a gnawing fear in the pit of his stomach. The frightening reality — that he and Otto were really on their own — finally confronted him. Until then, they had been under the responsibility of a family to whom their parents had sent them. Now they faced an uncertain future in an unknown place for the duration of the war.

Karl rested his head on the back of the seat and closed his eyes. Something his father had taught him from the Talmud sprung to mind now. If one has food enough for one day, and he worries about what will happen on the morrow, he is lacking *bitachon*, his father said. Karl found his own situation to be a parallel with that *dvar Torah*, and realizing that set his mind at ease. Who but Hashem knew what the future held in store for them? And in that case, how could one worry if one knew nothing yet? "But still," Karl murmured to himself in German, "I hope we arrive at our destination in time for Shabbos." It was already past noon.

A fair-haired boy sitting across the aisle suddenly tapped Karl on the shoulder. "Excuse me," he said politely. "Do you speak English?"

"Yes, I do."

"I could not help overhearing you just now when you were talking to yourself in German. Did you just say the word *Shabbos*?"

"Yes, I did," Karl replied, studying the boy. "Are you Jewish, by any chance?"

The boy beamed. "Yes, I am." He held out his hand to Karl. "My name is Miles Benjamin."

Karl leaned across the aisle and shook his hand warmly. "I am Karl Alexander, and this is my brother Otto, and a friend of ours, Erich Bildmann." He gestured toward the two boys who sat beside him. "Unfortunately, they do not speak much English."

Miles smiled over at the two younger boys. "Hello," he said, and then turned back to Karl. "This is my friend Joshua King. And this is Kurt — he has been staying with us for a few days. I believe he comes from Austria, but he doesn't speak any English either, so we haven't been able to find out much about him."

"Oh!" Karl exclaimed, sitting up straighter and peering at Kurt, who sat staring straight ahead, stony-faced. "I remember seeing him on our train. Perhaps I can help. I could speak to him in German."

Miles and Joshua clapped their hands with excitement. "Please do! We want to be able to help him!"

Karl leaned across the aisle. "Kurt!" he called. "Are you from

Austria?'' he asked him kindly in German.

"*Ya*," Kurt replied, turning slightly toward Karl but avoiding his gaze.

"Where are you from in Austria?"

"*Wein.*"

"I am from Germany," Karl went on. "I come from Ruhenwald on the outskirts of Berlin." Kurt was silent. "I think we came to England at the same time. Do you remember me from the train?" Karl ventured again.

There was a slight flicker of recognition in Kurt's eyes.

"How are things for you?"

"Not good."

Karl sat back again, and exchanged a look with the two English boys. "Not much luck?" Miles asked.

"No. He doesn't seem to want to talk. How did he come to stay with you?"

"It was all very strange," Miles explained, recounting the incident of how the little boy was discovered unconscious, half-starved and injured. "So you see, we really know nothing about him."

"Perhaps when he gets to know me a little better he might tell me what happened to him," said Karl, studying the boy with concern.

"Look!" cried Otto, pointing excitedly to the green fields rolling past outside the window. "*Ach*, there's an orchard a little like ours, Karl! And there, in the distance..."

"Yes, I see, Otto. The scenery is beautiful, isn't it?"

"It looks like home."

"I suppose it does a little."

"Is *this* the vacation then?"

Karl studied his brother's eager face. "Yes," he replied gently. "It is." And he joined his brother at the window. No, the scenery was not like his home, but still, it reminded him...open fields, and trees, and rolling hills. His heart too lifted a little.

"Excuse me!" A voice broke into Karl's reverie. A stout

woman wearing a pair of glasses attached to a chain around her neck seemed to be addressing him. Karl recognized her as the teacher of Otto and Erich's would-be class. "Are you the German boy?" she asked Karl.

"One of them," he replied, smiling.

"These two are the others?" She pointed to Otto and Erich. "Yes, that's right."

"And where is the Austrian boy?"

"Over there," he said, indicating the silent boy across the aisle slouching in the corner of his seat.

"Do they speak English?"

"No."

"I see. Well, what I have to say concerns all of you, so please convey the message to them when I have finished telling you. When you arrive at your destination, it would be in your best interests to say that you are Polish rather than German."

Karl raised his eyebrows. "Why?" he asked, taken aback.

"With the situation as it is, you will find that anti-German feeling is running high."

"But we're *Jewish!* We are ourselves victims of the Nazis."

"Believe me, *I* understand that, but the people in these small villages are very provincial, and may not. Some of them may not ever have seen a Jew before, let alone know what being a *German* Jew means. I would strongly recommend that you take my advice."

It was late afternoon by the time they arrived at the tiny train station with its name blacked out. It consisted of one double track and a small station house, and was a far cry from the hustle and bustle they had left behind in London.

"This is the middle of nowhere," Joshua whispered to Miles as their class was told to alight from the train. The train was to continue further down the line and deposit the rest of the children at other villages along the way. Karl was relieved that they were one of the first classes to reach their destination — in less than two hours it would be sunset, and Shabbos.

The platform was empty, except for one middle-aged lady with rosy cheeks who introduced herself to them. "I am Mrs. Beanshaw, your billeting officer," she announced. "Welcome to Swanstone." She then proceeded to explain to the small gathering that it was her job to dispatch them to the various families in the village who had agreed to take in the evacuees from London.

The village of Swanstone in Norfolk, they soon discovered, was a picturesque English village which might have come straight off an illustrated postcard. There were a few quaint shops situated around the village green, and some basic amenities. Aside from the five or six cottages in the center of the village, most of the villagers lived scattered about the surrounding area, many of them on farms.

Karl studied his new surroundings, gazing at the open stretches of land and greenery spreading as far as the eye could see. He took deep breaths of the clear country air, and closed his eyes and listened to the silence. Only the voices of the children and the chirping of the birds could be heard. For the first time since coming to England, Karl felt at peace. Whatever the future held, no one could ever take away from him the intense pleasure of seeing once again the beautiful countryside he so missed from his home, and the pervading sense of calm that he experienced. Otto squeezed his brother's hand and smiled up at him. He too appeared to be soothed by the surroundings.

"Listen," Karl said to Miles, who was standing near him.

"Listen to what?" Miles laughed. "I can't hear anything but a few birds singing."

"I know! Isn't it wonderful?"

"No! I miss all the noise, all the sounds of the city. It feels as if something is missing...it's too lonely, too quiet."

"This is the Willows' home," Mrs. Beanshaw said to Karl and Otto, the only two boys yet to be taken to their quarters. "They only anticipated one boy, so I don't know whether they will be prepared to take you both."

Karl felt at home simply looking at the cozy stone farmhouse surrounded by acres of farmland. He knew how fortunate he was to have come here. The country had always been his place.

A plump woman wearing an apron opened the door with a bright smile. She wiped her hands on the apron and then extended them in a gesture of welcome. "Hello, Mrs. Beanshaw!" she said warmly. "I have just put a couple of cakes in the oven. Would you like to stay for a cup of tea?"

"No, thank you. I am only here on a quick visit. I've brought you your billets. We have a slight problem, though. I know you said you would take *one*, but these two boys are brothers and do not want to be—"

"It will be no problem for us to take both of them," she said promptly, smiling at the boys. "I am sure Jack won't mind..." She nodded to Karl and Otto kindly. "Come on, dears."

Karl and Otto followed her inside.

"Do sit down, boys," Mrs. Willow said. "Leave your suitcases in the corner — we can take them up later. I am Fay Willow, and please, call me Fay. What are your names?"

"My name is Karl and this is my brother Otto," Karl replied.

"Your names certainly don't sound very English! And you have an accent too. Where are you from?"

"We're from...uh...Poland." Karl flinched at having to lie.

The kitchen door opened and a tall, broad-shouldered man in dungarees strolled in.

"Boys, this is my husband Jack," said Fay Willow. "Jack, I would like you to meet our two new billets: Karl and Otto. Karl was just telling me that they are from Poland."

"Oh, yes?" said Mr. Willow with genuine interest as he took a seat opposite the two boys at the round wooden table in the kitchen. "Whereabouts?"

"Um...near...near Warsaw. We had a farm there."

"You don't say! So you are familiar with farm life?"

"Oh, yes, sir."

"Don't bother with formalities — I haven't been knighted

yet! You can call me Jack. I heard the terrible news about the invasion earlier. There's no going back now, you know. The Germans have overstepped the mark this time."

"What do you mean?"

"Haven't you heard? Germany invaded Poland today."

"No."

"Do you still have family there?"

"Yes. Our parents."

Jack Willow shook his head and sighed. "It's going to be a messy business out there. You boys were lucky to get out when you did."

"Jack, sorry to interrupt," said Fay, "but I was wondering if I could offer Karl and Otto something to eat. What do you say, boys? You must be hungry after your long trip. Could I cook something up for you perhaps?"

"No thank you," Karl answered quickly. "I'm really not hungry."

"Are you sure? What about your brother?"

Karl bent down and said something to Otto in an undertone, in rapid German. Otto shook his head.

"A drink perhaps? Some homemade apple juice?"

"Yes, thank you, that would be fine."

Fay Willow was pouring two glasses for them from an earthenware bowl even before Karl had finished answering. "Here you go, dears."

Karl and Otto drank thirstily.

"How old are you Karl, if you don't mind me asking?" Jack resumed the conversation.

"Sixteen."

"I thought they were only evacuating up to the age of fifteen."

"They are, but I asked for permission to come with my brother. You see, until we came to England, he had never been away from home on his own before, and besides that, he does not speak any English."

Fay and Jack nodded sympathetically. "It can be tough coming to a foreign country. But he'll soon learn English once he starts at the school. It doesn't take long to pick it up when you're young. Your own English is very good. And what are your plans, Karl?''

"Well, I don't know what I can do if I'm considered too old for school. I'm not really trained for any profession, although I am familiar with farm work. I always helped my father." Karl quickly pushed away the memories of his father and their farm, which flooded him suddenly.

"I could offer you work on the farm, Karl. I wouldn't be able to pay you much, but I'm sure a bit of pocket money would come in handy."

"Oh, thank you," Karl said, smiling. "I would like that."

"Good!" Jack exclaimed, noting to himself how pleasant it was to see a smile and some light come into Karl's expression. Both boys seemed so stiff, and so...unhappy, poor fellows. "I have a few casual laborers, and my sons, of course, help me when they're not at school, but I can always do with the extra help. How about if I give you a couple of days to settle in, and then you can begin on Monday when Otto starts school."

"That would be great," Karl said, and then stood up nervously. "I'm sorry if I appear a little rude, but my brother and I are very tired. It has been a long day and we could both benefit from an early night."

"Probably a good idea," Fay agreed, nodding at them maternally. "Jack, would you mind carrying the suitcases up to the boys' room, and I'll make up the extra bed."

Fay showed them to a little room on the second floor containing two wooden beds. There was a matching bedside table in between, and a high wardrobe, which almost reached the wooden beams which were laid across the ceiling. "It's not the Ritz," laughed Fay, "but I hope you'll be comfortable here." She fluffed up the pillows.

"It's a lovely room," Karl said. "I am sure everything will be just fine."

"Sleep well, then, and we'll see you in the morning."

"Thank you for everything. Good night."

Karl and Otto listened to the Willows' footsteps descending the stairs and then, as if on cue, changed into their Shabbos clothes and davened *Kabbalas Shabbos* and *Ma'ariv* in the fading light. There would be no Shabbos candles, *Kiddush* wine, or challah, and their empty stomachs attested to the fact that it had been a long time since they had eaten a proper meal. There was no hope of a hot Friday night dinner awaiting them. Nevertheless, Karl explained to a pale and confused Otto, it was Shabbos and there were many things to be thankful for. At least they had not been separated. Karl thanked Hashem that he had been able to accompany Otto. It would have been a perilous mistake had Otto come on his own.

In whispers, the two brothers sang "*Shalom Aleichem*" and in their minds' eye saw themselves in the brightly lit dining room at home, with their father, mother, sister Charlotte, and numerous guests around the long Shabbos table, covered with a pure white tablecloth. On it stood two tall shimmering silver candlesticks, at the top of which two crimson flames glowed. The crystal decanter of wine sparkled; the velvet challah cloth covered two large crispy golden challos liberally sprinkled with poppy seeds, which their mother had baked; and the table was set with the finest crockery and cutlery they possessed. Their parents' smiling faces, suffused with the glow of the candles, beckoned them. Karl and Otto slumped down on the two beds. "Good Shabbos, Otto," Karl said.

"Good Shabbos, Karl," Otto whispered with a choked voice.

"What do you think of the Willows?" asked Karl.

"They seem kind and honest people," Otto replied. "We are very lucky, I guess. I feel sorry for Erich, though."

"What do you mean?" asked Karl, leaning forward with interest.

"I don't like that lady he is staying with."

"Why? You don't even know her."

"I know! But she didn't seem very likeable."

Karl shrugged. "Let's go and visit him tomorrow and see how

he's doing. Maybe everything is alright.''

The sun was streaming in the kitchen windows when Karl and
Otto hesitantly entered the room. "Good morning!" Mrs. Willow said heartily. "I'm sure you two must be starving by now. Did
you sleep well? What would you like to eat? A nice cooked
breakfast, perhaps?"

Karl quickly glanced at what he realized was bacon sizzling in
a large frying pan on the stove. "Uh..." he stammered, "we are
not really used to big breakfasts where we come from."

"Fancy that!" Fay raised her eyebrows in surprise. "And
coming from a farm, too! What do you usually have then?"

"Um...tomatoes, carrots, apples and fruit juice," Karl replied
quickly.

Mrs. Willow looked at him curiously, but the wide smile
remained. "That should be no problem! I'll soon get used to
your preferences and habits. Have a seat. It will be along in a
minute."

The four children already sitting around the kitchen table
stared as Karl and Otto joined them. "Silly me!" Fay exclaimed.
"I completely forgot to introduce you to each other. This is Karl,
and this is Otto," she told her children. "As I told you earlier,
they come from Poland and will be staying with us for the time
being. You can speak English with Karl, and you can teach a little
English to Otto."

Then she turned to her guests. "And these are our four
children. Peter is the eldest, at thirteen." She pointed to the
serious-looking boy with wide-set eyes and a freckled face. "Then
there is Tom — he's eleven, and he's the joker of the family."
She gave him a soft dig in the ribs, which set him off in a fit of
giggles. "April is seven, and a proper tomboy." April promptly
gave Karl and Otto a mischievous smile. "And this little sweetie
is Enid. She's almost two." Enid giggled and hid her curly head
in April's lap.

"What are you planning to do today?" Fay asked, as the boys
dived hungrily into their food.

"I thought we might go down to the village and visit a few of our friends," Karl replied.

"That's a good idea. Do you know the way there?"

"Not exactly."

"I'll tell you then. The narrow path to the left of our front gate leads straight down to the village. Keep going down for about ten minutes, and don't turn off anywhere. If you cannot remember where all your friends are staying, ask Mrs. Beanshaw. She runs the general store, and you can't miss it. Would you like to take along some lunch?"

"No, no," Karl hastened to answer. "We will be all right. Thank you anyway."

"As you like. And one more thing. Don't forget to shut the gate whenever you come in or go out — otherwise the cows will go wandering off."

"We won't," Karl said, smiling.

Miles and Joshua were delighted to see Karl and Otto. Even Kurt looked pleased. They introduced them to their hosts, Mr. and Mrs. Berrin, a childless couple in their mid-fifties who lived above the post office, which they also ran. Then the boys set out for a walk. As soon as they were out of the Berrins' earshot, Karl asked, "How has Shabbos been?"

"As you can imagine!" Miles replied. "But the Berrins seemed interested in my explanations of Shabbos and kashrus. I think we are the first Jewish people they have ever met! But they are being quite decent and understanding about it."

"Actually, they were a little frightened when they originally found out," Joshua added, "and I think they expected us to place a spell over them or something! But I think it will be all right. How have things been with you?"

"Complicated. We're staying with the Willows, who live on a farm some distance from the village center. They seemed like genuinely good people, and it is getting to be awkward making up excuses about not eating, especially since Mrs. Willow goes out of her way for us. I'm reluctant to tell her we're Jews though, after the warning we got about not stirring up anti-German feeling. What did you tell the Berrins about Kurt?''

"We said he was a Polish Jew and they simply accepted it,'' Miles said.

"Hmm.'' Karl nodded. "I'll have to think about what to tell the Willows.''

"I'm a little concerned for Erich,'' Joshua remarked. "He must be finding things quite difficult on his own.''

"Especially with that elderly widow he's staying with,'' added Miles. "I have my suspicions about her.''

"You as well? Otto said something similar last night.'' Otto nodded.

"Let's go and see him.''

They approached the small cottage and Miles swung open the little wooden gate.

"Are you sure this is the one?'' Karl whispered. "They all look alike to me!''

"I couldn't forget this garden,'' Miles whispered back. "Look at it!'' It was indeed a sight to see, with its rows upon rows of blooming flowers, planted in a tidy and organized color scheme, perfectly spaced out and all the same height. Wild roses climbed the outside wall on both sides of the front door, almost reaching up to the low overhanging thatched roof. Surely such a beautiful and cared-for garden was evidence of a kind and caring hostess!

Mrs. Redley opened the door and gave the five boys a disdainful glare, her eyebrows knotted and mouth turned down. She peered from one to the other with the distate she might show to a gang of street urchins. "What can I do for you?''

"We are some of Erich's fellow evacuees,'' Miles began, "and we have come to visit him and see if he can come out for a walk with us.''

"Wait here,'' she ordered. "Erik! Erik!'' The boys noted the harshness in her shout and looked at each other gravely. Then Erich appeared at the door, and an expression of relief crossed his serious face.

"Would you like to come out for a walk with us?'' Karl asked him quietly, while Mrs. Redley inclined her ear, trying to catch what he was saying.

Erich nodded eagerly.

The boys set out down the tree-lined lane. They chatted together, the sun warm on their pale cheeks, the country air full of the sweet smell of flowers, hay, and earth. A group of Jewish boys — English and European — set down in a remote English village made a strange sight to the occasional passerby, but the boys were unaware of this.

The excitement of seeing each other, and the beauty of the Shabbos morning, dispelled momentarily the dark memories that filled Kurt, Erich, Karl and Otto. Vienna, Berlin, violence and dread; Jews shoved on trucks; synagogues burning; shattered windows; threatening Nazis; and then the unfamiliar, teeming streets of London, and a language not their own; fear for their beloved families they'd left behind. It all seemed to fade, and become unreal, like something dreamt. They had stepped out of that ominous world and into this one.   The talk turned to their respective hosts.

"And how's Mrs. Redley?'' Karl asked Erich.

"I haven't eaten anything since I arrived! She handed me a plate of *treif* sausages last night, which of course I could not eat, and since I didn't know how to explain to her in English why I didn't want them, she was extremely offended. Furthermore, she watches every single thing I do. I constantly feel her eyes on me, studying me.'' And then, without warning, Erich suddenly burst into tears.

"Erich, what is it?'' asked Joshua.

"This morning I did a terrible *averah*.''

"What did you do?''

"Mrs. Redley wanted me to weed the garden for her. I couldn't explain to her that it's forbidden on Shabbos, so I pretended I didn't understand. Then she gave me a demonstration, to show me what needed to be done. Still, I didn't do it, but she forcibly grabbed my hand and made me.'' Erich's tears came again. "I had no choice."

"It wasn't your fault," Karl said, putting his arm around Erich's shoulders.

"But I still broke Shabbos," Erich insisted. " I feel terrible. I cannot stay here. I have to leave."

"Where will you go?"

"I'm thinking of writing to the Firestones after Shabbos and asking if I can go back to stay with them."

"But it might become very dangerous to stay in London."

"I am already in danger," Erich replied mournfully.

13

SUNDAY, THE THIRD of September, was a day which would be etched forever in the minds of everyone who was old enough to remember. For most people, their lives would never be quite the same again.

The day began as usual on that beautiful late-summer morning. Jack Willow gave the Alexander boys a tour of his farm, while Fay prepared a large Sunday roast in the kitchen, humming to the music on the radio.

"Will you be wanting to go to church?" Jack had asked them earlier.

"Um..." Karl was lost for words. He certainly could not agree, but what would the Willows think if he refused?

"To tell you the truth," Jack continued, "though I'm a little embarrassed to admit it, we don't go all that often."

"Neither do we," said Karl quickly, flooded with relief.

"Well, then, we'll all stay home!" joked Jack. "But if you change your mind, I'll be happy to take you. We're not against religion, but we've become a bit lax over the years."

Mrs. Redley pursed her lips and looked critically at Erich as he came down the stairs in his plain pair of shorts, a gray shirt, and shoes which were scuffed at the toes. She pointed her finger toward the stairs and ordered him to go back up, with her following on his heels. While he stood mystified, Mrs. Redley rummaged around in his small cupboard until she found the white shirt and dark pants he had worn the day before — Shabbos. Satisfied, she took them out, handed them to Erich, saying, "Today is Sunday!" and left him alone to change.

When he reappeared several minutes later, Erich found her scrubbing furiously at his shoes with a brush and tin of brown shoe polish. Mrs. Redley handed him his shoes, wiped her hands on a cloth, and straightened his hair and shirt, muttering as she did so. She left the room and returned wearing a straw hat with a bunch of decorative artificial cherries. She donned a pair of white gloves and then took him by the hand and led him out of the front door. There were three locks to close and she tried the door to make sure it was firmly shut. Only then did she decide it was adequate. It began to dawn on Erich what was happening.

They met many of the villagers on their way. Erich noted that they all appeared to be heading in the same direction, confirming his suspicions. Mrs. Redley paused to talk to several people on the way, and Erich noted that she did all the talking, and her neighbors replied with one or two words.

The moment came. In front of them loomed the village church. Erich fought for breath and glanced wildy about. He had to get away! He tried to wrench his hand away from Mrs. Redley, but she grasped it tighter still, and he found himself being dragged inside the forbidding building, all the while the voice inside his head crying, "No!"

Fay Willow sang along to the music on the radio and danced around the kitchen clearing up while the roast baked in the oven. Suddenly the music abruptly stopped and a broadcaster's voice came crackling over the radio: "We interrupt this program to bring you a special announcement by the Prime Minister, Mr. Neville Chamberlain."

Fay leaned out of the kitchen window. "Jack!" she shouted. "Jack! Come quickly!" She caught sight of Peter in the flower garden. "Peter, go and call your father! Hurry!"

Jack burst in, with Karl and Otto right behind him. "What is it, Fay? What's the matter?"

"Sh-h," said Fay, putting her finger to her lips, and turned up the volume knob. All eyes turned to the little brown radio sitting on the kitchen table.

"I am speaking to you from the cabinet room at Ten Downing Street. This morning the British Ambassador in Berlin handed the German Government a note, stating that unless we heard from them by eleven o'clock that they were prepared to withdraw their troops from Poland, a state of war would exist between us. I have to tell you now that no such undertaking has been received and consequently, this country is at war with Germany. We are ready. We can only do the right, as we see the right, and reverently commit our cause to God.

Stunned, they all stared at each other. Fay dabbed at her eyes with a handkerchief. "Go save England," she whispered.

"Does that mean the mail between England and Germany will be blocked?" Karl asked, thinking of the single letter he and Otto had received from their parents, in the first week of their arrival in England. Since then, they had heard nothing. Karl was also worried because he had not yet informed his parents of their change of address, and if there was to be no postal service between the two countries, how was he going to let them know where they were?

"I suppose so," Jack murmured, "but what do you care about Germany?"

"Well...I...suppose Poland is considered to be Germany now."

"Karl, don't ever think like that!" Jack sat up straight. "We have only just begun the war. We have not been defeated yet! Our boys will reclaim it from the Germans, you'll see."

Karl smiled weakly. He would have to watch his words more carefully in the future.

The Sunday dinner was over. The younger children were playing quietly in the garden, and Karl, Otto and Peter had just gone out to do some farm work with Jack. What nice boys her guests were, Fay thought to herself. But they were such poor eaters! They hadn't touched the roast, though they had seemed to like the vegetables. Well, she thought, soon I'll get to know more about what they like and I'll make their favorite dishes for them. Poor things, they're probably worried about their folks back in Poland, too, and haven't much appetite.

Suddenly there was a knock at the door.

"Why, Mrs. Redley, what a pleasant surprise. Do come in. Please take a seat in the parlor and I will make us a pot of tea."

"Thank you, Mrs. Willow."

Mrs. Redley wandered around the parlor, a little-used room which was reserved mainly for guests. She wiped her finger across the mantlepiece, checking it; finding it dust-free, she gave her grudging approval. She pulled out a couple of books from the bookshelf to read their titles and stared closely at each of the family photographs on the mantlepiece.

When Fay entered with a tray of tea and cake, Mrs. Redley was sitting in the high-backed armchair casually gazing about her.

"How are you, Mrs. Willow?" she asked.

"I am very well, thank you. And yourself? Tea?" she questioned, indicating the teapot.

"Thank you. All I can say is that I am very worried."

"About the war, you mean? Yes, indeed, it is distressing news."

"Among other things. I heard the declaration in church this morning. I have hardly been able to think of anything else since. I am also quite concerned about the boy I have staying with me. They have sent some very bad elements up here, Mrs. Willow. Did you hear that the Berrins have some Jewish boys staying with them?"

"No, I hadn't heard."

"I simply do not know how they could agree to take them."

"Why not?"

"Jews are not the kind of people I would like to take into *my* home. You could wake up one morning and find that they had gone, taking most of the contents of your house with them.''

"Oh, now, Mrs. Redley, I don't think so.''

"Well, would you have taken them in?''

"If I'd been asked. They might have a different religion, but they're still people, you know.''

Mrs. Redley snorted. "Mrs. Willow, I think you ought to go to church more often, if you'll excuse my saying so. One can so easily become confused if one does not go regularly.''

Mrs. Willow smothered a smile. "You were saying something about having problems with the boy who is staying with you?''

"Oh, yes! So I was. He behaves very curiously indeed. I have my suspicions,'' Mrs. Redley said, lowering her voice and fixing a piercing stare on Mrs. Willow, "that he might be a German spy.''

Fay could not suppress her laughter this time. "A German spy? But he's only a little boy! That's absurd.''

"Mrs. Willow, I do not know about you, but I take this war very seriously. There is talk that they have sent agents over here.''

"That may be so, but surely not eight-year-old boys!''

"Why not? The fact that they are young puts them under less suspicion.''

"Come now — how would they have gotten into England?''

"On false passports, of course, and by posing as *Polish* refugees.'' Mrs. Redley pronounced the last two words slowly, nodding her head.

Fay smiled tolerantly. "I think you are mistaken. Your guest is simply a little boy, far from his family in Poland, who can't even understand what you're saying to him.''

"Then how do you explain the fact that when I looked through his address book, I found that most of the addresses are in Germany? And I don't believe for a minute that the language he speaks with your two boys is Polish. Furthermore, he is extremely ungrateful toward me. He hardly touches any of the food I give him, and yesterday, when I wanted him to help me weed the garden, he would not do it until I literally forced him to. Can you imagine?''

''Maybe he simply did not understand you.''

''Oh, he understood all right. Today, in church, when we were listening to Chamberlain on the radio announcing war, the little sneak fled outside and was promptly sick. If you ask me, the little Nazi is scared now that we're going to fight back and the likes of him will get exactly what they deserve!'' Mrs. Redley was quite worked up by this time. With red cheeks and eyes blazing, she went on. ''Another thing! Do you know that I practically had to drag him into church this morning? It is a known fact they are anti-religion.''

Mrs. Redley helped herself to a piece of homemade ginger cake and had a sip of tea, which calmed her down somewhat. ''You cannot say that you have not noticed odd behavior with your two?''

''I haven't, really. They don't eat much, and they don't seem to be religious either, but other than that...''

''There you are!'' Mrs. Redley exclaimed, claiming victory. ''Take my advice: watch them carefully, and do let me know if you notice anything else which is irregular.''

''What did Mrs. Redley want this afternoon?'' Jack asked, as they sat in the kitchen over mugs of hot cocoa that evening, with the radio playing softly in the background. ''She basically came to warn me to keep a close watch on Karl and Otto,'' Fay replied, smiling.

''Whatever for?'' Jack asked, putting down his mug.

''She thinks that they, and her boy too, might be German spies.''

''What a load of rubbish! That woman is off her head. She just loves to stir up trouble.''

''That's what I thought at first, Jack, but you know, she did make a few valid points.''

''Such as?''

''The fact that they are not religious.''

''We're not exactly prime examples ourselves.''

"They hardly eat anything."

"What does that show? They're probably homesick."

"She said that she found some German addresses in her boy's address book."

"If they weren't written in English, how could she even read them?"

"I didn't think of that." Fay smiled, ashamed of herself.

"Mrs. Redley talks a load of nonsense. These poor kids have fled Poland because of the Germans, and I'm sure the last thing they would want to be called is German."

"You are probably right."

"I know I am, Fay! Take what that woman says with a pinch of salt. Mrs. Redley is an old gossip with nothing else to worry about."

"Are Karl and Otto awake yet?" Jack asked his wife. It was only five o'clock in the morning but Jack was already dressed and prepared for the day ahead.

"Yes, I called them a few minutes ago," Fay replied, pouring his coffee.

"Would you mind going up and telling Karl to come down now if he's ready. I'd like to show him how to milk the cows before breakfast. I understand he has never had the experience. His parents dealt mainly with agriculture."

"Of course."

Fay climbed up the stairs, puffing as she went. She knocked on the boys' door but received no reply. She could hear no sounds coming from their room. "I do hope they haven't gone back to sleep," she murmured to herself, turning the handle quietly and peeking in around the door.

Her mouth dropped open when she saw Karl. She clapped her hand over her mouth, slammed the door shut and fled down the stairs in terror.

"What's happening? Is he coming now?" Jack asked.

"Jack!" she said breathlessly. "Jack! Oh, Jack, I just saw something so terribly awful!"

"Calm down, catch your breath, Fay. Now tell me, what are you talking about?"

"I knocked on the door, but there was no response, so I looked in to check that they hadn't gone back to sleep. Karl was standing there with a kind of..." Her eyes widened, and she lowered her voice. "...*black box* on his head, one on his arm, and something — a wire maybe — was wrapped all the way up his arm. I don't know what it was. Perhaps it's something for sending messages." They stared into each other's fearful eyes. Neither voiced their apprehensions, but both knew what the other was thinking.

"I'm going up there to see what's going on," Jack said decisively.

"Be careful," Fay warned.

Jack flung open the door, as Karl was guiltily winding up his *tefillin* and placing them into their velvet bag. "I want you both downstairs, now!" he ordered. The three descended silently. Karl put his arm around Otto and walked beside him defensively, into the kitchen where Mr. and Mrs. Willow faced them. Their eyes were filled with accusation. "I think it is time you told us the truth, young man." Jack said. "You are not really Polish at all, are you?"

Karl's eyes were downcast. "No," he replied.

"She was right!" Fay whispered to her husband.

"Where are you from then?"

"We are from Germany," Karl said in a steady voice.

Simultaneously, Mr. and Mrs. Willow gasped.

"We are Jewish."

"Jewish?" Jack echoed.

"Jewish?" Fay asked, confused.

"Yes. We came to England to flee the Nazis. I am not sure what you have heard, but they are treating the Jews very badly there."

"Yes, we have read all about it," Fay said. "But why didn't you tell us right from the start? Why did you pretend to be Polish?"

"We were advised to do so by a teacher who came with us on the evacuation. She told us that the people here in the village might not want us if they heard we were German, even if we explained that we were German *Jews.*"

"Oh, you poor dears, carrying this distressing burden around with you! I don't know what to say except that I am sorry. Especially for not trusting you."

"And the same goes for me," added Jack. "But what on earth was that contraption with the boxes and wires that you had on just now?"

Karl's face broke into a smile. "They're called *tefillin* — that's a Hebrew word that means 'prayers.' You see, we must wear them when we say our morning prayers..."

"Some spies!" Jack said softly to Fay, who blushed.

"Inside the boxes are verses from our Bible...I can explain to you, later perhaps, what is written..."

"As long as you're explaining," Fay broke in, "perhaps you'll tell me why you won't eat?!"

Karl smiled again, and rapidly explained to Otto the gist of the conversation. Turning back to fay, he said, "Your food looks delicious and, you've been most generous. It isn't that we don't appreciate it. But you see, we must eat only what is kosher..."

"Ah," Jack said, "I've heard of that. No pork, right? No bacon for them, Fay, hear?"

"That's right," Karl said. "Actually meat in general is a problem for us. But vegetables and bread are just fine..."

"Well, Fay," Jack said softly. "We've learned a thing or two this morning, haven't we?!"

"Indeed we have," Fay gently answered.

"And..." said Karl, suddenly looking away, studying a distant tree from the kitchen window, "you don't mind now that you know the truth?"

"Mind? Not at all! It's a pleasure to have you with us," Jack boomed. "And I can understand why you were given such advice. There are some bigoted people about." Jack suddenly exchanged a look with Fay. "And I suppose that Erich, that boy staying with Mrs. Redley, is also a German Jew?"

"Yes, that's right. He is."

Fay looked down. "Poor little boy — he must be having a terrible time of it there."

"Yes. We are very concerned about him. He is so unhappy that he's even talked of going back to London."

"He certainly can't do that, now that war has broken out!" Jack cried.

"What other choice does he have? He's really suffering where he is."

Jack and Fay exchanged another glance. "Leave it to me," Fay said quietly.

That evening when Karl returned from his first day of work on the farm, he entered the kitchen to find Erich sitting there with Otto, eating a heaping plateful of bread and farm vegetables for supper.

"Erich has come to live with us," Fay explained, smiling proudly.

Karl shook his head incredulously. "How did you manage that?" he asked.

"Let's just say that I did not quite tell Mrs. Redley the whole story. I told her that you were Polish Jews, but I suspect that she still thinks otherwise. I want to warn you, Karl, to be very careful not to do or say anything that would ever give her the slightest reason for suspicion."

"Is she dangerous?" Karl asked, his face suddenly clouded with worry.

"Not really. She's just a gossip." Fay hesitated. "But she has been know to stir up trouble in the past."

14

BY THE TIME Rosh Hashanah came two weeks later, things had settled down. Karl, Otto, and Erich were careful not to refer to Germany to anyone, and not to speak German loudly among themselves in public. Once the initial curiosity about the new Jewish children wore off, the villagers appeared to accept them. They acknowledged that they were different from themselves in some ways, but they were fellow human beings all the same and certainly not freaks. As for Mrs. Redley, the boys hardly ever saw her, except perhaps on the rare occasions when they went to run errands for Fay in the village, or went to visit Miles, Joshua and Kurt. Even then they barely took any notice of her.

All six of them ate only what kashrus observance would allow, and their diets basically consisted of fruits and vegetables. Both the Willows and the Berrins were very understanding and accommodating, and did everything they could for their young boarders. They even bought them separate cutlery and dishes.

Karl found working on the farm satisfying and enjoyable. He worked mainly with the fruit trees and field crops, which were what he knew best. In the late afternoon when the others finished school, all the boys would meet and go for walks through the country lanes and fields of Swanstone, discovering and delighting in their new surroundings. Sometimes they would simply sit in the haystack on the Willows' farm — a favorite place — and talk for hours. On Sunday afternoons they were permitted to take Jack's old rowboat onto the narrow river that bordered the farm. They were golden days. Otto thrived in the countryside and hardly ever mentioned going home. Color came to all their cheeks, and the sorrowful look in their eyes slowly faded. Erich was back to his old happy self and had almost erased from his memory the few miserable days he had spent with Mrs. Redley. Even Miles and Joshua were growing accustomed to the tranquil life of the countryside and were beginning to see that life outside the city did have its advantages. They adjusted well to their new school and found the other children friendly and helpful. The war news that was broadcast all day on the radio somehow did not shatter the boys' new-found peace during these days of late summer.

Only Kurt remained aloof and silent. He rarely joined them on their excursions, preferring to go for long walks on his own. All Karl's coaxing and questioning about why he did not participate more in their activities met with a sharp reply in return.

For Rosh Hashanah, Jack had very thoughtfully cleared out an old barn for them, where they could pray and eat their holiday meals together without being disturbed. On the first night of the Festival, the six of them sat on bales of hay around a table made from logs, which was covered with a piece of white cloth. Two bottles with candles fixed into them stood in the center. It was very basic, but they all agreed that it looked and felt like *Yom Tov*. Mr. and Mrs. Firestone had sent up a package of cakes and kosher cold meats for all of them. Joshua's mother had sent up two home-baked round challos, which surprisingly had remained intact. Miles' parents had sent some grape juice for *Kiddush*.

Karl handed around the pieces of apple dipped in honey. "And may it be His will that it be a sweet New Year for all of our People, for us, and for our families," he said emotionally.

"Amen," the others replied. How far away their parents seemed at that moment! What was real was this Rosh Hashanah in a peaceful barn in the English countryside. Thoughts of

Europe, of their parents and relatives, seemed dreamlike, unreal, and clouded.

"Let's hope the war really will be over soon," Miles said.
"Nothing much seems to be happening anyhow." He was referring to what American journalists soon termed the "phony war."
Contrary to what most people expected, bombs had not started
falling immediately and life continued the way it always had. In
fact, the only fighting that was taking place at all was at sea.

"Mr. Berrin thinks this is the lull before the storm, and we'll
still cop it," Joshua commented.

"Isn't that morbid?" Miles asked.

"I don't think so. War cannot end until Germany is defeated,
and we've given them what they deserve. Then Karl, Otto, Erich
and Kurt will be able to go back home again. Not that I'm trying
to get rid of them!"

"I can't picture going home again," Karl murmured, instantly sorry he had said it, and hoping Otto had not understood
the English.

"Why not?" Miles asked.

"I'm not sure what will happen when the war ends. Everything is so uncertain right now."

"Does it worry you?"

"It's always at the back of my mind, but I try not to think
about it too much. At any rate, there's nothing I can do except
pray, hope and wait. It is all in the hands of Hashem."

On Yom Kippur, as they recited the moving and solemn
U'nesaneh tokef, the prayer had never seemed so meaningful, or
so fearful, before. "...On Rosh Hashanah it is inscribed, and on
Yom Kippur it is sealed, how many shall pass on and how many
shall be born. Who shall live and who shall die...who will remain
tranquil and who will be disturbed. Who shall reap enjoyment,
and who will be painfully afflicted..."

"When's your next Festival, boys?" Jack asked Karl while they
milked the cows the morning after Yom Kippur.

"In three days."

"My goodness! Which one is this?"

"This one is called Sukkos, and it lasts a whole week. It is when we remember how we lived in temporary dwellings, huts, while we wandered through the desert."

"The desert? I thought you said you came from Germany. I didn't think it was that hot there!"

Karl laughed. "This happened a little while before we got to Germany — about three thousand years ago! Shortly after we left Egypt..."

"Oh, I think I know that story. Isn't it the one with Pharaoh?"

"Yes, that's when we were slaves in Egypt. God brought us out and we wandered in the desert for forty years before we were allowed to enter our homeland, the Land of Israel."

"Interesting...you know, I learned all that stuff in Sunday school, but I never connected it with Jews today, with you and Otto. Never thought about it, I guess. It must be great to have such an interesting past, to know what your ancestors did and who they were. You know, I hardly even know what my great-grandfather did or where he came from. I admire your people."

Karl smiled bitterly. "Try telling the Germans that."

Jack shook his head sadly. "So what do you do to celebrate this Festival? Live in a hut?"

"Actually, we do."

Jack chuckled to himself. "I'm learning fast, aren't I? Will the barn be good enough? It's pretty big for a hut."

"We'll need something which doesn't have a real roof. Then we put branches over the top of it."

Jack was pensive for a while. "I've got it!" he exclaimed, rising to his feet. He examined the large bucketful of milk the cow had given and patted her flank. "Good girl, Bess," he said, and then turned to Karl. "Come along with me."

Jack strode to a storage shed nearby. "This is what I call my repair room. I keep spare parts, tools, and plenty of timber in here," he explained. "You boys are welcome to use anything you like from here to construct your hut."

*   *   *

The next day the village of Swanstone was privileged to have the first *sukkah* ever built in its midst. When Miles, Joshua and Kurt dropped by after school to lend a hand with the *sukkah*, they found that it was almost finished.

"How did you manage to make it so quickly?" Miles asked.

"Well, I used to help my father every year making ours at home, and Jack helped by carting the heavy logs across the farm on the back of his tractor."

"He is such a kind man," Joshua said.

"Yes, he is. We were very fortunate to come to the Willows."

"I'm disappointed that you've finished most of the *sukkah*," Erich said. "I was looking forward to helping."

"There's still plenty to do. We need to cut down some *sechach* for the roof, and make decorations."

"Well I'm no good at artwork, so I'll look for the *sechach*," Joshua said.

"I'll go with you, Joshua," said Erich. "I know a good place to look."

"And I'll start the decorations by making the *Ushpizin*." Miles said. "Come and help me, Otto!"

"What would *you* like to do, Kurt?" Karl asked, turning to the sullen boy standing a little distance away.

"I don't care," he replied indifferently.

"The only sad thing about Sukkos is when you have to take the *sukkah* down again," Erich said as they dismantled it the morning after Simchas Torah before going to school.

"Did you enjoy our *Yom Tov*?" Karl asked.

"Yes, it was really great. I missed not being in shul, though, especially on Simchas Torah. Well, next year, *b'ezras* Hashem."

"*B'ezras Hashem*," Karl echoed softly.

"Karl!" Fay called from the kitchen window. "A letter has just arrived for you."

Karl was off at once. "I'll be right back!" he called behind him to the other boys.

He was breathless when he reached the kitchen. He had not received a single letter from anyone since coming to Swanstone, but he hadn't lost hope that a letter from his parents might somehow get through.

"It looks quite official, and I thought that it must be important," Fay said.

Karl tried to hide his sharp disappointment, and took the brown envelope with its English postmark. His disappointment soon gave way to fear and panic as he read the contents once, then twice. "Oh, no! What am I going to do?" He put the letter down on the table and stared at it.

"Karl, what is it?"

He handed Fay the letter, and she scanned it quickly. "I'll go and fetch Jack," was all she said.

"What's going to happen to me? They won't put me in jail, will they?" Jack put a firm hand on Karl's shoulder. "Now just calm down," he said. "Nothing bad is going to happen to you. This is purely a precautionary measure. You are not the only one who has been requested to attend a Tribunal. I understand that literally thousands of people in England who were born in Germany and Austria and are over the age of sixteen, have also received the letter. The fact of the matter is that there probably *are* some Nazis or Nazi sympathizers in the country, and they must not be allowed the freedom to commit atrocities on behalf of Germany or to stir up their propaganda. The only way to find these people is to try everyone. This method is fair, you know, for it means that there can be no doubt who is the real enemy and who isn't."

"But it says that I'm not even allowed to have a lawyer."

"That's right, but you're allowed to bring someone along with you — see, it says so right here. I will come with you next week. I know you and can vouch for you better than any lawyer." Karl was about to voice another torrent of uncertainties but Jack prevented him. "Karl, everything is going to be all right. But if you're still feeling a little uncertain about this, I can ask the local constable, P.C. Morrow, to come over. He'll put your mind at rest.''

Karl shook hands with the tall policeman and Jack showed him into the parlor.

"Now, what exactly is the problem?" P.C. Morrow asked, coming straight to the point.

Karl cleared his throat nervously. "This morning I received a letter telling me that I must attend an...an Enemy Alien Tribunal, since I was born in Germany."

"I see," he replied politely, as if he were waiting to hear what the problem was.

Jack took up the story. "Karl, here, is naturally a little apprehensive about it, but I told him that he has no need to be."

"Well, that really depends on whether he has anything to worry about," P.C. Morrow replied.

"I'm not a *Nazi*, if that is what you're trying to say!" Karl exclaimed, his cheeks flushed.

"Did I say that you were?"

"No, but..." If anything, this encounter was causing Karl to feel more uneasy than ever.

"Karl has more reasons to dislike the Nazis than you or I," Jack said softly, coming to his assistance.

"You do not need to defend him to me. This is not the Tribunal yet."

"True," Jack replied. "Can I offer you a cup of tea, Constable?"

"No, I'm afraid I can't stay."

"Perhaps some other time then. Thanks for coming 'round."

P.C. Morrow tilted his hat. "Good evening, Mr. Willow."

After seeing P.C. Morrow to the door, Jack and Karl went back into the living room and were joined by Fay. "What did he say?" she asked.

"Not much," Jack replied, frowning. "He has changed somehow. Maybe it's because of the war. I don't know..."

"Changed? How do you mean?"

"I can't put my finger on it, but he seems somehow...oh, colder and more formal."

"Not the old 'Morrow' we used to know?"

"Not at all." Jack shook his head. "Not at all."

"Well, there's nothing we can do at the moment and we'll not know anything until the case has come to trial, so we might as well put it out of our minds until then." Fay turned to Karl. "Don't worry about it, Karl. All right?"

Karl nodded, putting on a brave face for everyone and trying to seem as normal as possible. But inside he was in turmoil: how utterly absurd and ironic that in Germany he had been looked upon first and foremost as a Jew and an enemy of the Germans, and here he was regarded as a German!

On the morning of the Enemy Alien Tribunal, Karl awoke with a heavy heart. He felt like a prisoner about to go to the gallows. He was to appear at the Town Hall in Cromer at 9:30, and on their way to the train station they ran into the last person they would have wanted to meet: Mrs. Redley.

"Good morning, Mr. Willow!" she said, glancing quickly at Karl too. "It *is* unusual to see you around here at this time of the day."

"Yes, I suppose it is," Jack replied and continued walking with Karl; but Mrs. Redley was not about to let them go that easily. "Are you two off to anywhere in particular?"

"Just to Cromer," Jack said offhandedly.

"What are you doing there?"

"Not much. I need to pick up a couple of things and thought Karl might like to come along. Now, if you'll excuse us, we must hurry or we'll miss the train."

"Of course, Mr. Willow! Good day."

"Hm-m," Mrs. Redley mused to herself as she strolled home, "I wonder what Mr. Willow wants to get in Cromer." It was her habit to take a walk to the village center every morning to see who was about and learn what was happening in Swanstone. She was so absorbed in her thoughts that she did not even notice P.C. Morrow or hear his "Good Morning." He tapped her on the shoulder. "Are you all right?" he asked.

"What?" she said, looking up. "Oh, I'm sorry, Mr. Morrow, I was miles away. I just met Mr. Willow with that Polish boarder of his. They told me that they're off to Cromer. Most strange, you know...I don't think Mr. Willow goes there from one year to the next."

The Constable nodded, to show his polite interest, but then suddenly his face clouded over and he furrowed his brows.

"Something wrong, Constable?"

"Did you say the boy was *Polish?*"

"Yes — at least that's what I and the rest of the village have been led to believe." Mrs. Redley pursed her lips and arched her eyebrows. "I don't know if it is my place to say, Constable, but I have my doubts."

"What do you mean?" P.C. Morrow asked, with open curiosity.

"For a start," she whispered, "I think he's German, not Polish. Yes, I have my suspicions about the boy."

"*Really?*"

"P.C. Morrow, I have some lovely honey cake inside. Could I tempt you at all?"

"Yes...yes, I could do with a cup of tea and a piece of honey cake."

Jack and Karl sat beside each other on the wooden bench in the large waiting area. "It looks like it's your turn now," Jack whispered, as a man in a dark pinstriped suit approached them.

"Karl Alexander?"

"Yes, that is me...um, I am he."

"And you are accompanying him?" He turned to Jack.

"Yes, I am," Jack replied, standing up.

"Follow me, please."

"Good luck," Jack whispered. Karl acknowledged his words

with a weak smile. They entered the room where the Tribunal sat, and the door was firmly shut behind them.

Karl was one of seventy-three thousand people called to the Tribunal between October 1939 and February 1940. They were classified and each person was put into one of three categories: Category A was for people who posed a potential security threat. These risk cases were interned almost immediately. Category B was for those who, although their loyalty to England was suspect, were allowed their freedom, subject to certain restrictions, such as not being allowed to own a camera or a large-scale map, or to travel more than five miles from their home. Category C was for those who posed no risk and were allowed to remain at liberty at least for the time being.

Karl was classified as a C.

15

IT WAS STILL DARK outside when Jack and Karl heard a little tap on the kitchen door. They had only just sat down for a quick breakfast before getting an early start and milking the cows. They looked at each other, wondering who it could be at that time of the morning. Jack yawned. "It's open," he called. "Come on in!"

"Mr. Berrin, what are you doing here so early?" Karl asked, as the man entered the kitchen and stamped his feet on the mat to shake the snow off his boots.

"Take off your coat, sit down, and have a hot drink with us," Jack urged him.

Once Mr. Berrin was seated, and thawing his hands on his mug of hot cocoa, he explained the reason for his visit. "It's Kurt," he sighed. "He's disappeared."

"What, again?" Karl asked. Every so often Kurt would wander off on his own without telling anyone where he was going. Sometimes he would stay out for a whole day, leaving early in the morning and not returning until nightfall. They never knew where he went, and he never explained his disappearances. At first they had all been worried, especially the Berrins, since he was their responsibility, but after it had happened several times they began to grow accustomed to it. They realized that he just needed to be alone at these times, and they tried to understand. It was difficult for the Berrins to communicate with him, but they had become very fond of the boy. They were troubled when he went off alone, and were always relieved when he returned home again.

"I'm sorry for bothering you at such an early hour," he went on, "but my wife and I were a little worried. You see, he left early yesterday morning but he didn't return at night like he always does. We thought he might have come over to stay at your place."

"No, he didn't," Jack replied. Mr. Berrin rubbed his red eyes. "You look exhausted. Have you been up all night?"

"Yes," he said in a low voice. "To be honest, we were more than a little apprehensive. I'm afraid that he might be in real danger. Who knows, perhaps he had an accident in the snow, or was caught up in a blizzard and forced to sleep outside. He could be half-frozen by now..."

"Oh, I'm sure nothing like that has happened," Jack said quickly.

"Well, I hope not. Miles and Joshua are already out looking for him."

"Karl and I will go and search for him too. Right now," Jack said, getting up. "Maybe you should go home and try to sleep a bit."

"I don't think I could sleep,worrying that something terrible might have happened to him."

"I doubt that it has. At least lie down and rest for a while. We'll surely find him soon — that is, if he hasn't gone home already. Will you manage to get home all right?"

"Yes. I came with the car."

"In that case, be careful on the roads."

"Thank you, Jack. And you too, Karl."

"We had better bring the first-aid kit along," Jack said, as soon as Mr. Berrin was gone.

"Do you think that he might have had an accident then?" Karl asked nervously.

"Hard to say. I didn't want to worry poor Mr. Berrin, but I

must admit that there is a distinct possibility. After all, he's gone now for almost twenty-four hours, probably without food or drink, and he's been exposed to this hazardous weather. But Mr. Berrin did not need me to compound his fears. Anyway, put on a few warm layers and we'll get going immediately.''

They went down into the village and asked a few passersby whether they had seen Kurt at all that morning. They did not mention, however, why they wanted to know, or the fact that he had not returned home the night before. No one had seen him.

Their next stop was the Berrins, to check if there had been any news. Miles and Joshua had already been home once to let them know that they had not yet seen any sign of him, and they went out again to continue their search. Since they were concentrating on the area in and around the village, Jack and Karl decided to comb the surrounding countryside and neighboring farms.

By lunchtime they must have covered a radius of at least five miles but he was still nowhere to be found. Karl, too, was beginning to fear the worst.

"Let's go home and have something to eat," Jack suggested, "and after that we can discuss where to try next. Although I would prefer not to, I am seriously considering whether we should call in P.C. Morrow. In a few hours it will be dark and if Kurt has been injured, I don't think he could survive another night out in the cold."

"Please don't call him yet. Let me go and have a look here and there."

"All right, but if you don't find him, I really think that we must get outside help. It is getting too risky to leave things as they are any longer. Would you like me to come with you?"

"No, but thank you. I'll be fine. I have an idea...where he might be."

"Well, if you need me at all, call me at once. I'll be in the house." He touched Karl's arm. "Good luck," he said.

                    *   *   *

Karl had been thinking a great deal about where Kurt might
have gone. He knew that the boy could be a little irresponsible,
but he certainly was not stupid. Thus it had occurred to Karl that
he might not have been out in the cold that night at all. He had
probably gone for one of his walks, gotten caught in the blizzard,
and decided to take shelter somewhere for a while. Then, seeing
how thick the snow was getting, he had probably decided to stay
there for the night. Karl knew of a very likely shelter — and a
good one.

He trudged back to the farm and through the snowy fields,
to the little barn where they had held the *Yom Tov* prayer services.
Over the winter it had been used to store the winter feed for the
animals.

He made his way to the barn door quickly, with mounting
excitement. Karl quietly pushed open the door. Compared to
the glare of the white fields, the barn seemed wrapped in
darkness. Karl stood for a moment, straining his eyes, bringing
them to rest on a shadowy bundle in the corner. Sure enough,
there was Kurt, lying on a bed made up of bales of hay and
covered with more hay for warmth. He was still sound asleep,
but he looked fine. The barn was a little drafty but the hay had
kept him warm.

Karl reached for Kurt's hands to make sure they were warm,
and while he was doing so, Kurt awoke. Immediately alert, he
wrenched his hands away from Karl. "What are you doing here?"
he asked angrily.

"We were anxious about you, Kurt. You did not return home
last night, and I came to search for you."

"What business is it of yours? It's my concern."

"Well, it's my concern when Mr. Berrin comes over to us at
five o'clock in the morning worried sick about you!" Karl replied.

"Oh, I'm sure you were all worried about me," Kurt muttered
sarcastically.

"Kurt, I am becoming quite fed up with your behavior!"

"Then leave me alone!"

"It wouldn't bother you if I did?"

"Not really." Kurt looked away.

"Don't you think anyone cares about you?" Karl asked softly.

"I *know* they don't."

"Well, for your information, Mr. Berrin did not sleep a wink all night, out of worry over you."

Kurt met Karl's eyes and Karl could see that he was surprised.

"Miles and Joshua have been out looking for you since early this morning," he went on, "and Jack and I went out as soon as we heard you were missing. You are acting ungratefully and unfairly toward the Berrins, who care about you. And aside from that, you always act so coldly toward us, who want to be your friends, and tell us nothing about yourself. In fact, you never talk to us at all unless you're asked a question." Karl's anger and hurt came out now. "You're not the only one who has left his family behind and come to a strange place, you know. We are all going through the same thing."

Kurt stared at him but remained silent.

"Don't you trust us?" Karl went on, not knowing if Kurt was angry with his outburst.

"No."

"Why not?" Karl was taken aback by the utter honesty of his reply.

"Because..."

"Because what?"

Kurt was silent.

"Have we ever let you down? Have we ever not included you in anything, even after the way you have acted toward us?"

Kurt said nothing.

"Have we, Kurt?"

"N...no."

Karl could see that he was beginning to reach Kurt somehow and perhaps even gain his trust. He decided to seize the opportunity now — for it might not arise again — and ask the question which was on the tip of his tongue. "What did happen to you,

Kurt? Why are you so bitter?''

Kurt's face got very red. His eyes filled with tears. What he had bottled up for so long now came rushing out. He told Karl about Helga, about his grandmother, his flight from the Nazis through the back streets of Vienna, being in hiding, about his parents, and finally about the Kilerns and his escape. When Kurt had finished, Karl was dumbfounded.

"Kurt — I don't know what to say. I'm so sorry. I didn't realize—" Karl could not finish his sentence. A cry suddenly burst from Kurt and his whole body shook with loud and uncontrollable sobs. Karl sat beside him for twenty minutes, his arm tightly around the younger boy. Finally it seemed that Kurt had almost exhausted himself.

Karl hugged him and realized that for all his prowess, the boy's build was slighter than Otto's.

"Karl," he whispered hesitantly.

"Yes?"

"There is one thing that I did not tell you. Do you promise not to tell anyone?"

"Of course."

Kurt took a deep and ragged breath. "I...I am responsible for the death of many Jews in Vienna," he murmured, his face in his hands.

"What?"

Now he lifted his head and met Karl's eyes. "Do you remember I told you how my grandmother was humiliated and how the Nazis chased me?"

"Yes."

"I left something out. That afternoon they rounded up many Jews into the square and shot them." He bit his lips trying in vain to prevent the tears which were already falling. "My mother told me what had happened that night when I returned home. She didn't say that I was to blame, but I wondered if she thought it. I have never told anyone, but since that day I have carried it with me. All those people who lost their lives because of me. And here I am, managing to escape from Vienna, while my parents, and the people who lost their loved ones because of me, are left to face the Nazis.''

"Don't ever think like that!" Karl cried. "No, you are not responsible! You were a little boy who wanted to defend his grandmother, and that is all! How could you have known what was going to happen? It might have occurred anyway, for such things occurred all the time. In the Torah we learn that to embarrass someone is like killing him. You *saved* those old people from humiliation — it was a very brave thing to do, a little boy fighting the Nazis for the sake of his grandmother's honor. I am sure your parents understand that.''

"Thank you, Karl." Kurt smiled shakily and wiped a tear away. "I have never been able to tell anyone this before. You have helped me. You won't mention it to anyone, will you?''

"No, of course not." Karl stood up and brushed himself off. "I should get you home now. Kurt, one thing — please don't run off without telling anyone again.''

"I won't!''

"And if you ever need to talk to anyone, remember that I am always here.''

"Thank you, Karl. I will remember that.''

"Kurt! Thank God you are safe!" Mrs. Berrin cried when she saw him standing beside Karl, looking a little pale and drawn but healthy enough otherwise.

"I am very sorry for all the trouble I have caused," Kurt replied — in English.

16

APRIL 1940 MARKED the end of the so-called "phony war," with the invasion of Norway by Germany. This was followed a month later — on the 10th of May — by German attacks on Holland, Belgium and Luxembourg. On that very same day the British Prime Minister Neville Chamberlain resigned, and the king asked Winston Churchill to form a new government. He called his first cabinet meeting for the 11th of May at 2:30 P.M. This was on a Saturday.

While Karl, Otto, Erich, Joshua, Miles and Kurt were eating their Shabbos lunch together, they were blissfully unaware that at that very moment the Vice-Chief of the Imperial General Staff was summing up a decision the Cabinet Committee had already taken: "In light of the possibility of invasion, it [is] very desirable that all enemy aliens in Counties of the South-East...should be interned..."

Sunday afternoon, the 12th of May, found the boys all rowing on the river in two small boats. One of them belonged to Jack Willow, and the other had been made by the boys themselves in the few days since the weather had become warmer. It was little more than a raft really, but the boys were proud of the fact that it was water-tight.

"Do you remember how we used to do this back home?" Karl asked Otto suddenly, as he gently paddled his oar.

Otto smiled at the recollection. Dipping his hand in the clear water, he asked, "Do you remember the time I fell in?"

"Of course I do! That was how you learned to swim. By the time I'd jumped into the water to save you, you'd already reached the boat."

"And we both came home dripping wet!"

"And is this the first time you've gone boating?" Karl asked Miles, who was sitting beside Otto on the homemade boat.

"We aren't that backward in London!" he laughed. "Joshua and I used to go rowing often in Regent's Park, or in the Serpentine in Hyde Park. They have artificial lakes especially for this."

"Really?"

"Yes. I hope one day I'll be able to show you." Miles looked across to the right bank of the river. "Hey, look over there," he said. "It's Jack!"

The boys all turned to look. Jack was running toward them, waving his arms in the air. Karl and Otto laughed at him and waved back at him. "He can be so funny sometimes!" Karl said to Miles.

"Karl!" Jack shouted. "Karl!"

"What is it?"

"I need you in the house a moment."

"Fine!" Karl called back. "I'm coming." He moored the boat to the right bank and stepped out, handing the oar to Miles. "Do you want to take over? I'll just go and see what Jack wants, and I'll be back in a few minutes."

He caught up with Jack and fell in step with him. "Is anything wrong?" he asked.

Jack was still trying to catch his breath after his sprint. "It's P.C. Morrow," he panted. "He's up at the house. He wants to see you."

"Any idea what it's about?" Karl's voice was low. He stared gravely at Jack.

Jack did not need to say a word. They both knew.

*   *   *

As they entered the kitchen, P.C. Morrow rose from his chair at the table. "Good afternoon, Karl," he said in a friendly tone of voice.

Sehr falsch, Karl thought to himself. The policeman's friendliness was clearly not genuine.

"Karl, I'm afraid you'll have to go away overnight," the policeman went on in the same matter-of-fact way. "If you could just pack a few essentials, such as toiletries and so forth..."

"Why do I have to go away?"

"Oh, it's only overnight. Just a routine procedure."

"Where am I going?"

"I'll be waiting in the car for you," the policeman said, and was gone.

"Best do as he says then," Jack said gently, putting his arm around Karl's shoulders.

"I don't like it, Jack."

"Neither do I!" cried Fay, who had been silently standing at the sink the whole time.

"Never mind," Jack said. "It won't be for long. Do whatever it is he wants you for, and come home."

Karl went up to his room. Why did he feel such foreboding? P.C. Morrow had said it was only for one night, after all. He took down his brown leather suitcase from the top of the wardrobe, and opened it. He packed his pajamas, a spare change of clothes, some money, his official papers, and his washbag with all his toiletries. And, since he would not be back until at least the next morning, his *tefillin* and a *siddur*.

"Karl's taking a long time, isn't he?" Miles remarked to Otto. "Perhaps there really is something the matter. Do you think we should go up to the house and find out what's happening?"

"Yes, let's," Otto replied.

"Joshua!" he called across to the other boat. "We're going to see what's taking Karl so long. Are you coming?"

*   *   *

They arrived at the house in time to see Karl climbing into the back seat of P.C. Morrow's police car.

"Karl! Karl! Where are you going?" Otto shouted.

The engine had already started up. "I'll be back!" Karl called, and the car sped off.

"Karl!" Otto cried again. "Karl!" The car disappeared in the distance. "Oh, where is he going? Why is he leaving me?"

The others stood behind him, dumbstruck, and then Kurt walked up to his side and put his arm around him. "It's all right, Otto," he said. "We are all here. You are not alone."

The barracks to which Karl was taken were located a few miles outside Swanstone. As soon as P.C. Morrow dropped Karl off, he sped away without so much as a good-bye or a word of explanation. The bleak buildings were surrounded by a barbed-wire fence, and a watchtower stood in the center of the yard. Lined up outside were men of all ages — some looked to Karl to be as young as he was, sixteen, but many were older. A few were even quite elderly, stooped over and walking with canes. Karl joined the end of the line.

Within a few minutes, Karl realized that everyone else was as confused as he was. The men questioned each other in German or English, while British soldiers watched them carefully. In front of Karl was a group of boys talking animatedly in German.

"*Enschuldigen Sie,*" Karl said. "Do any of you know what's going on?"

A tall boy with lank blond hair and crystal-blue eyes turned to him. "Nobody has told us anything, but we think they suspect us of being Nazi agents or something of that nature. It's absurd! A policeman was waiting for me when I came home from church with my grandparents this morning."

"Oh...then you're not Jewish?"

"No!" The boy smiled. "But I'm certainly not a Nazi, either. My father is German but my mother is British. They thought life would be safer for me here than in Germany, so they sent me to stay with my grandparents until the war is over. But look what happened — I was arrested here instead!"

"I wasn't told anything either," Karl said. "The local policeman told me I had to go, he brought me, and then he disappeared."

"Are you Jewish?"

"Yes," Karl replied. He glanced at the boy nervously, and wondered if he sympathized with the Nazis nevertheless.

"That's outrageous then!" cried the boy. "How could a Jew be accused of being a Nazi?"

"I don't know. I don't understand it either."

The boy held out his hand. "By the way, my name is Klaus."

"And mine is Karl." The two shook hands.

"I suppose you came here in the first place to escape the persecution in Germany?"

"Yes, I did," Karl nodded.

Klaus shook his head. "These people are such fools, and this is such a ridiculous business. There may very well be some Nazi sympathizers among the Germans in England and I can understand their being arrested. But you? And I?"

"Do you really think there are some?" Karl glanced around.

"Sure — but I don't think they could make any trouble. Why, they wouldn't even be able to say *'Heil Hitler'* without being jumped upon."

The two boys were so engrossed in their conversation that they did not realize that they had reached their turn in the line. "Hey!" shouted the soldier processing them. "What did you just say?"

"I was only explaining that— " Klaus began.

"Sure, sure...I know your type very well," the soldier said, looking at Klaus with disdain.

"I am no Nazi, if that's what you mean!" Klaus said hotly.

"That's what they all say," murmured the soldier. "Can I have your Alien's Registration Certificate?"

Klaus withdrew it from his canvas bag. The soldier held out an open palm for it but Klaus made no move to hand it over. "Why do you want it?" he asked.

"Listen, you, if you make trouble I can cause a lot more for you, so I would suggest that you follow orders." Klaus was about to protest but thought better of it. What was the use? "I want yours as well," the soldier said to Karl.

Karl opened his case and handed it to him. The soldier snatched it out of his hands. In the meantime another soldier grabbed their luggage for searching, and confiscated certain items, such as toiletries, including Karl's precious bar of soap. "What do you think you are doing?" Klaus cried. "Give us back our things!"

Karl breathed a prayer of thanks for the foresight he'd had when he took his mother's engagement ring out of the bar of soap and sewed it into his jacket lining while he was in Swanstone.

"Some of them act as badly as Germans," Klaus whispered quietly in German.

"What could they want with our certificates?" Karl asked. Before Klaus even had a chance to reply, the soldier returned the certificates to them. They had been stamped with the word "Internment."

That night as he settled down on a blanket on the cold concrete floor, Karl could not fall asleep. He lay there listening to Klaus talking animatedly with his newfound German friends. Karl had been asked to join them but had declined the invitation. Klaus was pleasant enough, but Karl knew he would not feel comfortable among them all. Besides that, he wanted time to gather his thoughts. Things had happened so quickly, he still couldn't grasp them fully.

His Tribunal had taken place so many months before that he had pushed it to the back of his mind and all but forgotten about it. In any case, it had been decided that he was no security threat. He smiled ruefully to himself at the thought of those words possibly applying to himself. Yet now he had been arrested and no one would tell him for how long he was going to be held. The one thing he was sure about was that he would not be back in

Swanstone the next day.

"Are you having trouble sleeping?"

Karl looked up, trying to find where the voice in the darkness had come from. An elderly man with a German accent was smiling down at him.

"Yes, I am," Karl replied, sitting up.

"Let me introduce myself. I am Rabbi Lurmann," he said. "I come from Frankfurt."

Karl's face lit up. He had found a kindred spirit, another Jew! He rose quickly and extended his hand. "I am Karl Alexander, from Ruhenwald. It is a suburb of Berlin," he replied.

"Yes, I know it well," Rabbi Lurmann said, nodding. "Many years ago I had a good friend from there. His name was also Alexander — Joseph Alexander."

"Joseph Alexander? He was my grandfather!"

"Really?" Rabbi Lurmann was excited. "What a small world! We were in yeshiva together, many, many years ago. I was saddened when I heard that he had died. Unfortunately, I was unable to come to the *shivah*. Do you still remember him a little?"

"Oh, quite well! I was nine when he died."

"*Ach*, he was a wonderful person," said Rabbi Lurmann softly. "He was my *chavrusa* for a long time."

"Could you please be quiet?" someone called out. "I am trying to sleep."

"I am truly sorry," Rabbi Lurmann apologized, and then to Karl he added quietly, "Perhaps you would like to learn with me tomorrow."

Karl's face brightened. "Oh, yes! I would like that very much."

"Otto, you must go to school," Fay said gently. But Otto sat on his bed and adamantly shook his head.

"I want to see Karl."

"You will see him when you get home."

"But I want to wait here until he comes."

"He may not return until this evening, and in that case you

will have missed a whole day of school for nothing. Erich and the others are waiting downstairs for you. You don't want to make them late.''

"Fay, if Karl returns before I come home from school, will you ask him to come to school and fetch me?''

"That's a deal,'' she replied, patting him affectionately on the head.

The one bright spot in Karl's first day at the barracks was studying Mishnah for two hours in the morning with Rabbi Lurmann. It had been many months since he had studied with someone older, and it brought back such clear memories of the hours he used to spend learning with his father. How he had missed it! He also discovered that there were a few other Jewish boys there, and Rabbi Lurmann agreed to give them all a *shiur* in the evening. Perhaps things would not be so bad after all.

In the afternoon he sat down to write two letters: one to Otto, and the other to Jack and Fay, who were probably worried about what had happened to him. To his brother he made no mention of the fact that he had been interned. He simply wrote that he had been sent to the barracks for questioning, as a routine procedure, but since there were so many people there it was going to take longer than he had expected and he was not sure when he would be back. He told him that the conditions were quite comfortable and he had made many friends — and he had even found a man who had been in yeshiva with their beloved grandfather. He ended his letter telling Otto to be good and not to forget to say his prayers or make *berachos* when he should.

To the Willows he wrote of his uncertainty about when he would be released, and his poor living conditions. He explained that he was sure there had been some sort of mistake and that he would be released in the near future but he asked Jack if perhaps he could find a way to help him.

Later in the afternoon, when Karl tried to hand the letters to a soldier, asking him to mail them for him, he was told that it was forbidden to send any letters.

                    *   *   *

"How are you, Karl?" Klaus asked, smiling.

"Fed up. How about you?"

"Pretty much the same." Klaus lowered his voice and pushed back his straight hair. "You know, I would escape if I thought I stood half a chance, but those soldiers watch us like hawks."

"Be careful, Klaus," he warned, "and don't make any trouble for yourself. We'll probably be out of here within the next few days anyway."

"Don't worry, I won't make trouble. Believe me, I want to get out of here as soon as possible. My grandparents must be frantic about me."

Fay looked up from her sewing machine as Jack entered the room. "Well, did you ask P.C. Morrow again?" she asked.

Jack sat down on the sofa, and closed his eyes wearily. "Yes, I did."

"And what did he say?"

"He still won't tell me anything!" Jack sat up angrily. "When he came for Karl, he said he would only be away for one night. It's been over a week now, and he refuses to give me an explanation. I can't imagine what could have happened to him. How's Otto this morning?"

"I think he cried himself to sleep again last night, poor kid. His eyes were all red and puffy this morning. It's really hard on him."

Jack nodded sympathetically. "His brother is the only family he has here," he said.

Karl awoke to the sound of a shrill whistle. He rubbed his eyes and sat up. "Everybody up!" a soldier shouted. What could they want with the men at this unearthly hour? It was the middle of the night. "Attention, please. Attention, please. In ten minutes you will be leaving. Pack all your belongings and be ready to leave in ten minutes."

Leave? Immediately, the barracks were a hub of activity, as everyone prepared...for what? For going, but to where exactly, they did not know. Karl, now fully alert, was ready in five minutes. In high spirits, he followed the line of men into the waiting truck outside. He assumed that they were about to be released, and looked forward to being back in Swanstone by mid-morning, reunited with his brother.

He could not have been more wrong.

17

THE MOMENT KARL walked through the barbed-wire gates at Huyton, something died in him. He looked around at the unfinished housing project with its shacks and piles of building debris scattered over the grounds. He found that the scene matched the way he felt: utterly hopeless.

Indifferently, he handed his suitcase over for inspection. He was given a sack to fill with straw, for a mattress. Aimlessly he did as he was instructed. By now he could have been back in Swanstone with Otto and the Willows.

The camp was already quite full when Karl's group had arrived. Almost all of the sparsely furnished buildings were filled to capacity, so most of the new arrivals — including Karl — were allotted two-man tents. Karl entered his tent, carrying the straw-filled mattress, and met the other occupant, a middle-aged German doctor in a dark suit, immacutely polished shoes and small, gold-rimmed round glasses. Nodding politely at the doctor, he put down his belongings and went outside again.

Without specific direction, Karl wandered around the camp, taking in the dismal houses and tents which had been erected on the muddy ground. For the first time he felt truly a prisoner, but what made it all the more terrible was that he had committed no crime.

He returned to his tent and remained there for three days, leaving only when necessary, such as for roll-call or meals. On the morning of the fourth day, as Karl lay on his side propped up on one elbow, staring listlessly into space, he had a visitor. He was not even aware that Rabbi Lurmann had entered the tent until he felt a tap on his shoulder.

"You were not at the *shiur* again last night," the rabbi said softly, withouth any hint of rebuke. His comment was phrased more as a question, inviting Karl to confide in him. No reply was forthcoming, however. "The other boys were concerned about you," he went on. "They were all asking where you were. And even that young German boy approached me today, Karl, and inquired about you. He told me to tell you that he came to visit you last night, but you were already sleeping and he didn't want to disturb you."

Karl rose, and brushed off his clothing. "I wasn't sleeping," he mumbled.

"Oh." Rabbi Lurmann sighed. "I see. So you knew that he came?"

"I knew, I just didn't feel like talking to anyone, that's all."

Rabbi Lurmann changed the subject abruptly. "Some of the boys are going to start growing their own vegetables, you know," he said. "It will improve our food situation somewhat, since there is a shortage of kosher food. They asked whether you might like to lend a hand. They could use your help, especially since you lived on a farm and know how to grow vegetables." He paused and looked at Karl. "How about it?"

"I don't think so."

"Why not?"

"Oh, what's the use?" he blurted.

"Karl," the rabbi said gently, putting an arm around his shoulders. "It isn't necessary to make things worse for yourself than they already are, you know."

"Things couldn't be much worse!" Karl cried. "My little brother is all on his own. He doesn't understand what is happening at all, or where I am. I'm stuck here indefinitely, for no valid reason. I haven't even had a proper trial and I don't even have the opportunity to lodge an appeal. Why, it could be years until

I am released!"

The rabbi nodded. "Let us discuss first things first — *al rishon rishon,* as our Sages said. From what I gather, your brother is with very good people who will look after him until your return. He has many caring friends and I am sure he will be fine. As for you being here for a long period, you don't know if that will be the case. Nothing is certain. Just think — a few weeks ago, did any of us imagine we would be interned? Just as we have been imprisoned, we might be free tomorrow. Who knows what Hashem has in store for us? Remember what the Geonim said: 'Heaven's rescuing help comes in the twinkling of an eye.'

"Even though we may not understand why this is happening, we must have *bitachon.* That does not mean we can rest assured that everything is going to be just the way we want it to be, Karl. Of course we don't know. But we must believe that whatever Hashem does is ultimately for our good, even if it may not appear so at the time. As Rabbi Akiva said—"

Karl interrupted him. "'Everything that Hashem does, He does for the good.'"

"Yes," the rabbi said, smiling. "You see, Karl, the most important thing is that we don't lose our spirit. Trying to improve our condition is the only way we can fight. Even in the worst situation, one can make something good." The rabbi noticed that Karl seemed more alert, and the sparkle was returning to his eyes. "I remember you telling me how you regretted the fact that when you came to England you were unable to continue your education. This could be an ideal opportunity for you to catch up on some of that lost learning."

Now Karl met the older man's eyes. "Rabbi Lurmann..." he began.

"Yes, Karl?"

"Would you...if you wouldn't mind...go over with me what has been studied in the *shiurim* I've missed?"

Fay was busy rolling out a ball of yeast dough, intent on her bread-making, and did not hear Otto enter the kitchen. Until he stood right beside her, she was quite unaware of his presence. "Fay...can I...perhaps talk with you?" he asked in hesitant, heavily accented English.

Fay did her best to hide her surprise. "Yes, certainly, Otto," she replied, wiping her hands on her apron. "Come, let's sit down."

Otto sat upright at the kitchen table, looking pathetically formal. "Fay— " Otto began again, in an attempt to muster his courage. "Why...why did Karl lie to me?"

"Otto! Whatever do you mean?"

"He said that he would only be away for one night, but it has been many weeks now and he has not come back. Why? Where did he go? I am all alone. I was sent away from my parents, and now my brother has left me! Don't any of them care about me anymore?" His voice broke.

"Oh, no, it is nothing like that, dear. Poor boy, we should have explained it to you better. Of course Karl did not want to leave you! He was forced to."

"Why?"

"Well, it's very confusing. Now that there is a war on with Germany, the government believes that German-born residents in England might be a threat. Do you grasp when I am trying to tell you?"

"No. I don't understand. Did we not have to leave Germany because we are Jewish?"

"Yes, that's right."

"Then why do the English people think that we could be one of those bad Germans who do not like Jewish people?"

Fay smiled sadly. "I think you understand the situation very well," she said. "It is indeed a dreadful mistake, but that is what they take him for."

"Do you know where he is?"

"No, but believe me, Otto, we are trying to find out. I am sure we will learn something soon."

"So Karl didn't want to leave me..."

"Of course not! He loves you so much, and he must be

missing you a great deal.''

Otto got up, and began to leave the table. "Thank you for helping me to understand," he said solemnly.

"Please come to me any time you want to talk," Fay replied, blinking away the tears as she watched the brave little figure walk stiffly out of the kitchen.

"I really enjoy Rabbi Lurmann's *shiurim*," Karl told Franz — a new friend — as the two of them slowly waded through the mud on their way back to the tents. They held on to each other for support, as there was no outside lighting and in the darkness, only the dim outlines of the tents were visible.

"So do I," replied Franz. "They are about the only redeeming factors of this place. I have learned so much in the short time we've been at Huyton. The fact is that I was not a particularly observant Jew in Germany, or after coming to England, but since meeting the Rabbi and going to his *shiurim*, I have begun to feel that living a fully committed Jewish life is the only option for me."

Karl and Franz suddenly froze, as a sharp cry echoed through the night.

"What was that?" Franz whispered.

"I don't know," Karl replied, as the shadowy figures of three youths emerged from one of the closer tents and stealthily ran off into the night. The two boys stood stock still until the figures were out of sight. "Come on, let's go see what's happened," Karl said.

They entered the tent and found someone doubled over on a mattress, whimpering and groaning in pain. He looked up at the two astonished boys, clutching his stomach.

"Klaus!" Karl exclaimed. "What happened? Who has done this to you?"

"It...it...was Helmut and his mob," Klaus said with difficulty.

Karl and Franz exchanged a look. Helmut was well-known among them. A confirmed Nazi sympathizer, he always did his

best to cause discomfort to the Jewish inmates by giving the Nazi
salute when he walked past. Everyone was wary of him and kept
out of his way as much as possible.

"What did he want with you?"

"I...I don't know. He said this was a warning."

"Against what?"

"'Fraternizing with the enemy,' he said."

"What enemy? Does he mean us? The Jewish prisoners?"

Klaus looked away, not meeting their eyes. "Who knows?"

"He means us, doesn't he?"

"Yes," he admitted. "He told me that although I'm only part
German, he still considers me a member of the 'Master Race,'
and as such...oh," Klaus tried to smile through his pain, "never
mind. It's all so foolish."

"Go on," Karl urged him. "What did he say?"

Klaus sat up on his mattress. "I don't know...oh, you can
imagine..." He looked away again. His pain was easing up, and
he could breathe more easily and talk without a strain.

"Perhaps you should not be seen talking with us then," Karl
suggested. "This is serious — I don't want you getting hurt
because of us, God forbid."

"Don't be ridiculous! They have no right to tell me what to
do. I won't stand for it! I said that to them, too — and that's
when they punched me! Look, Karl, I am determined not to
become like them. Our differences — yours and mine — don't
prevent us from being friendly with one another, and I'm going
to keep it that way. If no one takes a stand, then *they'll* be able to
get away with anything."

"You are to be admired," Franz said quietly.

"There is nothing admirable about my behavior. I am only
doing what is correct and what I believe in."

"You are paying a price for it," Karl added. "And that *is*
admirable."

"Are you feeling all right now?" Franz asked.

"Yes, thanks. I'll be all right."

"Goodnight, then. We'll see you tomorrow."

"Take care of yourself."

As they left the tent, Franz turned to Karl, unable to conceal the fear in his voice. "Now they're starting here."

"It doesn't necessarily mean anything," Karl replied, his voice even. "It's only one incident. They just want to frighten us. If we don't pay any attention to it, I'm sure they'll get tired of it and leave us alone."

Franz remained very grave. "No, I think it's something more than that. I have the feeling that they know something. While we're all in the dark about what's happening in Europe, and don't have access to any newspapers, they appear to be receiving information, thought I can't imagine how. I heard something: there are rumors that Holland and Belgium have been invaded by the Nazis, that France has been conquered and that parachutists have landed here — in England."

Karl gasped. "Can it be true?"

"If it is, and the Nazis here know that...well, it explains a lot. And there is room for our serious concern."

The next morning two soldiers approached Karl's tent. "Karl Alexander! Karl Alexander!"

"Yes, I'm here."

"Prepare to leave in a quarter of an hour. You may take one suitcase."

"Where am I going?"

They ignored his question and left.

Karl quickly packed his few personal items and left the tent. He wanted to find Rabbi Lurmann, Franz, and the other boys to ask whether they too were leaving, but there was no time. Before he knew it, he was being ushered out of the barbed-wire gate and onto one of the waiting trucks. Whatever lay ahead, he told himself, at least he would be out of Huyton.

The truck came to a halt, and Karl smelled the sea. As all the passengers alighted from the trucks, he realized they had come to a port. The ocean was gray and the air smelled tangy.

"We're at the Liverpool Docks," he heard someone say. They were all headed to a pier where other people were waiting. In front of them loomed a large white vessel which looked like a cruise ship.

"You as well?" Karl heard a familiar voice behind him.

"Klaus!" he exclaimed, relieved to see a friendly face. "Do you know where they're taking us?"

"Some say to the internment camps on the Isle of Man. But I've also heard that we're going overseas."

"Overseas! Where?"

"I haven't the faintest idea."

"Tell me, have you seen Franz and the other boys?"

"No, I haven't. Look! We're being taken on board!"

The *Arandora Star* was once a luxurious cruise ship but there were constant reminders that it was now a prison ship. Certain exits were prohibited to the passengers, and barbed wire shut them off. They were not allowed to walk on the promenade deck and the ship was constantly patrolled by armed guards. Most of the passengers were German and Italian (though not all of them were Nazis or Fascists), and there were a few Jews on board, perhaps thirty in all. The curious thing was, Karl discovered, that all of them had been given the A classification, and he was apparently the only one with a C. Obviously there had been a dreadful error.

At 4:00 A.M. on Monday, the 1st of July, 1940, they set sail. Karl heard that their probable destination was Canada. It seemed that he was constantly being taken further and further away from his family and all the friends he had made. But he resolved to make the best of what he had. The food was fresh and abundant and there were plenty of vegetables available for the few who were trying to maintain a kosher diet. Despite the growing distance between him and all that was familiar, Karl nevertheless felt heartened. He gazed at the vast blue sea and the receding shores of England, and felt hope stir in his heart that they would understand in Canada, and release him.

After their first full day at sea, Karl was extremely tired. Since he had not had much sleep the night before, he decided to turn in early. He had been allocated a cabin which he shared with three others. It had been intended as a cabin for two, but two additional mattresses had been placed on the floor. Apart from this, the cabin was comfortable and the stylish design made him smile ironically. Mrs. Samson would have approved, he thought.

A hollow rumbling penetrated Karl's deep sleep. At first he stirred slightly, turned over, and went back to sleep. Gradually he became aware of the sounds of excited voices and running feet. He rose and switched on the light, but nothing happened. The cabin remained dark. His roommates began to wake up too, and they quickly threw their clothes on over their pajamas. The voices in the hall and above were hysterical. Karl opened the cabin door, and cried, "What's wrong? What's happened?"

"A torpedo has hit the ship!" came the frenzied reply. "We are sinking!"

Charging back into his cabin, Karl found his life jacket and tied it firmly around himself. He joined the rush up to the deck. Some of the passengers were screaming. In the predawn dimness, he could already see that the ship was tilting. It was beginning to go down. He spied an empty lifeboat and made for it but a guard barred his way. "These are only for British soldiers," he barked.

"What are we supposed to do?" Karl cried desperately. There were some life rafts still available but they were attached to the walls with wire, and try as he might, he could not undo them. A few men came to his aid, but it was no use: they would need some tools and there was no time to go hunting for any now.

Karl quickly realized that he had no choice but to follow what many of the other men were doing: to jump overboard. He found a large plank of wood and threw it down into the dark swirling water. As he stood looking down from the railing, he was joined by another Jewish man, who stood beside him, hesitant of what to do. "Jump!" Karl cried. "It's the only way to save yourself!" Then Karl recited the first paragraph of *Shema Yisrael*, and heeded his own advice.

As he clung for dear life to the piece of wood in the black, oily water, he tried to swim as far away as possible from the ship. Twenty minutes later, he stopped, gasping for breath, and turned toward the ship. Listening to the distant cries, he watched the dawn break and in the first morning light the *Arandora Star* slowly sank to the depths of the sea.

On the evening of July 3rd, as Otto, Erich and the Willows sat listening to news on the radio, they heard of a certain ship named the *Arandora Star* which had been sunk off the West Coast of Ireland with fifteen hundred German and Italian internees on board en route to Canada. The impression given was that only Nazis and Italian Fascists were on board, but as they sat there taking in the details, they looked at one another, the same terrible unvoiced fear in all their eyes. The final fatality count, the announcer reported, was not yet known, but over half the passengers were thought to have lost their lives.

Otto spent a sleepless night tossing and turning in mounting fear and anxiety. Had his brother been on that ship, and if so, what had happened to him?

It was not until several days later that Otto received the first piece of correspondence from Karl. It was a simple postcard with a message of only three words: "*I am safe.*" But it was all Otto needed to know.

18

A WEEK AFTER being rescued by a Canadian destroyer and taken to Greenock, a part in southwest Scotland, Karl found himself back on the very same wharf in Liverpool where he had departed on the *Arandora Star*. He made his way, along with hundreds of other people, to the boarding area of the HMT *Dunera*, a low gray ship which lay at the pierhead. It looked small and scruffy to Karl, and he wondered how they would all fit.

Tired, impatient soldiers subjected each of the passengers to a brutal search. Karl was horrified to watch a middle-aged man in front of him being forced to turn all his pockets out. The ginger-haired soldier searching him ripped open his suitcase like a hungry scavenger, taking anything that might be of value, including items such as soap and writing paper. When the soldier caught sight of the man's passport, he held it up in front of him and callously ripped it in two.

"No!" The man cried, his hand stretched out, pleading to have it returned.

"You won't be needing this anymore — after the war you'll be sent back to Germany where you belong," snarled the soldier, roughly pushing him aside. The man bent over to salvage the remains of his personal belongings. "That's what I like to see: Germans crawling," the soldier remarked to his companion before turning on the next in line.

Karl was roughly grabbed by the collar by another soldier.

"Where's your luggage?"

"I don't have any," Karl replied simply.

"Don't lie to us. Where is it?"

"I lost it all on the *Arandora Star*." The soldier grunted, but insisted on giving Karl's clothes a thorough search. Karl tried to look aloof and hoped he would not be betrayed by his guilt; he succeeded. "Next!" shouted the soldier, giving him a hard shove and ordering him to move on.

Karl and the other passengers were herded up the gangway to board the depressing ship. Since they had heard nothing about their intended destination, Karl assumed that they were bound for Canada once more. He paused for a moment at the entrance, and looked out to sea. As he inhaled the salty air, he wondered how Otto was faring and when he would next see him, or at least be able to send him a letter. Like the rest of the *Arandora Star* survivors, all he had been permitted to send to his family was a postcard informing them that he was safe. He hoped that Klaus had also been rescued. He had not seen him before the ship had sunk, but he wanted to think that he had survived. Klaus was a German, but he was a good person, and he had shown great kindness toward Karl.

"Get a move on!" shouted a soldier, prodding Karl with his rifle butt. "You're holding everyone up!"

On board, Karl was appalled by the conditions. It was already overcrowded and there were still many more passengers streaming onto the ship. Unlike the *Arandora Star*, where most of them had slept four, or at maximum six, to a cabin, on the *Dunera* there was so little space that the men were forced to sleep on the decks and on the stairs.

Some men were fortunate enough to be allocated with hammocks which were strung across the ship. The rest had to make do with sleeping wherever they could find space to lie down. Every available space was occupied. Some of the men argued over the prized hammocks, but Karl did not think it was worth the effort and found himself room in a corner.

In the middle of this chaos, an officer held up his hand for silence. "To those of you who have survived the Arandora Star," he began, "I have some reassuring words: If this ship should be torpedoed, we have made sure that none of you will get out."

Karl looked around, and realized that this was true. His position was indeed helpless. Almost every porthole on the entire ship was firmly closed and locked up. No natural light or air was able to filter in. The passengers were forbidden to go up to the deck at all, except for their set exercise period of a few minutes every day.

At midnight the ship left Liverpool and set off at full speed. Karl lay in his corner, indifferent to his surroundings, lost in memories and thoughts. It was almost a year to the day since he had last seen his mother and father. What was happening to them now? He prayed they were safe. And Otto — when would he see him again? Karl wiped an unbidden tear from his eyes.

As the ship rocked and lurched over every wave, most of the men felt seasick. A boy about Karl's age staggered across the deck. He looked extremely ill and from the way he was tripping over all the sleeping passengers, he appeared to be very dizzy. Gasping for breath, he was trying to inhale fresh air but there was none to be had. Much to the annoyance of the other passengers, who shouted their protests at him, he appeared to be experiencing severe difficulties regaining his balance.

Karl rose from his mattress and made his way over to the boy. Taking his hand, he led him back to his own corner, where he told him gently to sit down with his head between his knees. After a short time the boy felt much better and raised his head. It was the first time that Karl was able to get a good look at him in the darkened ship, and an expression of surprise crossed his face as he did so. "*Willie?*" he whispered in disbelief.

Hearing his name, the boy lifted his head more and stared closely at the vaguely familiar face. "K...Karl?"

Karl nodded. Willie gasped, and hugged his old friend. It had been three whole years since he had last seen Karl, three long years since Willie and his family had suddenly left Germany. Willie and Karl had been neighbors, best friends and classmates, and had grown up together.

"What are you doing here?" Karl asked him. "I didn't know you were in England."

"We fled Germany to Holland. But when Holland was invaded, my...my parents were arrested." Willie paused, looked down, and drew a deep breath. "I was saved by a very kind non-Jewish family who hid me and then helped me to get on a train bound for England. But shortly afterwards," Willie went on, gaining strength as he spoke to his friend, "I was arrested and sent to the internment camp at Seaton. Then yesterday, I was put on a train with a few hundred other men and sent here. What about you, Karl? How did you come to be here?"

"I'll tell you. It seems there is no refuge, no safe place at all for us to be, Willie. Last July I came over on the *Kindertransporte* with Otto. When war broke out I managed to be evacuated with him to the countryside, where we were taken in by a very kind non-Jewish family. Everything was fine until three months ago, when I was arrested, and after a few days sent to Huyton. I was on board the *Arandora Star*...did you hear about it?"

Willie nodded. "Yes, of course."

"*Baruch Hashem* I managed to survive and, a week later, here I am."

Willie let out a ragged sigh. "Are your parents still in Germany?"

This was a subject that was so painful to think about that both boys developed a matter-of-fact tone as a defense. "Unfortunately, yes. And have you heard any news regarding *your* parents?"

"Not a thing," Willie replied quickly.

"Have you heard any recent news about the war? What's happening?"

"The last thing I heard was that British troops were forced to evacuate Dunkirk in France, and Mussolini has declared war on the Allies, namely England and France.''

"Really! I hadn't heard," Karl exclaimed. "Does that mean we're losing?''

"I don't know. But it's all in Hashem's hands, isn't it?''

"Yes...yes...''

The following morning while Karl was rolling up the prized pair of *tefillin* which was shared by the two hundred or so religious Jews on board, he heard a sharp grating sound followed by a dull thud. He froze in terror. "It's happening again.'' Other began to cry out, and several men panicked and tried to force their way up the staircase. At that moment the all-clear siren sounded to signify that there was no danger, but Karl remained where he was, standing at the foot of the stairs, gripped with fear. "No...'' he murmured. "No...''

Willie took him by the arm and led him gently back to his mattress. "Nothing is going to happen.''

"Thank you, Willie,'' Karl whispered.

The Jewish passengers on the *Dunera* subsisted mainly on root vegetable, onions, and dried fruit, whenever it was available. They took their advice from one of the rabbis on board, who informed them of what was kosher. Karl was certain, though, that even if the rest of the food were kosher, he would not have been able to eat it. The bread was often so stale and old that it was green with mold, and once he saw maggots in someone's soup. It was no wonder that a great majority of the passengers were suffering from disease.

After a few days at sea, they were forced to go up on deck, in groups, to exercise, encouraged to do so with the extra incentive of rifle butts when they did not run or walk fast enough. What made conditions even worse was that they were forced to walk barefoot. On one occasion a soldier had thrown a glass bottle across the deck, the shattered glass leaving sharp splinters everywhere. They had all walked on broken glass, and every one of them had cut his feet.

When Karl felt particularly low, and fears and worries overcame him, he would call to mind the encouraging words Rabbi Lurmann had said to him at the detention camp. Heaven's help could come in the twinkling of an eye. And what else did they have but hope?

The human spirit can be very strong, especially during difficult and trying times. This was the case among the Jewish passengers on the ship. *Shiurim* were given daily, and generally conducted from memory, since most of the Jewish passengers' books had been confiscated prior to embarkation. Some, though, had managed to save a few pages of *Chumash* here and *Gemara* there, which they fervently taught from. They even established regular Friday evening and Shabbos morning services on Deck Four.

Two weeks after their departure, the *Dunera* docked at Sierra Leone, a British protectorate on the west coast of Africa. Though they were forbidden to leave the ship and were barely able to sight land through the closed portholes, they were excited about having reached a port. During the journey, many of the passengers had tried to make calculations as to their intended destination, and the theories were many.

"How are you feeling?" Karl asked, when he returned from his mission of gleaning some information from some of those who had been attempting to plot the *Dunera's* bearings. Willie tried to prop himself up a little. He had suffered particularly badly from the dysentery which was rife on the ship. Although he was over it now, it had left him feeling very weak. "A little better now. I think I slept for a while," Willie replied. "So did you manage to find anything out?"

"Yes, I did," Karl nodded.

"Is it good news?"

"That depends on how you look at it."
"Does anyone know where we're going?"
"Yes...and it's certainly *not* Canada."
"Then where are they taking us?"
"Australia."

On August 6th they arrived at Cape Town, South Africa. As Karl peered out of one of the only open portholes and caught his first glimpse of Table Mountain, he could not help but be disappointed to find it shrouded in mist. He had seen pictures of it and was looking forward to seeing it. By the next morning the cloud had lifted, and when they set sail that evening, it was a beautiful sight to behold.

"Come and take a look," Karl urged Willie, who heaved himself up while Karl held his arm for support. Willie was much improved but still found that he needed to lean quite heavily on Karl. They gazed in silence at Cape Town which was bathed in the golden evening light, the majestic mountain towering over the town.

"It's breathtaking..." Willie murmured.

"Yes," Karl agreed. "The work of a very talented Artist."

After their departure from South Africa, conditions eased up slightly on board the *Dunera*. The soldiers were not quite so hard on them and the passengers were now permitted to exercise with their shoes on! Those who were ill were allowed to spend up to an hour on the deck in the fresh air each day. Slowly but surely, Willie regained his strength, and color returned to his pallid face.

On August 27th the *Dunera* slid into the Indian Ocean port of Fremantle in Western Australia. Their nightmarish journey was nearing its end.

Customs officials boarded the ship and each of the passengers was fingerprinted, photographed with his internment number around his neck, and issued a Certificate of Registration. It was here that Karl learned that all the former passengers of the *Arandora Star* would disembark at Melbourne, while the rest would continue to Sydney. That meant he and Willie would be separated, a thought that Karl found difficult to bear.

Karl approached one of the customs officials, and explained his reunion with his former friend, and Willie's illness. He asked politely whether, under the circumstances, he might be permitted to sail on to Sydney with the rest of the passengers.

The Australian official turned out to be understanding and helpful. "It is irregular to allow this," he said, "but I'm sure something can be arranged." He gazed sadly at the drawn, anxious face of the young boy and he could not see any way to consider him the slightest possible threat.

After a short stop in Melbourne, the *Dunera* finally dropped anchor in picturesque Sydney Harbor on the morning of September 6th — fifty-seven days after leaving Liverpool.

Once the initial formalities and procedures were over, and they had been served a hurried lunch, the passengers were asked to disembark. In a final act expressing defiance toward the British soldiers, Karl joined some of the passengers in forcing open the portholes which had been sealed throughout the entire voyage. With few exceptions, the British soldiers had insisted on making life miserable for their prisoners until the end.

Karl walked down the plank of the *Dunera* without turning to look back for a last glance. He had to shade his eyes from the bright sunlight, and he suddenly felt so light-headed and giddy from the rush of fresh air that his legs almost gave way beneath him. He had not realized how weak he had become.

The behavior of the Australian soldiers waiting on the pier in their wide-brimmed hats could not have been in greater contrast with their British counterparts. They greeted the passengers warmly and showed them to the train waiting to take them to the camp. "You all right, mate?" one of the soldiers asked Karl with concern when he noticed him tottering unsteadily on his feet.

Karl had never heard the distinctive Australian accent before, and it took a minute before he figured out what the friendly soldier was saying. "Oh...oh, yes! Thanks!" he replied.

These soldiers were actually treating them like human beings!

At regular intervals during the train trip they stopped at various stations along the way where each prisoner received fresh fruits and vegetables. They had not eaten fresh food in weeks and Karl thought that he had never eaten any that were more delicious than those.

As they headed inland from the blue sea and the bustling harbor, the vast Australian landscape stretched out before them, unlike anything Karl had ever seen before. There appeared to be empty land as far as the eye could see. As if out of a picture book, wild kangaroos hopped along beside the train.

He would have enjoyed the adventure had he not been beset by a terrible, weighty guilt — though he could not be held to blame — for the day they arrived in Sydney had been Shabbos.

19

THE INTERNMENT CAMP at Hay was built on the sight of an old airstrip. At first glance, it looked to Karl like the most uninhabitable place on earth — and he was not far from wrong. Hay was situated on a harsh arid plain. The oppressive heat sometimes exceeded one hundred degrees Fahrenheit. The only relief was provided by the cool waters of the Murrumbidgee River and a local sheep farm shaded by a lone gum tree. The camp itself was divided into two compounds, which were called Camp 7 and Camp 8. Camp 7 was entirely for Jewish prisoners and it was here that Karl and Willie were sent.

A double barbed-wire fence surrounded Camp 7, and four watchtowers fitted with machine guns faced down on the thirty-six wooden huts which were set in a semi-circle, containing approximately one thousand prisoners. The camp was equipped with a hospital, a canteen, and a football ground. The religious Jews, who numbered no more than about three hundred, were allocated separate huts, their own kitchen, and a dining hut. It was not long before they had established a shul and a yeshiva as well.

However, they were refused permission to receive new dishes and they certainly did not want to eat out of the old ones, which had been used for non-kosher food. The rabbis of Hay discussed the matter, and came to the decision that the men would simply have to kosher the dishes themselves.

Kurt and Willie helped build the large bonfire needed for the koshering but they did not get very far before the soldiers came rushing down from their watchtowers and surrounded them. "Put that fire out at once!" one of the soldiers shouted in his heavy Australian accent, and ordered some of the men to bring buckets of water in order to quench the flames.

Rabbi Meirer made an attempt to explain. "But we were only trying to —"

"It's quite obvious what you were trying to do," snapped the soldier.

"But we had no choice! You refused to give us new—"

"No choice?" the soldier was incredulous. "That's a good one! Did you really think you would be able to get away with it?"

"Yes," replied the rabbi simply. "You see—"

"Let me tell you something: You wouldn't have gotten very far. All of us are armed, you know."

"I'm afraid I don't understand what you mean," the rabbi replied, frowning. "We already had the fire going."

"I wasn't referring to *that*. I was talking about what would have happened if you actually had managed to get outside the camp."

"Get outside the camp?" echoed the rabbi.

"In my language, when you *escape*, you leave the place you are confined to — you do not remain there."

Rabbi Meirer studied the soldier. "Excuse me, but what are you talking about?"

"Your attempted riot."

"Our attempted *what*?"

"I think we have our lines crossed, mate." The soldier almost smiled. "Were you or weren't you trying to set the camp on fire?"

"We were simply trying to kosher our dishes!"

Karl and Willie sat on their flea-infested mattresses doubled over in uncontrollable fits of laughter. "And did you see the look on that soldier's face when Rabbi Meirer could finally get a word in edgewise and tell him what we were doing?" Willie gasped.

He took his glasses off to wipe away the tears.

"Yes, and the poor soldier obviously felt like such a fool and didn't know what to say," Karl replied. "But he was a pretty good sport, wasn't he? I just hope a fully functioning kosher kitchen is set up for us soon, like he promised."

"So do I. You know, Karl, they're going to need quite a few people to staff it. Are you going to volunteer?"

"I'm not sure. How about you?"

"I think I might. Between studying in the yeshiva and helping out in the kitchen I'll have plenty to keep me occupied. Besides, it might be quite useful."

"Yes — you'll learn important survival techniques, such as how to boil an egg," Karl joked.

"Careful, or you might find all your meals seasoned with lots of black pepper!" Willie gave him a playful punch, and then yawned. "I'm feeling a little tired, Karl...I think I might go to sleep for a while."

"Do — you look as if you could do with a rest. But let me ask you first — would you mind if I borrowed some paper and your pen? I want to write a letter to Otto. It's been months since we've been in contact."

"Of course. Just rummage around in my suitcase and you'll find a few sheets of paper somewhere in there. And here's my pen."

"Thanks, Willie."

Karl rested the piece of paper on Willie's suitcase and began to write. He wrote and wrote, telling his beloved little brother of all his experiences over the past few months, all that had happened to him since that Sunday afternoon in May when P.C. Morrow had come for him. Outside there was a clap of thunder and a sudden torrential rain poured down, soaking the dusty, parched earth. To Karl the hammering of the rain on the tin roof sounded like a burst of bullets.

Willie was awakened by the rain. He stirred and glanced at his watch. Karl was still writing, completely absorbed in his letter.

"What are you writing — an epic?"

"Something along those lines," Karl replied.

"It must be almost time for *Minchah* now. Are you coming?"

"Yes, I'll just sign off."

Karl had been so involved in his letter that he hadn't noticed that the rain stopped as suddenly as it had started. When they left the hut, the sky was golden and the setting sun a ball of fiery crimson. Karl and Willie stood speechless. They had never witnessed such a stunning and dramatic sunset. For a few moments the two boys stared in awe at the splendor, feeling a pervading sense of calm. "We might be on the other side of the world," Karl said to himself, "but we are not alone." Hashem's protecting hand would always be with them.

The *Yamim Tovim* fell shortly after their arrival. On Rosh Hashanah, Karl could not help recalling how, the year before, he had spent the High Holy Days in Swanstone, and the year before that he had been home — in Germany — with his parents. He wondered where he would find himself the following year... Who knew what lay ahead?

Practically every person in Camp 7 attended the shul on Yom Kippur. There was a powerful feeling of togetherness that day. Whatever their differences, these Jewish prisoners who had fled from Germany to England, only to be sent to this strange and empty land on the other side of the world felt a growing bond among themselves.

From scraps of old wood, with neither nails nor tools, a few of them managed to erect a *sukkah*. Karl naturally helped to build it, and in a letter to Otto, described it all, adding that he hoped that Otto and the others had managed to build one too. Karl had still not heard a word from his brother. For "security" reasons, the prisoners had been prohibited from receiving any mail for the time being and it frustrated Karl terribly. He longed to hear from Otto and be assured that he was all right. He worried a great deal about him.

At night it was freezing in the *sukkah*, while during the day it was blisteringly hot. In Europe they would be approaching winter, but here in the southern hemisphere they were only beginning the Australian summer. Karl could not imagine how much hotter it would become. In Germany, he mused, the year had properly defined seasons: in summer it was warm and sunny, and all their fruit and vegetables ripened. In autumn the days became cooler, the trees lost their leaves, and they harvested all their produce. In winter it snowed, they fixed what needed mending, and they cleared the land. His eyes momentarily filled with tears as he remembered that winter was the time his father could turn to Torah study. In spring the days grew warmer and buds on the trees became sweet blossoms.

Here the weeks seemed to pass one after the other without any major contrasts. It was either warm, hot, or very hot during the day and the nights always cooled down tremendously. The colors of the landscape never changed. The red and dusty plain remained the same. When it rained, it poured, and the ground turned to mud. It was difficult to walk around, especially since many of them had no shoes. But within days after a downpour the ground would be dry and cracked again. Sometimes strong winds blew, and dust swirled thickly around the camp.

The Festival of Simchas Torah was one of the most memorable days of Karl's whole stay at the camp. There were Chasidim in the camp and they led the lively singing and dancing in the shul for hours and hours. A shul in Sydney had kindly lent them a *sefer Torah*. They may have been imprisoned, but this could not dampen the high spirits and joy of the Chasidim on that day. No one could help but be affected by it and Karl personally felt that he had never experienced such a Simchas Torah, or indeed enjoyed one as much.

''Letters! Letters!'' was the shout which reverberated

through the camp. Karl was washing his face when Willie came looking for him. "Karl, they're giving out mail!" he cried. Karl stared at Willie, dropped his towel and the two boys ran to the dining hall where all the letters had been spread out across a long table. Hundreds of people were gathered around it and the noise was deafening as they pushed and shoved each other in an effort to find the letters addressed to themselves. It took Karl some time until he was able to get anywhere near the table. In vain, he rummaged through the piles time after time. Other people, as desperate as he, kept turning the letters over and mixing them up, and Karl discovered that he kept seeing the same ones over and over again. Finally, under a large heap, he found what he had been yearning for. He snatched it and raced back to his hut.

Willie found him there a while later, sitting on his mattress and holding the letter limply in his hand. But instead of looking happy at having received news from home, Karl was staring into space with a closed and sullen expression on his face.

"Well?" Willie prompted him.

The sight of Willie fired renewed energy — and anger — into Karl and he stood up to face him, his green eyes burning. "Do you know, I'm not even supposed to be here! I'm not supposed to be in this wretched place! It was all a mistake! All these long months of suffering need not have happened!" he cried in a loud voice.

Willie was a little frightened. He had never seen Karl in such a rage — in fact, never had he seen him angry at all.

"I don't understand what you mean, Karl. Please explain," he said gently.

"Otto has written me that Jack Willow discovered that Mrs. Redley — a callous woman, a terrible gossip, whom Erich stayed with for a few days — spoke to P.C. Morrow on the day of my Tribunal telling him that she was suspicious of us and especially of me. She said that we had hidden the fact that we were German by claiming we were Polish, a deception which showed that all was not as it should be. She also told him that it was strange that I, who was sixteen at the time, should be evacuated with the primary school when in any case the age limit was fifteen. She told him of a mysterious hut we had built, and how she had heard, while out walking one night — though I don't know what she was doing out so late trespassing on private property — how she had heard us speaking in German, and that it was 'blatantly obvious' we were plotting something."

"But, Karl, if none of it is true, why should the words of a silly gossip worry you?"

"Ah, but that's just the problem! There *is* a basis of truth to everything she informed the policeman about. It's just that she chose to twist everything around. We *did* tell everyone we were Polish, but that was only because the teacher who accompanied us from London warned us to, in order to prevent something like this from happening! It *was* unusual that I should be evacuated with children of eight and nine but I received special permission from the headmaster of Otto's school, to go with him. As for the 'mysterious hut,' why, that was nothing more than a *sukkah*! Otto writes that after P.C. Morrow arrested me, he decided to do a 'good deed' by telling higher authorities all that Mrs. Redley had disclosed to him. Can you imagine, Willie? It was all because of that 'report' that I was placed on the *Arandora Star* with all the other classification-A passengers." Karl groaned. "Do you realize that I could have been drowned on that ship — all because of her?"

"Karl," Willie began, gently putting an arm around his friend's shaking shoulders. "Listen to me. I know it must be difficult for you to learn about this, but try to keep in mind that everything that happened was meant to happen...otherwise it would not have taken place."

"But if Mrs. Redley had not tried to be such a 'good citizen,' this would *not* have happened!" Karl declared stubbornly.

"How can you know that? If something is meant to be, it is meant to be. Mrs. Redley was only a catalyst for making it happen. That doesn't mean she is any less to blame, you know.

For she had the choice. She didn't have to do it. Something else might have happened to you instead. You could have drowned on the *Arandora Star,* true — but you didn't. That has nothing to do with Mrs. Redley. It has to do with Hashem. *He* was the one who saved you. He had *His* reasons for wanting you to come here, for wanting all of us to come here, and only *He* knows why. So, its true, you do have a right to be annoyed with Mrs. Redley, Karl, but you mustn't let yourself feel bitter over your situation. And even though it may be tough, and no one's denying that, you must accept it. We all must. The same way you did before you received the letter."

Karl sank back onto his mattress and rubbed his eyes. Then he gazed up at his friend with eyes full of admiration for him. "You are right," he said simply.

Willie smiled warmly at him. "Besides which, you finally received the long-awaited letter. Your brother must have written about other things too."

"Yes," Karl said, sitting up again. "He says he is very well but misses me a great deal. He is progressing at school and his English is quite good. The five boys — Erich, Kurt, Miles, Joshua and Otto — have grown extremely close. They're supposedly inseparable now, and they study Torah together every day. Otto says they spent the summer boating, hiking, and helping Jack on the farm. Jack also added a few lines of greeting, as did Fay, their two oldest children, and the rest of the boys. Otto writes that when Jack Willow's children heard I was in Australia, they asked whether we walked upside down since we are 'down-under'." Karl laughed. "You know, when I was younger I used to wonder about that too. Who would have dreamed that I would actually end up in Australia? In England the weather is getting cooler now, and here the sun is beating down. It's a funny life, Willie. Everything is upside down. Our very lives have been turned upside down."

"But things are not that intolerable, are they?" Willie said, smiling.

"No. I have truly got a lot to be thankful for. Even here there have been good times. And you are a very special friend, Willie. Thank you for making me see sense.''

"No, you did that. All I did was cheer you up a little.''

"Don't belittle yourself. You taught me a very important lesson today. I can't question my situation. I was meant to come here and that is all there is to it. And you know, if I had not, I might never have seen you again. Oh, and Willie, I didn't even ask. Did you get a letter?''

"No.'' Willie looked away.

$$20$$

MILES STAMPED HIS feet, rubbed his hands together, and blew on them in an effort to keep warm. "Where are they?" he asked the others. "They said they only had to buy a few items for Mrs. Willow, but they've been in the General Store for almost half an hour."

"Well, you know how Mrs. Beanshaw is — once she starts talking, she doesn't stop." Joshua replied. "Maybe I should go in and see what's taking them so long. If I stand here any longer I'll turn into a block of ice."

"Whoops, look who's just walked out of the General Store," Kurt said.

The three of them turned to watch Mrs. Redley, her string shopping bag bulging with groceries, striding purposefully in their direction, though she had not yet noticed them. "Come on, let's go. If she sees us waiting around like this she might accuse us of being spies!"

Miles swiftly glanced about. It was too late to walk away — she was bound to see them. With silent, mutual agreement, the three of them turned and walked through the door of the second-hand shop they had been standing next to. The bell above the door tinkled softly. The three boys stopped in their tracks as Mr. Tarlon, the proprietor, glanced up from his seat behind the counter at the front of the shop. They had never met Mr. Tarlon personally, but they had heard a great deal about him. It was said that he was a sort of recluse and did not have much to do with the other villagers, nor they with him. He opened his shop first thing in the morning and closed it when it grew dark, hardly ever leaving the shop; even his home consisted of two rooms on the second storey.

Mr. Tarlon peered at the boys. "May I help you?"

"Uh...no thanks...we're only browsing," Miles replied brightly.

"Mind you don't break anything."

"We'll be careful."

As the three of them wandered around the cluttered shop, their interest was drawn by the countless objects piled high everywhere. An old bicycle rested against the wall in a corner; a dusty china doll was balanced precariously on the bicycle seat and a basket of dried flowers hung between the handlebars. A heavily carved, solid oak table, and four moth-eaten but elegantly upholstered chairs were stacked upside down.

The front panel of the counter was made of reinforced glass. Kurt and Joshua stared, fascinated by the old coins, stamps, and war medals set out on trays inside it. Miles, meanwhile, was rummaging through a large crate of tattered books. For underneath the great pile Miles had caught a glimpse of something which was not a book at all — not in the literal sense.

He quietly called the others to come and verify his finding, hardly able to contain his rising excitement. There was no mistaking it: it was definitely a *sefer Torah*. The three held a huddled conference, and then Miles, cradling the *sefer Torah* in his arms, carried it across the room to the counter. "Excuse me," he began, and Mr. Tarlon looked up from his paperwork. "What is this?"

Mr. Tarlon pushed up his glasses and studied closely the weighty roll of parchment wound around two posts, which had been laid before him. "It's a Jew's scroll," he finally replied. "Would you be wanting it?"

"Uh ... I'm not sure. How much are you asking for it?"

"I am asking fifteen pounds."

Miles was taken aback. That was about as much as his father earned in a week! They would never be able to raise that much money. "I don't think so," Miles replied cooly. "That's quite a steep price for what it is."

"Thirteen?"

Miles shook his head. The man was becoming interested in making the sale, just as the three of them had hoped.

"All right, then — ten pounds. But that's my final offer."

Miles was pensive.

"Are you going to take it or leave it?" Mr. Tarlon asked.

"You won't go any lower than ten pounds?"

"No, I won't, and I'm sure it's worth even more than twenty. I certainly won't come down to less than ten."

He does not realize how right he is! Miles thought to himself.

"Come on, I haven't got all day."

"I would like it, Mr. Tarlon. But I don't have the money on me right now. Could you hold it for me until I return with the money?"

"For how long?"

"Oh, I'd say...a few weeks."

"A few weeks! I have a business to run, young man. I couldn't possibly do that. But all the same, we've agreed on a figure and if the scroll is still here when you're ready to buy it, you can have it for that price."

"Thank you very much, Mr. Tarlon."

"Oh, here you are! Where have you been?" Erich asked when he saw his friends emerging from the shop. "We've been waiting for you for ages."

"Likewise," Joshua replied. "We waited a long time for you, and were about to see what was taking you so long when we suddenly saw Mrs. Redley coming out of the General Store—"

"But what were you doing in the second-hand shop?" Erich asked.

"We ducked in there to avoid Mrs. Redley..." Kurt began.

"And we made the most amazing discovery in there," Miles

continued excitedly. "Let's go back to your place, Otto, and we'll tell you all about it."

While they thawed out in front of the fireplace in the Willows' living room with steaming cups of hot cocoa, Miles told his friends all about the discovery of the *sefer Torah* and the deal he had struck with Mr. Tarlon.

"Ten pounds! That's still very expensive," Otto murmured. "How can you possibly raise the money?"

"Perhaps if we pool all our savings we could do it," Miles suggested.

Otto brought some paper and the boys added up their collective savings: they had barely a pound all together!

"It's impossible," Joshua said glumly. "We'll never be able to do it."

"There must be a way," Miles insisted. "There has to be. I just can't bear the thought of that *sefer Torah* lying under a pile of worn books, collecting dust in a second-hand shop. Why, it doesn't even have a cover."

"Perhaps we can borrow the money?" Joshua suggested.

"From whom?"

"Jack Willow is a very kind man. Perhaps he would be able to help us out."

"Oh, I don't think he has that kind of money to lend," said Kurt, "and besides, how would we ever be able to pay him back?"

"Kurt has a good point," Miles said.

"Oh, if only my violin were not broken!" Erich exclaimed. "I'm sure that if I could sell it, we'd have more than enough to buy the *sefer Torah*."

"Never mind, Erich. But it's a generous thought anyway," Miles comforted him.

"I have an idea!" Otto cried, his eyes suddenly shining. "You know, whenever we work for Jack he gives us a bit of pocket money. Why don't we see if he needs us to work more, in all our spare time! Eventually we might make enough money."

"You know, that's a good idea," Kurt said. "And we could

inquire whether there's work available on the neighboring farms too.''

"That's it!" Miles announced. "That is exactly what we'll do. And God willing, the *sefer Torah* will soon be in our hands." He leapt out of his chair and headed for the door.

"Where are you going?"

"To start work, of course!"

"But it's freezing out there. You said so yourself."

"So what? We have a job to do. Don't put off to tomorrow what can be done today! And, as our Sages said in *Pirkei Avos*, 'If not now, when?' Come on! What are you all waiting for?"

Karl lay on his mattress, staring at the application form in his hand, hoping that in some way this might help him make up his mind. In any case, it was good to be resting inside. The heat outside was unbearable. Karl had never experienced such a summer, although — after a few initial mistakes such as getting badly sunburned, and suffering from heat exhaustion in mid-December — he had learned to take precautions such as not being outside without wearing a hat, and preferably not being out at all at midday if he could help it.

Chanukah had been an interesting experience. It was quite strange and disconcerting to be celebrating it in the middle of summer. The prisoners had fashioned menorahs out of wood scraps and other materials lying around.

Apart from that, the summer had passed rather uneventfully. Karl enjoyed his *shiurim*, worked in the kosher kitchen, partici-pated in camp sports, kept up a lengthy and regular correspon-dence with Otto, and spent a great deal of time with Willie. Now it was almost the end of March and the long Australian summer was coming to an end. Karl welcomed the thought of finally being free from the relentless scorching heat. The waning sum-mer contributed a great deal to improving the mood of everyone at Hay. Another factor was the arrival of Major Layton, an official representative from England who had come to see what condi-tions were like at the camp.

It turned out that their days at Hay were numbered. Major Layton had come to the conclusion that their camp was totally unsuitable and that all the internees should be moved to Tartura, the internment camp near Melbourne, where most of the Arandora Star passengers had been sent. However, the Major had also presented them with another proposition: He was willing to send back any internees who wished to return to England — provided they join the Pioneer Corps, a military unit which served as a civil guard on the home front.

Karl had taken an application form, though he had still not filled it out. Although joining the Pioneer Corps would be his only chance to see his brother again after a separation of almost a year, he was nevertheless filled with uncertainty. He well remembered the brutal and unsympathetic treatment he'd received at the hands of the British authorities.

Willie entered the hut and sat on his mattress opposite Karl. "Well?" he asked. "Have you come to a decision yet?"

"No, and I'm still not sure what I should do," Karl replied.

"You've been saying that for two days. You'll have to decide, Karl."

"Won't you reconsider and join up with me, Willie?"

Willie sighed. "We've been over this time and again, Karl. What is there for me in England? I would only be going from one prison to another. I would rather stay here with what I know, until they release me. For you, of course, it's different. You have your brother to think about, and this is a great opportunity for you. It might be the only one you get for a long time."

"I know."

"Why don't you speak to Rabbi Zoller about it?" Willie suggested.

"That's an excellent idea. In fact," he exclaimed, jumping up, "I think I'll go immediately."

Rabbi Zoller, one of the rabbis who had been interned at Hay, was a teacher in their yeshiva, and Karl had always valued his advice. Karl found him sitting at a table so absorbed in his books that he hadn't even noticed his approach.

Karl cleared his throat. "Excuse me, Rabbi Zoller...could I speak to you for a few moments?"

The rabbi looked up and upon seeing Karl, his face lit up. "Oh, hello, Karl! Yes, of course...please sit down."

Karl explained his dilemma to Rabbi Zoller, who listened intently to what he said, and looked pained at his young friend's plight. On the one hand, Karl explained, he knew of few people who had decided to join up and it would entail leaving Willie, his best friend, behind. However, there was his younger brother to think about. He had not seen him in almost a year, and for all that time he had been living with a non-Jewish family. They were very good people, he stressed, but the fact remained that he wasn't living in a Jewish, family environment. And who knew? Perhaps when Karl reached England he would manage to be discharged from the Pioneer Corps.

When he had finished expressing all these thoughts, he looked gravely at the rabbi. "Well, Rabbi Zoller, can you help me? What do you suggest I do?"

Rabbi Zoller stroked his long, gray beard. His brown eyes were soft and compassionate. "At the moment, Karl, you are in a very difficult state: you are sitting on the fence. If you take one option, you might regret not taking the other, and vice versa... and these days, who knows what our decisions may lead to? I'm sorry, Karl, but I cannot give you a definite answer. The only advice I *can* give you is to pray that Hashem guide you to make the right choice."

"You can't tell me?"

"No, Karl. You must decide that for yourself, but you will have my *berachah* whatever you decide upon."

21

JOSHUA DROPPED THE bale of hay which he had been trying to lift and flopped down onto it. "That's it, I'm finished for today!" he announced. As if on cue, Fay appeared, carrying a tray with a jug of home-made lemonade and some glasses on it. "Time for a break, boys," she called. The five of them gratefully and thirstily drank and sat for a few minutes under the warm sun, to rest from their strenuous work.

Now that they were on their summer vacation from school, they spent practically all day, five days a week, working on Jack's farm and occasionally on one of the neighboring farms if Jack did not have enough work to go around. The work was strenuous but it was worth the effort. Since the beginning of their campaign, they had earned almost eight pounds, and Miles had calculated one evening that if they continued at the same pace for another two or three weeks, they would be able to meet their goal and purchase the neglected *sefer Torah* which still lay in Mr. Tarlon's second-hand shop. Every few days Miles or one of the other boys would return, to see that it was still there — not that there was much chance that anyone else in the village would find it of interest — and each visit infused Miles with an even greater determination.

"Otto," called Fay, pointing out toward the road, "would you mind going to see what that man over there wants? He's probably lost, or seeking casual labor." Otto turned to the direction in which Fay was pointing and could just about distinguish a tall young man in the distance heading toward them with a bag slung over his shoulder.

"Of course, Fay," he replied. He leisurely made his way across the field, but then suddenly broke into a fast sprint.

"What's got into him?" Fay asked, watching.

"Karl! Karl!" Otto shouted. Karl put down his bag and stopped several feet away from him. The two brothers were face to face. They stood in utter silence, taking in the changes in one another. Karl's complexion still bore a deep tan. He looked a little thinner but otherwise appeared fit and well; Otto was a couple of inches taller and had a healthy glow to his cheeks. Then all at once Otto fell into Karl's arms and the two brothers burst into tears.

"I can't believe it! I can't believe it!" Otto repeated over and over. "You've returned at last. *Baruch Hashem!*"

Karl wiped his eyes and smiled at his brother. "Yes, Otto," he said shakily. "*Baruch Hashem.*"

"When did you get back to England?"

"Early this morning. I came straight here."

Otto did not have a chance to ask anything further, for in the next instant the others joyously crowded around them to welcome Karl.

"How did you get here?"

"When did you come?"

"How did you get so tanned?"

"Did you escape?"

Karl was not able to answer the barrage of questions fast enough, as question after question was thrown at him.

Fay had walked up to them and she was beaming at Karl. Then she turned to the group. "Boys, I am sure Karl and Otto have plenty to talk about. Let's give them time to catch up and we'll talk with him later. Now off you go," she said, shooing them away. Then she turned to Karl. "It is wonderful to have you back. We will talk soon. In the meantime, can I get you a drink or something to eat?"

"Thanks, Fay. I'll just have a cold drink. Oh, it's great to be back!"

When they were alone, Karl hugged his brother once again, then held him at arm's length and smiled at him. "I have missed you so much, my little brother."

"I have missed you too, Karl. But you know, I am not so little anymore."

"No, you aren't," Karl laughed. "Tell me, how have things been here?"

"Oh, fine. You know, I've thought every day how much I'll have to tell you, but suddenly I cannot think of a single thing to say. Oh, it will be wonderful having you here again."

"Otto," Karl said hesitantly, "I want to talk to you about that, actually."

"Yes?" Worry crept into Otto's voice.

"You see, the reason I was allowed to leave Australia was because I agreed to join the Pioneer Corps. I have not been totally freed."

"Oh," Otto replied slowly, "I see." He frowned, trying to comprehend fully what Karl was telling him. "What exactly does that mean?"

"It means that I'll be working for the British army, mostly doing menial tasks — such as clearing the debris from the bomb damage in London."

"So you will not be living here then?" Otto could not keep the disappointment from showing in his forlorn face.

"No."

"For how long will this be?"

"I'm not sure. I suppose until the war ends."

"That could be years!" Tears began to well up in Otto's eyes.

"I know." Karl looked away.

"When...when do you have to go?"

"I have to report for duty first thing tomorrow morning. I'll have to take the late evening train back to London tonight."

"That soon! Oh, Karl! But you've only just come!"

"Listen, Otto. We must be strong for each other. I was lucky that I was allowed compassionate leave to come and see you today."

"True. I only wish you could stay longer. We've been parted for so long."

"It will be easier now. I'll come up to see you as often as I can. But listen, I'm here now, so let's make the most of the few hours we have together."

The time went too fast. With Jack, Fay, their children, Erich, Kurt, Miles, and Joshua all wanting to know the details of Karl's experiences in Australia, Otto had little opportunity to spend more time with Karl by himself. But he felt no resentment. Everyone was fond of Karl and they too had missed him. He was willing to share him — after all, he'd only be in London, and that was still closer than Australia!

The two brothers embraced as the train pulled into the station.

"At leat I've seen you, Karl! I would rather have this than not to have seen you at all."

Karl rumpled Otto's hair. "You've settled in quite well here, haven't you?"

"I guess so." Otto smiled. "I've been here almost two years already."

"Two years! It's hard to believe. And you're happy here?"

Otto was silent. "The Willows are kind to me, Karl. I have good friends and I am safe from air-raid attacks."

"Do you...do you still think of home?" Karl asked, keeping his voice steady.

"Oh, not really. I guess I'm used to things now."

"Do you remember Papa and Mutti?" Karl asked in a low voice.

"Of course I do! How can you even ask? Is that what you mean when you ask if I think of home? Oh, Karl, I have not stopped missing our parents. I think of them constantly. It is *Germany* that

I don't miss, and I'm not sure I could still regard it as home. When the war ends I don't know if I would like to live there again. I think I would prefer that we all go to live somewhere else. Perhaps here in England.''

Otto has really grown up, Karl thought to himself.

The sound of the whistle blowing signaled the imminent departure of the train. Karl clasped his brother's hand warmly. ''I'll miss you!''

With that he was gone, as suddenly as he had arrived. Otto waved until the train was out of sight, imagining for a fleeting moment how his parents must have felt when they saw their two sons onto the train in Berlin. Was it only two years ago?

''Ten whole pounds!'' Joshua cried excitedly. The boys had reached their goal — they had raised enough money for the *sefer Torah*. It was a day of great excitement and satisfaction, and the very next morning they all went to the second-hand shop in order to purchase it together.

''I told you we would do it, didn't I?'' Miles said, exhilarated, as they entered the shop. He was enjoying their moment of glory. They were quite unprepared for what Mr. Tarlon had to tell them.

''Sorry, boys, but it's gone.''

''Gone?'' they echoed.

''Pardon?'' Miles asked in astonishment.

''It's gone, I said. Someone bought it.''

''When?'' Joshua asked, finding his voice.

''The day before yesterday.''

''Who was it?'' Kurt asked.

''Oh, a gentleman who's not from around here.''

''Did you get his name?''

''Now look, boys, I don't ask the name of every customer who walks into my shop.''

''Can't you give us any more information, Mr. Tarlon?'' Erich pleaded. ''It's very important to us.''

Mr. Tarlon paused for thought. ''Yes, I think I can. He paid by check...so his name would be on the check if I haven't sent it to the bank already..."

"Please look and see if you still have it!"

Mr. Tarlon rummaged around in his cash box while the boys stood watching with bated breath. "Here it is! It was a Mr. C. Canning. I believe he comes from London and was passing through here on business."

"Is there anything else you can tell us?" Kurt asked.

"I'm afraid not. As I said, I did not know the man. He simply browsed around my shop for half an hour and bought a few objects of interest, including the scroll. Did it really mean that much to you, boys?"

"Even more."

The five boys left the shop despondently. "After all that hard work...all those long hours," Miles said forlornly.

"And we were so close to being able to buy it, too."

"We did try our best."

"Perhaps this Mr. Canning is Jewish, and had the same motive we did for buying it."

"It would be comforting to think that even if we didn't get the *sefer Torah*, that it has gone to the right place."

"But maybe it's with someone who doesn't know how to treat it with the right respect."

"That might be."

"Then we have to do something," Miles said firmly.

"What can we do from here?" Joshua asked.

"Not a thing," Miles replied. "And that is why someone is going to have to go to London."

22

"THE BERRINS AND the Willows would never agree to it," Joshua said as he leaned against the sloping trunk of the weeping willow. The boys watched two swans gracefully gliding on the river.

"I know," Miles replied.

"Are you suggesting, then, that one of us go to London without telling anyone?" Erich asked.

"We have no other option. With all due respect, I don't think they would be able to understand our motives for wanting to go. They would surely tell us that it was not all that important — considering the dangers of bombing in London — and put an end to our plans."

"But they'll be extremely angry when they find out," Otto warned.

"They need not find out at all! If the one who is going leaves on the earliest morning train, he'll be in London by ten or eleven in the morning. He only needs to go and find Mr. Canning, see if the *sefer Torah* has fallen into safe hands and if not, try to buy it back, and then return immediately on the next train to Swanstone. He would be back here by the evening."

"Who will be the one to go?" Otto asked. They looked at one another questioningly.

"I want to go," Kurt announced.

"Are you sure?" Miles asked.

"Yes...I must go."

"I'll go with him," Joshua said suddenly. "Kurt doesn't know his way around London, and I do."

"That's a valid point, but you have to be absolutely certain that you want to do this," Miles said.

"I am."

"What about you, Kurt?"

"Positive."

"All right, then that's settled. Kurt and Joshua will go."

"When?" Joshua asked.

"As soon as possible. How about tomorrow morning?"

"I think you may have a slight problem there," Otto pointed out.

"What?"

"Where are they going to find the money for the train fare? We only have ten pounds and that's for the *sefer Torah*."

"Otto's right," Miles admitted. "Does someone have a suggestion?"

"Well, we can earn more money by working for a few more days," Erich proposed.

"An excellent idea. Shall we agree then that you'll go next Tuesday?" They all nodded in agreement. "Next Tuesday it is then."

Tuesday morning dawned, a clear bright day. Miles poked his head out of the bedroom door and looked up and down the hall. Joshua and Kurt crept down the steps behind him, careful not to make a sound that would wake Mr. and Mrs. Berrin. "Right, are we all set then?"

"Do you have everything? The money? Some food?"

"Yes, and don't worry so much," Kurt said. "Anyway, we'd better make a move now or we'll miss the train."

"*Hatzlachah rabbah*, and be careful."

"Thanks. *B'ezras Hashem*, we'll meet you back here this evening with our prized treasure." Joshua grinned.

As the train approached London, the boys stared open-mouthed through the windows. Signs of devastation were everywhere: shattered windows, fallen walls, and whole buildings reduced to rubble. "Reading about it in the newspapers and hearing about it on the radio is one thing," Joshua murmured, "but I never expected it to look as bad as this. Being away for so long, I somehow imagined that when I came back everything would still look the same."

"It certainly looks a lot different from when I was here last," Kurt agreed, trying to silence the small voice in his head that whispered, And what does Vienna look like?

"What do we do now?" Kurt asked. The boys were standing in Liverpool Street Station watching the crowds of soldiers and tense civilians rushing by.

"Good question," Joshua replied. "If we can find a telephone box we can look up Mr. Canning's address. I only hope it's listed."

Joshua flicked through the C's in the telephone book inside the cramped red booth. "Have you found him yet?" Kurt asked.

"Yes and no — there are six C. Cannings listed here! How do I know which is the right one? We won't have time to visit them all."

"Why don't we telephone them?"

"Simple! Why didn't I think of that first?"

Joshua dialed the first number. It rang several times before someone answered.

"Hello? Is that Mr. Canning?"

"Yes, it is."

"Uh...could you tell me please whether you were in the village of Swanstone last week?"

"What on earth are you talking about? You must have the wrong number."

"No luck?" Kurt whispered.

"No."

"Never mind. Try the next one."

"Hello? May I speak to Mr. Canning?"

"No, I'm afraid he is out at the moment," replied the woman at the other end. "May I help you?"

"Perhaps you can. Would you happen to know whether he was by any chance in Swanstone last week?"

"Oh, I don't think so. Charlie never goes out drinking at the pub."

"I see," Joshua giggled. "Thank you very much."

The telephone rang and rang. "I don't think anyone's at home," Joshua said. After the seventh ring, the fourth Mr. C. Canning answered the telephone.

"Hello, Mr. Canning?"

"Yes?"

"I have come up to London today from Swanstone, in Norfolk. I am trying to locate a Mr. C. Canning who was in Swanstone recently."

"Well, I was."

"You *were?*" Joshua was hardly able to contain his excitement.

"Yes, but I do not remember meeting anyone in particular. Did I speak to you there?"

"No, we have never met. The owner of the second-hand shop, Mr. Tarlon, gave me your name. I believe you purchased a few things from him."

"Yes, that is correct."

"Um...there was one item in particular I am interested in talking to you about. It's the...um...scroll."

"Oh, yes. By all means."

"Could my friend and I come to see you today?"

"Certainly. About what time?"

"Well, um...now, if possible. We are only in London until later this afternoon."

"All right. Let me just give you my address. I live in Montrose Place, in Belgravia. Look for a house named 'Excalibur.' Where are you now?"

"At Liverpool Street Station."

"All right — take the Underground to Hyde Park Corner,

and it is less than a five-minute walk from the station."

"Thank you. We should be there within the hour."

"And your name?"

"Joshua King."

"Excellent, Joshua. I look forward to seeing you."

"Excalibur!" Joshua exclaimed as they read the plaque above the door of the three-storey Edwardian townhouse. "Wasn't that the name of King Arthur's legendary sword?"

"Haven't a clue. Who was King Arthur, anyway?"

"Don't worry about it, Kurt. Just ring the bell!"

A distinguished-looking gentleman with graying hair, wearing a dark suit and silk tie, opened the door. "May I help you?" he asked.

"Yes...we have come to see Mr. Canning."

"I am he. And you are...?"

"Joshua King. I spoke to you earlier on the telephone."

"Of course! Please don't be offended, but I was expecting someone...uh, a little older. But never mind! Please come in. And you are?" He turned to Kurt.

"My name is Kurt. I am a friend of Joshua's."

Mr. Canning invited them into his spacious and elegant living room. The boys sank into the red leather couch and gazed around the room. A small abstract sculpture rested on the gleaming black baby grand piano. The walls were filled with old oil paintings in ornate gilded frames and on the mantelpiece above the fireplace was an array of curiosities: Kurt could make out an African tribal shield and a small, oriental brass urn. Mr. Canning caught Kurt admiring the ornaments. "From my travels I've managed to collect a lot of interesting artifacts. The scroll, though, has me stumped. I'm not quite sure what it is."

"We know what it is!" the boys chorused.

"You do?" Mr. Canning asked eagerly.

"Yes! It's a Torah scroll, a Jewish scroll of the law, or *sefer Torah*, as we call it in Hebrew."

"Really? Are you Jewish then?"

"Yes, we are."

"And tell me, what is it used for?"

"We live by it! We study it, we read from it, and, well, basically, it is what makes us Jews."

"Is it what's called the Five Books of Moses?"

"Yes, that's exactly what it is. You see, Mr. Canning," Joshua began earnestly, "we found it in Mr. Tarlon's shop among a pile of books earlier this year. Now, a *sefer Torah* is something we treat with the greatest respect and care. It is a holy object, certainly not something to be left lying about and treated like any old book. Therefore, we had been working hard to raise enough money to buy it. Finally when we had enough to purchase it, we came back to the shop and were told someone had already bought it! Luckily, Mr. Tarlon still had your check so he could tell us your name."

"And," Kurt chimed in, "that's the reason we have come to London today: to see you and ask whether we might possibly be able to buy it from you."

"I see," Mr. Canning said thoughtfully, rubbing his chin and looking seriously from one boy to the other.

"We would be willing to pay you ten pounds for it," Joshua said.

"Please wait here for one moment," Mr. Canning said, and excused himself from the room.

"What do you make of it? Do you think he'll sell it to us?" Kurt whispered.

"I don't know," Joshua whispered back. "He seemed very interested when we explained to him what it was. Perhaps now he realizes how valuable it is and will be *more* reluctant to part with it!"

Mr. Canning returned, carrying the *sefer Torah.* The boys' hearts ached to see the precious object in his arms. "Here," Mr. Canning said, smiling and handing it to Joshua firmly. "You can take it."

"Do you mean it?" Joshua asked in astonishment.

"Yes, yes. It rightfully belongs with you. That's obvious. For me, you see, it is just another unusual artifact. For you, it holds religious and emotional significance. As I said earlier, I am interested in other cultures and I have especially great respect for the Jewish People. Somehow, through all the persecution you have suffered throughout the ages, you have managed to survive as a nation. That shows a great strength...and more..."

Kurt handed him the money, but he waved it away. "No, no. I want you boys to have the scroll. Keep the money. You need it more than I do. Buy yourselves something nice with it."

The boys hurried to the Underground. "I can't believe that we really got it back!" Joshua said as he held on tightly to the precious *sefer Torah.* "And it was very decent of him not to accept payment."

"Wait until the others hear all about it."

"What do you think we should do with the money?"

"I have a few ideas, but I think we should wait to discuss it when we get back to Swanstone."

A sudden, loud wail pierced the air. "What's that?" cried Kurt above the noise as several people went rushing past them. "It must be an air-raid siren!"

"You mean there's going to be a bombing attack?" Kurt asked with alarm.

"I think so," Joshua replied fearfully.

"Where do we go?"

"I'm not sure. There must be some kind of shelter nearby."

"We'd better hurry!"

"But I don't know where to find it!"

"Let's ask someone then, and fast!"

"I'm scared, Kurt."

"There is no time for that now! We have to reach safety. Come on!"

They turned onto the main road, which was almost deserted by then. Joshua struggled to keep up with Kurt as they ran along the sidewalk. "Give me the *sefer Torah* to hold for a while,

Joshua,'' Kurt offered.

In the distance they heard the drone of aircraft.

''They're coming!''

''All right, don't panic!'' Joshua spotted a uniformed man wearing a tin helmet and a badge with the initials ARP — Air Raid Protection — on a strip wrapped around his arm. ''Where's the nearest shelter?'' Joshua called out to him.

''This way, boys.'' The shelter was full when they reached it, but the friendly Londoners made room for Kurt and Joshua on an already-crowded bench. The shelter warden shut the steel door firmly and not a moment too soon, for they could hear the airplanes approaching, and the horrible thudding sound as the bombs hit the ground, followed by an explosion.

''That was close,'' someone commented.

''How often do you have these raids?'' Kurt asked the man who had just spoken.

''Not from 'round these parts, then, are you, boys?''

''No,'' Kurt replied.

''Oh, every few days. Sometimes several times a day. They usually come at nighttime now, though...not much during the day anymore. I think the Gerries are beginning to see we're too strong for them, and they're too cowardly to come out in daylight. A bit like rats, you might say.''

''It's like a different world up in Swanstone,'' Kurt whispered to Joshua.

''You can say that again!''

Almost an hour later the all-clear siren was sounded. Kurt and Joshua emerged from the dark shelter and blinked in the bright sunlight. The acrid smell of smoke filled the air, and firemen were trying to extinguish the flames that still burned here and there. Single walls teetered where whole buildings had been standing only an hour before. Piles of brick and glass were everywhere.

''Our train leaves in less than twenty minutes,'' Kurt said.

''I know, and I'm sure we're going to miss it,'' Joshua replied.

"Then what are we going to do?"

"I know what...let's go back to my house. Oh, it's been so long since I've seen my parents, and now that my brother has been drafted, they must be very lonely. I've missed them so much. It would be wonderful to see them again."

"Fine," said Kurt roughly, his cheeks suddenly flushed. Joshua's innocent words has brought feelings to the surface that Kurt usually kept very deeply buried.

Joshua stared with open-mouthed stupefaction at his old street. Apart from a few children who were playing in the ruins and on the bomb sites, the street was empty. The houses looked as if they had been ripped apart by a giant hand. On one, a section of a room hung precariously from the single wall left standing. The front of another had been blown away, leaving the rest of the house exposed, like a ghastly doll house. On another, the ground floor was still intact but the second floor had been destroyed. Shards of glass and pieces of twisted metal littered the street and there was a large gaping hole in the center of the road.

Joshua walked slowly up to what had once been his home, but now all that remained of it was two walls and a mound of rubble. He let out a gasp. "My parents..." he whispered.

"Joshua," Kurt said swiftly, taking his friend by the arm, "do you have any other family nearby?"

"Yes, my grandparents. They live a ten-minute walk from here." Joshua spoke in a monotone and his eyes looked dazed.

"Come, we're going there. Perhaps they can tell you what's happened."

"Yes," Joshua replied distantly, unable to take his eyes off the ruins of his former home. "It's this way, down this side street."

"Joshua!" cried his grandmother in surprise. "What on earth are you doing here?" Without waiting for an explanation, she ushered him and Kurt inside. "Look who's here!" she announced as she entered the kitchen.

"Dad! Mum!" Joshua cried with relief. "I saw the house, and I thought...I thought..."

"Oh, poor boy!" cried his mother, as his parents hurried to him.

"It happened last night," said his father, "but *baruch Hashem*, we were in the Anderson shelter at the bottom of the garden at the time. The house is a complete write-off, but at least we're safe."

"Oh, It's so good to see you again!" Joshua exclaimed.

"And us, you, needless to say! But please explain: What exactly are you two boys doing here? You're supposed to be in Swanstone. And what on earth are you holding in your arms? It looks like a *sefer Torah*!"

Miles knocked on Otto and Erich's bedroom door. "Come in," Erich called.

"Well?" Otto cried anxiously.

"They weren't on the last train back from London."

"Oh, no!"

"I've been avoiding the Berrins all day, but I have to go back eventually, and it's getting late. I don't know what I'm going to tell them."

"What could have happened?" Otto asked.

"Hello, Mrs. Berrin," Fay greeted her cheerfully.

"Hello, Mrs. Willow. Sorry to disturb."

"Not at all. I'm happy to see you — please come in. Is everything all right?"

"Well, to tell you the truth, I'm a bit worried...have you seen the boys at all? I haven't seen them all day. First thing this morning when I woke up, they'd already left the house."

"Why, they're upstairs. I'll call them all to come down."

"Oh, Miles, there you are!" Mrs. Berrin sounded relieved. "I didn't see any of you this morning, and was rather concerned. Where are Joshua and Kurt?"

Miles' face flushed and he bit his lip.

"What *is* it, Miles?" Fay asked. "Is anything the matter? Do you know where they are?"

"Yes," he said in an undertone, staring at his shoes.

"Where are they?"

"In London."

"In *London? London?*" she repeated in dismay. "What are they doing there?"

Miles had no choice but to tell Fay and Mrs. Berrin the whole story, from beginning to end.

"Did you know about this too?" Fay asked Otto and Erich. They nodded guiltily, their eyes downcast. "Oh, how could you be so irresponsible?" she cried. "If it meant that much to you, why didn't you say something? Don't you know that Jack or Mr. Berrin would gladly have helped you or gone down to London with one of you! Who knows what kind of trouble they're in! There's no way we can even find out what has happened to them, and we are responsible for you all."

"There was another air raid on London this afternoon," said Mrs. Berrin with a tremulous voice. "I only hope no harm has come to them."

A cold shiver ran through Miles. He had never anticipated anything going wrong with their plan.

23

JOSHUA AND HIS PARENTS and grandparents were already eating breakfast when Kurt came down. "Good morning, Kurt. Did you sleep well?" Joshua's grandmother asked him.

"Yes, thank you," he replied politely. Then, turning to Joshua, he asked, "When would you like to leave?"

"In a couple of hours. I think we should try and catch the eleven o'clock train. Is that all right with you?"

"Uh, that's fine. Actually, I have to go out for a while." Kurt looked away.

"Oh?" The family looked at Kurt curiously.

"I must go to see someone," he murmured. It was clear he would not be volunteering any further information.

Kurt walked through the dismal streets, familiar and unfamiliar at the same time. They still teemed with ragged children. So many of the buildings had been destroyed. An improvement, Kurt thought wryly. He wondered whether he would still be able to find the right tenement block, but he recognized it immediately. The ones on either side had received severe damage but miraculously, this one had remained unscathed.

Kurt climbed up the rickety steps, remembering sharply his departure down them two years before. He knocked on the door. Inside he could hear screaming children and a woman shouting. He was sure no one had heard him so he knocked again, harder and louder this time.

The door was flung open. "What d'ya want?" There stood Mrs. Kilern.

"May I come in?" Kurt asked politely.

"No! Tell me who you are and what you want first," she replied.

"You know who I am, but apparently you don't recognize me."

"I've never seen you before in my life."

"Oh, yes, you have, but last time you saw me I was a newcomer to this country, and couldn't speak English. My name is Kurt Eisig."

"You were that German refugee?"

"Austrian, actually. And you are right, I was a refugee who came here not knowing a single soul, hoping to find some comfort and understanding after my unpleasant experience in Austria...only to be cruelly exploited by *you*." The words seemed to burst out.

"How dare you, you ungrateful boy! We took you in, gave you a bed and food to eat..."

"...took advantage of me and overworked me."

Mrs. Kilern began to protest, but to no avail.

"You didn't really care about me at all." Kurt went on bitterly. "Taking me in was very convenient for you. Not only was I cheap labor but you got paid to keep me, on top of that."

"Get out of here before I call the police!"

"I will go when I am good and ready, Mrs. Kilern. Do you realize that I could just as easily call the authorities and expose what you did?"

"You wouldn't dare!"

"Wouldn't I?"

"All right. What do you want?"

"I want to know whether a letter ever arrived for me from my parents in Vienna."

"No. We never got one."

"Thank you." Kurt was silent. "That's all I wanted to know.

I am going to give you my present address. If you ever receive a letter for me, be sure to let me know." Kurt jotted it down on a piece of paper and handed it to her. Mrs. Kilern scanned the address and then stuffed the piece of paper into the pocket of her dirty apron.

"Do you promise to contact me?"

"Yeah, yeah, now just get out of here!"

"Don't worry, Mrs. Kilern — I don't want to stay in this miserable place any longer that I have to."

With his head held high, he marched steadily down the stairs and heard the door slam shut behind him.

"I told you all to be quiet!" she shouted at her brood, who were having a fight on the floor. They looked up for a moment and then promptly ignored her, resuming their fight. Mrs. Kilern opened the top drawer of her dresser and removed the letter which lay on top. "I don't know why I kept this. I can't read it anyhow," she chuckled to herself, as she tore the letter up into tiny pieces.

"Where ever can Kurt be?" asked Joshua's mother. "You'll miss the train if he doesn't get back soon." She smiled warmly at her son. "You know, you really should not have come down to London without telling anyone. I hope they're not too worried about you in Swanstone. But it has been lovely seeing you again. We've missed you so much, and in fact Daddy and I wanted to tell you— "

"I've missed you too, Mum!" Joshua interjected. "Sometimes it's quite hard for me when Miles' parents and the Firestones come to Swanstone to visit. I surely don't mean to envy my friends, but I only wish we had the money for you to visit me too."

Mrs. King wiped her eyes. "Believe me, so do we. Who knows how long this war will go on...I cannot stand such a long separation from you either. That's why Daddy and I were thinking—"

"Oh, I wish I didn't have to go back!" Joshua blurted out.

"Have you suffered there?"

"No, no, in fact I've had a good time, but it isn't like being home with you."

"What I'm getting at, Joshua, is that we've talked it over, and suggest you come back to London to live at home."

"Do you mean that?" Joshua cried.

"Yes, yes. Daddy said last night, 'What do we have but each other?' We no longer even have a house. This war had caused enough separation. Daniel's in the army. Conditions are difficult, as you experienced yourself yesterday, but at least we will be together. We feel the dangers don't justify our being apart anymore."

"Oh, thank you, Mum! When can I come home?"

"Go back today to collect your things, and come back tomorrow." She opened her well-worn purse. "Here's the fare for the return journey."

The doorbell rang. "That must be Kurt!" Joshua hurried to open the door. "Is everything all right?" he asked him. "I was getting nervous."

"Yes, fine," Kurt replied. His face was set in a strange expression. "Are you ready to go?" His voice sounded distant.

"Yes, all set. Mum!" he called. "We're off now."

"Have a safe trip, boys. And I'll see you tomorrow, Joshua, God willing."

Joshua beamed.

"What did your Mum mean by saying she'll see you tomorrow?" Kurt asked, once they were out of the house. "Are they coming to visit?"

"No. I'm going back to live with my parents. My Mum and Dad want me home."

Kurt swallowed hard. "And how do you feel?" His voice sounded even stranger.

"We've had some good fun together, and it has been lovely getting to know you all, but of course I would rather come home.

Or to my grandparents' home, I should say."

Kurt nodded. "I understand."

Fortunately, there were no further bombing raids that day and they reached Swanstone safely and without any trouble. The "explosion" came when they returned to the Berrins, however.

"Don't you *ever* do anything like that again!" Mrs. Berrin cried.

"We're sorry. Really, we didn't imagine we'd get held up there," Joshua apologized.

"It's not only that! Going to see a complete stranger! Why, he might have tried to kidnap you, or worse!"

"You are right, Mrs. Berrin, and we really are sorry. It won't happen again, I assure you," Kurt said.

"I should hope not! How can we be expected to look after you if you run off and do as you fancy?"

"Please don't be angry anymore. It's all over and we're back now."

"I'm not angry, not really. We were only out of our minds with worry. If something had happened to you I would never have been able to forgive myself, or to face your parents."

Joshua felt extremely guilty for having to tell Mrs. Berrin right then and there that he would be returning to London immediately to live with his parents, but time was too short to pick the right moment, and he told her.

"Well, we are certainly going to miss you, Joshua. Whatever I have said, I've still enjoyed having you around." She smiled wistfully. "Let's go to the Willows," she suggested. "I'm sure Fay will be relieved to see you've returned safe and sound, and your friends will be delighted that you managed to find your...what's it called?"

"Our *sefer Torah.*"

"Yes, that."

"Oh, thank goodness!" Fay exclaimed when she saw Kurt and Joshua. "But no thanks to the rest of you," she muttered as she turned to glare at Erich, Otto, and Miles in turn. "I hope you never do anything so irresponsible again.'' They assured her they wouldn't and apologized again. ''All right. You had better go upstairs and share all the news,'' she said with a glint in her eye. They immediately flew upstairs into Otto and Erich's room. Fay sighed. ''Kids!'' she said in mock exasperation.

''What is most frightening during the air raid?'' Otto asked.

''The worst thing was trying to find the shelter. Once we were in there, it wasn't too bad,'' Kurt replied.

''Are the bombs loud?'' Erich asked.

''Louder than thunder.''

''Won't you be scared to go back there, Joshua?''

''I'll be with my parents. I'll be all right.''

''I still can't believe you actually managed to retrieve the *sefer Torah*!'' Miles said in admiration.

''And that man was so kind not to accept payment for it,'' Erich added.

''What should we do with all that money?'' Otto asked.

''Well...uh...'' stammered Kurt. ''Say, Erich, isn't that Fay calling you?''

''I'll go down and check,'' Erich said, hurrying down the steps. The others immediately huddled together.

The small group assembled on the platform watched as Joshua began to board the train. ''Thank you again for everything,'' he said, turning back to Mr. and Mrs. Berrin.

''It has been our pleasure,'' Mrs. Berrin replied. ''Look after yourself in London.''

''See you all very soon,'' Joshua said to the boys.

''Be sure to send my parents my love! And write!'' Miles shouted as the train began to move out of the station. They waved wildly until the train was out of sight. They could already feel an emptiness descending on them; and the boys could not prevent the sharp stab of pain that they felt. How they longed to be able to go home at will, or to send their love to their parents as Miles had done.

24

"WHEN CAN I OPEN my eyes?" Erich asked as Kurt led him by the arm.

"Not yet!"

Erich could hear muffled giggling. "Miles, is that you?" He heard more laughter but no one was saying anything. "Can't someone tell me what's going on?"

"Patience," Kurt said. "You'll find out soon."

He felt himself being seated on a chair, and a hard curved object was placed in his hands.

"All right, open your eyes now!"

Erich stared down in disbelief at what had been placed in his hands. "My Stradivarius!" he gasped. He turned it over, examining it in detail, but there was no trace of the damage it had suffered. The violin looked as good as new. Erich was at a loss for words. "How did you — I mean when — whose idea was it? Where—"

"It was Kurt's idea."

"But...how...?"

"Look, we all know how much this violin means to you, Erich. But even though it is so dear to you, you were willing to sell it, had you been able, to raise the money for our *sefer Torah*," Kurt said quietly. "When Mr. Canning refused payment, Joshua and I were wondering what we would do with the money. I came up with the suggestion of having your violin repaired. The others happily agreed, so that is what we decided to do.''

"A few days ago, when you weren't in your room,'' Otto confessed, "I took the violin out of your cupboard and gave it to Jack, who had it repaired.''

"Aha!'' Erich laughed, turning to Jack. "So those were the mysterious out-of-town trips you made!''

"That's right,'' Jack replied with a grin.

"Thank you so much, all of you,'' Erich said, becoming serious again. "You can't imagine how much this means to me.'' He looked lovingly at his violin again. "I don't know how I can ever repay you.''

"I do!'' Jack said.

"How?''

"Play us a few tunes.''

The audience — Miles, Kurt, Otto, Fay, and the four Willow children — took their seats in the living room. Jack stood beside Erich, acting as master of ceremonies. "Good evening, ladies and gentlemen! Tonight I bring you a special guest all the way from Germany: Erich Bildmann, world-famous violinist, who has kindly agreed to play for us. Take a bow,'' he whispered to Erich. Erich gave a dramatic, theatrical bow, much to the amusement of the others. "Let's have a big round of applause for Erich!'' Jack boomed. The audience participated enthusiastically. "Thank you,'' Jack said, making a sweeping gesture to present Erich. "I bring you Erich Bildmann.''

There was absolute silence as Erich tucked the violin under his chin and lifted his bow with shaking fingers. They were stiff from lack of practice, but after the initial few notes, everything came back to him. He played all the pieces he knew and loved, one after the other. The music seemed to transport him to another time and place and it was as if he could feel his parents close to him. He could see their smiles and feel their pride.

When Erich came to the end of his last piece, his audience broke into rapturous applause. Erich looked confused for a moment, as he was jolted back from his living room in Germany and his beloved parents, to the reality of the British countryside and his new friends.

"Bravo!" came a call from the far end of the living room. They had all been so engrossed in Erich's music that they had not noticed anyone coming in, and now turned around to see who it was.

"Karl!" A number of voices cried out at the same time. Otto ran to him and hugged him warmly. "How long do you have leave for?"

"Three days."

"It's so good to see you!" He stepped back to admire the impressive figure of his big brother, his khaki uniform making his eyes seem even greener.

"Wow!" Peter said. "Are you a real soldier?"

Karl grinned. "Yes, I guess I am."

"Do you have a gun?" Enid asked.

"No."

"How can you be a soldier then?"

"I don't need one for what I'm doing — helping to clear away the bomb wreckage in London."

"But soldiers are supposed to fight."

"Only some of them. Actually they do lots of different jobs." Karl began to look uncomfortable.

"That's enough, Enid," Fay said sharply.

"It's all right," Karl assured her.

"How's the situation in London?" Jack asked. "Come and sit down. Tell us what's happening."

"Things are improving, actually. The air raids are less frequent now."

"That's good. The Londoners have been through a tough time, haven't they?" Fay said.

"Yes," Karl nodded. "It hasn't been easy for them."

"But somehow they've kept their spirit," Fay continued. "I saw a picture in the newspaper of people in an air-raid shelter gathered in a circle and singing together. Quite remarkable. Now, what can we give you to eat, Karl?"

"Nothing, thank you. I...I think I'd like to go for a short walk with Otto."

"As you like. I'll make your bed up in the meantime."

The two brothers ambled across the fields together, the autumn twilight bathing everything around them in a soft golden glow. "How was Rosh Hashanah here?"

"Oh, fine," Otto replied. "How was it in London?"

"Well, I was grateful to be able to go to shul both days, and that was some compensation for not spending the holidays with you for the second year in a row."

They continued on in silence for several more minutes. "Okay, what's wrong, Karl?" Otto finally asked. He was aware that all was not as it should be and that something was bothering Karl. "There must be a reason why you were given this short leave. It wasn't just for nothing, was it?"

"No," Karl admitted, looking down.

Otto stopped and stood in front of Karl, forcing him to face him. "Karl?"

"I'm being sent overseas."

"What? Where?"

"I don't know yet. We haven't been told much for security reasons."

"Do you know how long you'll be away?"

"I have no idea. I suppose it depends on how the war progresses."

"In other words, it could be — years?" Otto's voice rose.

"It is a possibility, I suppose. I feel rotten having to do this to you, Otto."

"Please don't feel bad on my account. It's not your fault, Karl. I'll be fine. I really will."

"Maybe it would have been better if I'd gone to Tartura, instead of joining up."

"But then I wouldn't have seen you at all."

"Not necessarily. I hear that they're beginning to release some of them. Who knows, maybe I could have been freed and come back here for good.''

''What's done is done. How could you have known? Perhaps there's a reason why you must go. Only Hashem knows.''

Karl put his arm around Otto and together they walked back to the house. ''You've grown up a lot, my little brother.''

By the beginning of 1942 the bombings of London had almost come to an end and the children who had been evacuated to the countryside started to return to London. Miles' parents decided to bring him home, along with Kurt, who would live with them for the duration of the war. At the end of January, they came to Swanstone to collect the two of them. Around the same time Mr. and Mrs. Firestone wrote to Erich suggesting he and Otto come back to live with them. It was a tearful farewell on the blustery winter day when Jack and Fay saw them off. Fay cried openly and Jack dabbed at his eyes with Fay's handkerchief every so often. ''It's not going to be the same at home without you,'' Fay said.

''You've become part of the family,'' Jack added. ''Remember, there will always be a place for you here.''

25

KARL STIRRED THE pot of boiling soup and sniffed it. Not bad, he thought to himself. He had been with the Eighth Army in the Western Desert of North Africa under the command of Field Marshall Montgomery for eleven months now. He had been fortunate enough to be able to join the Catering Corps — his experience working in the kitchen in Hay had stood him in good stead. This meant he was able to observe *kashrus* easily. He knew what food there was, and he had even been able to kosher utensils.

The men were amaible enough, but being the only Jewish solider among them, he did get very lonely. No one there could possibly understand how he felt not experiencing a proper Shabbos for so long, not praying with a *minyan*, or ever listening to a *shiur*, or even ever seeing another Jewish person.

He waited anxiously for each letter from Otto and the other boys, and from his friend Willie, and read them avidly. The boys had been enrolled in a Jewish school and were very content. Their only discomfort was the rationing. After life in the country, they'd never dreamed of suffering from a lack of such items as milk, vegetables, and soap. Willie had returned to England and was living with a family he had stayed with before he had been interned.

Karl stepped outside the "camp kitchen" — a roomy tent — and gazed at the arid, rolling desert which stretched as far as the eye could see. A couple of boys from his unit were busy cleaning and repairing their rifles. Seeing Karl, they waved to him and he waved back. He watched them as they paused to drink from their large canteen and pour some water over their heads before continuing. Although it was September, the summer heat had not let up, and was, if anything, harsher. Karl brushed away a few flies which swarmed overhead and went back into the tent. He davened *Minchah* and sat down by himself to have an early evening meal, for it was the eve of Yom Kippur and the fast would begin in another two hours.

"Corporal Alexander!" the sergeant shouted as he entered Karl's tent the next morning. Karl quickly kissed his *siddur* and stood to attention. "Please collect your things and come with me. You'll be leaving the camp immediately. Another unit fifteen miles away is short of kitchen staff, so you, Corporal Williams, and Private Harley are being assigned there."

A fifteen-mile walk in the scorching desert when he was neither eating nor drinking! "I don't mean to sound insubordinate, but would it be possible to wait a few more hours, until..." Karl began.

"Unless you want to find yourself courtmartialed, Corporal Alexander, follow orders. Be ready to leave in ten minutes."

"How do you like the change of scenery?" joked Stephen Williams, an amiable boy from the North of England.

"Just think, a different stretch of sand and rocks!" added Jim Harley.

"I think the sand has gone to your head," Karl replied.

"You're probably right."

"Listen, on a more serious note, I need to ask you a favor... would one of you be willing to carry my backpack? This may be hard to understand, but today is Yom Kippur, the Day of Atonement, the holiest Jewish Festival. On our Sabbaths and Festivals it's forbidden to carry things in a public domain, and—"

"Well, I don't know," Stephen replied. "I'd like to help you, but my stuff is heavy enough..."

"I'll be willing to take your next three shifts of guard duty," Karl quickly added.

"Night duty?"

"All right, night duty."

"You've got yourself a deal."

Karl handed his kit over to Stephen. "Where's your flask?" asked Jim. "What are you going to do when you need a drink of water?"

"I won't. I'm fasting today."

"You mean you're going to walk through this desert without even having so much as a sip of water?"

"Yes."

"You're crazy! You'll get dehydrated, or worse."

"I'll be all right. I want to do this. It's important to me to observe the holiday."

"I understand you feel strongly about your religion," Stephen chimed in, "but aren't you taking this just a little too far? I am sure your God will forgive you if you have something to drink."

"You can't persuade me, but don't worry. I'll be fine."

Karl's throat was dry and parched. While he watched the others taking sips from their flasks, he attempted to concentrate on other things. He recited the Yom Kippur prayers by heart, humming the tunes to the rhythm of his boots as they made a soft crunchy sound in the sand. What would Otto be doing at that very same moment? He would probably be in shul. He wondered if Otto were taller now, and if he would look very different when he next saw him...he had already found a marked contrast on his return from Australia. And his parents? No! He would not let himself open that door in his memories.

Karl plodded on. The scenery hardly varied at all. The vast, parched desert was a fascinating place, both serene and dramatic at the same time somehow. His thoughts turned to the Patriarchs, to Moses, to the Children of Israel wandering in the desert before they reached the land of Canaan.

The sun beat down and the pale rocks and sand shimmered in the desert heat. Karl began to feel light-headed. How far was he from Palestine, from Eretz Yisrael, he asked himself. He liked to think that he was close to Yerushalayim. He had never been as near to Palestine before.

"How much farther do you think we have left to go?" Karl asked Jim.

"At least eleven miles, I'd say."

"That much? I thought we were almost there."

"No way. Are you starting to get tired?"

"No, of course not," Karl replied. But he was. The heat, flies, sand, and most of all, lack of water, were beginning to affect him and he found that he was having difficulty keeping up with the others.

A wave of nausea came over him and Karl was now barely shuffling along. He had begun to fall behind. The Sergeant turned around and noticed that Karl was at a distance from them. "Corporal Alexander...!" he shouted, but he never finished his sentence, for at that moment there was a terrific explosion. The force of it threw Karl several meters backwards in a cloud of dust and smoke.

Karl lifted his head and spat out the sand from his mouth. He noticed that his sleeve had been ripped and a wound in his arm was bleeding profusely. With his good arm, he picked himself up. The desert was still, except for a slight hot breeze, and strangely silent. The dust had settled.

Squinting in the intense sunlight, he suddenly recoiled in horror and disbelief. His three companions lay sprawled out, motionless, across the sand where moments ago they had been marching together. They must have stepped on a landmine, and Karl suddenly realized that had he not fallen a few paces behind, he too would have been lying there. He knelt beside them, calling their names and shaking them vigorously, becoming

more panicked by the minute. "Stephen! Jim! Say something!"
Soon he stopped shouting. He had to face the fact that he was
absolutely alone.

Karl found a large white handkerchief in his backpack and
tied it firmly around his bleeding arm for a tourniquet. Considering the alternatives, he decided that the only choice he had
was to keep going and pray that he find a friendly unit whose
soldiers would be able to attend to his fallen comrades and
provide him with medical attention. He was also afraid that if it
had been Germans who planted the mine, they might still be
nearby, and he did not relish the thought of being in German
captivity.

He trudged on through the relentless heat and tried not to
think of the consequences if he did not find anyone soon. It was
sheer determination which kept him going, one heavy step after
the other, his dry cracked lips gasping for breath.

The dry desert wind became stronger and whipped up the
sand with great force. Karl struggled to remain upright while the
sand swirled around him, stinging his eyes. Time and time again
he fell, but he dragged himself to his feet again.

"*Avinu Malkenu, Shema koleinu, Chus v'rachem alenu* — our
Father, our King, hear our voice, have mercy on us," he prayed
to Hashem. "...*Zechor ki afar anachnu* — remember that we are
but dust." This prayer had never seemed more relevant than
now, on this Yom Kippur, when he was but a small speck in this
vast desert. He could vanish without a trace. Who would find
him?

Severely weakened, he dragged himself on all fours. The
setting sun was a burning crimson flame in the sky. The sandstorm had died down and it was mercifully cooler. But soon the
freezing desert night would fall.

"...*Kabel b'rachamim u'veratzon es tefillasenu* — receive our
prayer with mercy and favor." Karl continued murmuring the
Yom Kippur prayers. "*Avinu Malkenu, chonenu v'anenu ki ein banu
ma'asim; aseh imanu tzedakah v'chesed, v'hoshienu* — our Father,
our King, be gracious to us and answer us though we have no

merits; deal charitably and kindly with us and save us.''

Karl collapsed on the sand. He could no longer lift his arms, could no longer crawl an inch. In the distance he thought he heard the sound of a shofar blast. With his last ounce of strength he tried to reach out toward it. ''*Le-shanah ha-ba'ah b'Yerushalayim ha-benuyah* — next year in Jerusalem,'' he whispered.

Then he passed out.

26

FOR DAYS KARL drifted between consciousness and unconsciousness. Sometimes he was aware of the distant echo of voices, but he could not discern the words.

One night, as he thrashed about in a pool of sweat, fever-racked, his body burning with a heat which threatened to engulf him, he cried out over and over, until something seemed to snap. The nightmarish images which had swum before him faded away. Karl opened his eyes and looked around. He found himself in bed, in a large room lined with other beds. A soldier sat beside him watching over him, and next to him stood a nurse. Karl thought that the soldier's uniform looked British, but he was still seeing things in a blur and could not be certain. "Are you British?" he whispered in English.

"Yes."

"Where am I?"

"You're in a military hospital in Cairo." Karl was silent while he tried to assimilate what he had just heard. His eyelids began to flicker and he drifted into sleep — but a peaceful sleep this time. His fever had finally broken.

It was a few days before Karl saw the British soldier again. In the meantime he was beginning to recover and regain his strength. When the soldier finally reappeared, he was accompanied by a higher ranking officer.

"My name is Commander Sadwell," he began. "I would like to ask you a few questions. Do you feel well enough to answer?"

"Yes," Karl replied.

The Commander drew up a chair and studied him with a fixed expression on his face. "What is your name?"

"Karl Alexander."

"Where are you from?"

"England."

"Your name does not sound English. Were you born there?"

Karl was afraid to answer. "I am a British soldier," he replied timidly.

"How is it that you speak German fluently?"

Karl was stunned. How did he know?

"While you were delirious, you were speaking German," he replied to the unasked question.

"I was born in Germany," Karl admitted.

"A German in the British army?" The Commander's tone had an edge of sarcasm and disbelief.

"I am a British soldier," Karl repeated, "but I am a *Jew* from Germany." He noticed a softening of the Commander's expression. "I left for England in July 1939, and was interned with German nationals in May 1940. I survived the torpedo attack on the Arandora Star, and was deported to Australia. The following year, I was given the opportunity of returning to England if I signed up for the Pioneer Corps. This I did, and served until I was posted to North Africa last October."

"You've been through a great deal, I see. Which unit were you with?" Suddenly the Commander seemed warm and friendly.

"I was in the Catering Corps attached to Captain Whiller's unit of the Eighth Army."

"What happened to you? Do you know that you were found alone and unconscious outside our camp?"

"So I've been told. I was being transferred to another unit, because they were short of kitchen staff. With two other men from my unit and our Sergeant, we set out on our way — a fifteen-mile trek. After a few miles, one of them stepped on a landmine, and the three were killed.'' Karl paused, his voice unsteady. ''I was only saved because I had fallen behind. You see, I was weak and couldn't keep up because I was fasting — it was the Day of Atonement, the most sacred day of the Jewish calendar.''

Was that a small twinkle Karl discerned in the Commander's eyes? ''The Sergeant was calling me to catch up with them,'' he went on, ''and I was thrown backwards by the blast. My arm was cut badly.'' Karl glanced down at the large white bandage wrapped around his arm. ''I decided to keep going, in the faint hope that I might find help, but I must have passed out. The last thing I remember was hearing something which sounded to me like the ram's horn we blow at the end of the fast — the *shofar*.''

The Commander turned to the other soldier. ''That must have been you blowing your ram's horn, Gideon!''

''What?! You mean I didn't imagine it?''

''Far from it, Karl. The eleven Jewish boys in our unit held a service together for the Festival. We did suspect that you might have been a survivor of the blast — your companions were found two days later, by the way — but I am sure you understand that we had to make sure.''

''Of course,'' Karl nodded. He was still trying to absorb the amazing information that there in the Middle Eastern desert he had heard a *shofar* blown by Jews on Yom Kippur!

''Now, you say you were on the way to the new unit to work in the kitchen — correct?''

''Yes.''

''If you agree, I would like to request your transfer to Cairo, for work of a different nature. Your skills make you the ideal candidate for translating the German radio messages we intercept. How would you feel about that?''

''Oh, I would be very interested,'' Karl replied excitedly.

''Excellent! I have been informed that you are well enough to be discharged from the hospital, but obviously you need some time to recuperate. I will therefore be granting you a seven-day leave pass as soon as you're released. You can have the choice of either staying here in Cairo, or — if you prefer — you can go to Palestine."

Karl's eyes shone. "Palestine?" he asked in wonder and disbelief.

The Commander smiled. "I think we have your decision then."

In the fading light of day the light aircraft landed on the small airstrip in Yerushalayim. Karl stepped out of the plane and gazed about, filled with awe. He bent to pick up a handful of the holy soil. Then he kneeled and kissed it, as his ancestors had done from time immemorial, when arriving in Eretz Yisrael. He looked at the setting sun and was overcome with emotion. Within weeks he had gone from the depths of fear and despair to the heights of euphoria. He hardly dared to believe it. With tears in his eyes, Karl recited the *shehecheyanu* prayer in a trembling voice, blessing God "Who has kept us alive, sustained us, and brought us to this time."

Karl was taken to the barracks where he was to stay for the duration of his leave, but he was filled with such excitement that he couldn't fall asleep at all that night. As soon as he saw the first hint of light, he said his morning prayers and left to explore Jerusalem.

The city was aglow with the radiance of the morning sun. Everything seemed made of stone, and everywhere he went he was surrounded by golden hills. Karl felt he was in an enchanted dream. Wandering through narrow streets and alleyways of the Old City, he saw Jews living in meager circumstances but they had a wealth Karl could only partake of for seven days. He strolled on through the oriental market in a daze, dazzled by the carpets, brassware, jewelry, colorful fruits and vegetables that he did not recognize. He was quite unprepared for the sight he encountered as he came to the end of a row of houses: In front of him rose the *Kotel Ha-Ma'aravi* — the Western Wall. Karl gazed at the remnants of the Holy Temple and slowly walked toward the wall to touch it. Resting his head on the ancient stones, tears streaming from his eyes, he prayed for the safety of his parents and of all European Jewry.

In seven days Karl managed to travel up to the north, to Safed high in the mountains of the Galilee, and to Tiberias on Lake Kinneret. He visited the ancient seaport of Akko and the modern town of Haifa on the slopes of Mount Carmel, rising from the sea. Then he traveled south again, through Jerusalem to Chevron and the Tomb of the Patriarchs. He walked along the beachfront in modern, vibrant Tel Aviv. All too soon it came to an end and he had to leave. It was with a heavy heart that he boarded the plane, but it was also with the resolution that, God willing, when the war was over he would return with his family to make Eretz Yisrael their home.

One afternoon, as Karl was routinely monitoring the German broadcasts, something came through on his headphones which made him sit up with a start. He listened intensely and as soon as it came to an end, he pushed back his chair and ran to headquarters.

"I must see the Commander immediately!" Karl blurted to the soldier who barred his way.

"I'm sorry, but he is at an important meeting at the moment and cannot be disturbed."

"Whatever they're discussing," Karl cried, "it isn't as vital as what I have to tell him."

Barging into the tent, Karl found the Commander and four other high-ranking officers sitting around a large desk studying a map. They glanced up to see what the disturbance was about.

"I tried to stop him," the soldier began, "but he—"

"Commander!" Karl interrupted breathlessly. "We must evacuate the camp immediately. I've just intercepted a message that German snipers have crossed into our lines. They're planning to surround and attack our camp!"

"When?" Commander Sadwell asked urgently.

"They did not say exactly, but very soon."

The Commander rose to his feet. "Get the men mobilized." It was decided that they would move to a higher vantage point which would give them an upper hand and enable them to launch a surprise counterattack.

As the British soldiers scrambled up the ridge, the Germans appeared and began to fire at them. Keeping low, Karl and the men continued to advance, pushing forward carefully on their hands and knees. Karl gritted his teeth and breathed deeply. He quickened his pace as another bullet whistled over his head, telling himself that they would soon reach safety. Suddenly he heard a cry from behind him. The Commander had been hit.

"Hurry!" Karl shouted to him. "We're almost safe."

"I can't," he moaned, clutching his leg in agony.

Karl looked up at the waiting sanctuary of caves above him and the Commander's pain below him. He crawled back down, doing his best to avoid the fusillade showering him overhead. Upon reaching the Commander, he ripped a piece of material off his shirt and tied it firmly around his bleeding wound. Then, he grabbed the wounded man's arms and placed them firmly on his own shoulders, carrying the Commander on his back for the rest of the precarious climb.

As soon as they reached the summit, the medics tended to him immediately while the remainder of the men in the unit began to retaliate. Commander Sadwell reached for Karl's hand. Although his grasp was firm, his voice was weak. "I shall be mentioning you in my next dispatch to London," he whispered. "I am eternally grateful to you. You saved my life down there."

27

KARL REMAINED in North Africa for another year and during that time missed the bar mitzvahs of his brother and all the other boys, which were celebrated in succession, within a few months of each other. Otto wrote that although no relatives had been present, all his "extended family" had attended. The boys indeed had become like brothers to each other by now. The Firestones had saved their rations for several weeks beforehand and were able to hold a modest but very enjoyable celebration. Perhaps most special and touching of all was that all the boys had read from "their" *sefer Torah.*

In June 1944 Karl was transferred to Italy, which had surrendered to the Allies. He was sent to recently liberated Rome, where he acted as an interpreter for the interrogation of German prisoners of war.

On the 6th of June, 1944 — D-Day — Allied forces landed on the coast of Normandy and invaded France. The massive onslaught against Germany was on its way. By the end of the year, France, Belgium, and Holland had been liberated and the British and American armies had advanced as far as Germany. Defeat of the Germans was imminent.

A few months later, Karl was transferred to Germany.

As Karl and his unit traveled through an utterly devastated Germany, he struggled with his feelings at being back. It was at once his homeland and an alien place. Since 1943, reports had been coming through of the widespread and methodical murder of the Jews by the Germans. Karl had heard no word from his parents for the five-and-a-half years he and Otto been gone. He had learned, too, of the existence of the concentration camps, since Auschwitz had been liberated in 1944. But nothing could have prepared him for the terrible reality, for the sights he would witness when he and his fellow soldiers entered the gates of liberated Bergen-Belsen.

No one said a word as they moved through the silent camp. The survivors wandered aimlessly around or stood behind the barbed wire staring blankly at the world outside. They were so emaciated that they looked to Karl like living skeletons. He had never imagined that human beings could look like that. Their sunken eyes were dull and reflected only dread. Some were too weak to lift themselves up and lay listlessly on the rows of wooden shelf-like bunks, barely clinging to life. Karl's heart pounded as he saw more and more of the inmates. Each scene was more horrific than the one before.

For the first half hour Karl was numb with shock. These were his people — his brothers. He wanted to cry for each and every one of them, but he would not have had enough tears. He began to move from person to person, speaking in German or Yiddish, telling them they were free, that it was all over now. He wanted desperately to relieve some of their hurt and suffering but it was embedded too deeply within them. Many were unaware that someone was even talking to them. They were desperately ill and had withdrawn into themselves. Some cried upon realizing that this tall British soldier was actually a German Jew, and Karl hugged their frail bodies as they clung to him. In the barracks he held the victims' hands, whispering soothingly to them, and helped the doctors who fed them with milk, as they were able to digest only liquids.

The register of inmates who had died was discovered in the offices. The Germans had kept their records efficiently. Drawn to the lists of names like a magnet, Karl read one name after another. Suddenly he froze in terror, staring at two names: *Alexander, Heinz. Alexander, Selma.* Cause of death: typhus.

The letters blurred before his eyes, and he began to tremble uncontrollably. For a long while he had acknowledged the possibility that his parents might not have survived the war, but he had suppressed his fears and tried to convince himself that his parents were fine and they would all be reunited soon.

To think that they had perished in this nightmarish hole! *Alexander, Heinz. Alexander, Selma.* Karl reread the words in a whisper several times over. Papa and Mutti! While Karl had been in Rome, his beloved parents had died. "*Baruch...dayan ha-emes,*" he murmured as he made the traditional mourner's tear in his shirt.

"Karl!" A soldier was calling for him. They needed him to act as an interpreter. Karl followed him in a dream-like state.

When he got to the offices, he found that a former guard had been captured and they needed Karl to translate for the interrogation. Karl sat, stiff and white-faced, expressionlessly translating the questions the officer posed. The guard sat with his head held high, with no sign of remorse. In mid-sentence Karl suddenly bolted from his chair, knocking it over. "Murderer!" he screamed at the guard in German, as hot tears streamed from his eyes. "Murderer!" The guard just stared back with a cold look in his eyes. Karl seized him and began to shake him violently. "You killed my mother! Oh, you have taken them away from me forever! My mother and my father! Do you hear me, you animal? You beast! Forever!"

It took three soldiers to hold him and restrain him. They led him away, still screaming hysterically and thrashing about wildly trying to break loose.

A few hours later he was sitting quietly with his Commanding Officer. "Karl, I was terribly sorry to hear about your parents," he began. "Naturally, we did not foresee this happening, and I really think that, under the circumstances, it would be better for you to return to England and continue your service there. It would clearly be a mistake to remain here. It is just too harrowing for you."

Karl nodded slowly.

"A car will be arriving shortly to pick you up and take you to the airfield."

Karl rose to his feet and saluted his C.O. "Thank you," he whispered. The Commander returned the salute and put his hand on Karl's shoulder, full of compassion for him.

As the military plane sped down the runway, Karl was glad to be leaving ravaged Germany and gruesome Bergen-Belsen, but he knew the memory would be forever imprinted on his mind.

It was not yet eight o'clock on the beautiful spring morning that Karl knocked on the front door of Mr. and Mrs. Firestone's house. After several minutes the door was opened by Mrs. Firestone. "Karl?" she asked incredulously, and then shouted up the stairs, "Otto!"

He stared at the brother who had left a boy and returned a man. Otto, at fourteen, had changed too and was almost as tall as Karl. Otto cried and hugged his brother warmly. "I can't believe it!"

"Otto, I cannot tell you how glad I am to see you again. It has been too long." Karl's voice trembled.

"I'm so relieved that you've returned safely, Karl. Are you back for good? Why didn't you write me that you were coming?"

"It was...rather sudden."

"Is everything all right?" Otto stepped back and studied Karl's serious face and sad eyes. "There *is* something wrong. What is it?"

Karl had difficulty finding his voice. "Do you have a few minutes to spare before school, Otto?"

"What a question!" Otto laughed. "Do you think I'd go to school today? After a separation of over three years, I'm sure they won't mind if I spend the day with you."

"Let's go for a walk in the park then," Karl said quietly.

"Why were you sent back to England? Didn't they need you anymore in Italy?" Otto asked him as they strolled arm-in-arm.

Karl took a deep and shaky breath. "I have just come back from *Germany*, Otto," he replied.

"*Germany*? What were you doing *there*?"

"My unit was sent to Bergen-Belsen. I was to act as an interpreter. Otto, it was terrible there. Never in my life have I seen more dreadful sights than the sick and starving people there. Our people. The German Jews."

He put his hands on Otto's shoulders, which had begun to tremble. "In the camp register I found the names of Papa and Mutti, Otto."

"Papa and Mutti!" Otto turned pale. "Are...they...alive?"

"No," he replied gently, weeping and grasping Otto's hand.

"When?"

"Last year."

Otto let out a heartbreaking sob, and the two brothers held each other and cried without restraint.

On May 1st, 1945, a news flash came over the radio: Hitler was dead. This was followed on May 7th by the complete surrender of the German forces. "This is your victory," Prime Minister Winston Churchill announced on the radio the following day. "Victory of the cause of freedom in every land."

V.E. — or Victory in Europe — Day was designated as a national holiday. In London, people took to the streets to celebrate. Karl had leave that day and he and Otto went with the others to watch the rejoicing, though their hearts were still heavy with grief. Time would help to heal the pain, but the scars would remain forever.

After five-and-a-half years the war was over at last. Now they would begin to rebuild their shattered lives.

28

MRS. FIRESTONE wordlessly handed the letter to Erich. He had been expecting it for some time already. It had been almost two months since he had written to the Red Cross asking for news of his parents. Nervously, he ripped open the envelope and read the letter. Then, his face flushed, his hands trembling, he whispered something incoherent, fled from the room, and thundered up the steps. From upstairs they could hear the sounds of heartrending sobs. Mrs. Firestone picked up the letter. Erich's father had died at Sachsenhausen, it said, and his mother had died at Buchenwald. Her heart went out to him and she brushed away the tears which had sprung to her own eyes. "The poor boy," she said sorrowfully. "I must go up and talk to him."

But Mr. Firestone restrained her. "Leave him be for a while. He needs to be on his own and let it all out."

Two hours later, Mrs. Firestone tapped on his door and entered softly. Erich sat cross-legged on the bed cradling his violin in his arms. His face was pallid, and his eyes red and swollen. "May I sit down?" she asked softly.

Erich nodded, his eyes still downcast. "I thought I had prepared myself for every possibility," he said in a barely audible, cracked voice, "but until this letter I could still hope. Now it is final. The end."

Mrs. Firestone did not know how to reply. What could she say in the way of comfort? She realized that there was nothing she could do but simply be there for Erich. After several more minutes she rose to leave. Erich was still staring absently at the violin, a thousand memories tormenting him. "Remember, Erich, we are always here for you if you need us," she said gently. Soon her husband would bring their rabbi and perhaps he would find the right words of comfort.

Karl checked the address on the ripped-off flap from the back of his envelope and compared it with the number on the gate. Yes, this was it. He ventured slowly up the garden path and rang the doorbell of the little semi-detached house. A young boy with muddy knees, dressed in shorts and a T-shirt, answered the door.

"Hello," he said to Karl, and his face instantly brightened when he saw that he was in uniform. "Wow!" he muttered under his breath.

"Hello," Karl replied. "Does Willie live here?" The boy continued to stand in the doorway with his gaze transfixed on Karl. Karl bent down slightly to the boy's level. "Does Willie live here?" he repeated.

"Willie? Oh, yes, he does. Please come in." He led him into the living room, turning around every so often to look him up and down. It wasn't every day that a real soldier came to his house. He couldn't wait to tell his friends at school the next day.

Willie was absorbed in a book and had not even heard the doorbell. "Hey, you've got a visitor, Willie!" the boy announced.

"Hello."

"Karl!" Willie jumped up and embraced his friend. "How great!"

"Can I get you a drink?" the boy asked Karl.

"No, thanks."

"All right," said the boy, "but call me if you change your mind." He left the room reluctantly.

"Sit down, sit down, Karl. How good to see you. When did you get back? I hadn't heard from you since January and was starting to get worried."

"I got back to England two months ago," Karl admitted. "I'm sorry it's taken me so long to come and see you, but...things have been a little difficult."

"I understand," Willie answered quickly.

Karl began to speak softly. "After a long stint in Rome, my unit was sent to Germany. We were at Bergen-Belsen shortly after its liberation. I cannot begin to describe to you, Willie, how horrible it was. The images still haunt me."

Karl drew a deep breath. "I wasn't there long. I found the names of my parents on the register — both of them had died. When I lost control of myself and tried to attack one of the Nazi guards who was being interrogated, my commander realized that I could not remain there, and had me sent back to England, where I've been ever since. I'm working in translations, and still living in barracks, but at least I'm near Otto. My officers have been very understanding and I've been given a great deal of leave. I've spent most of the time with Otto, and together we're trying to come to terms with what has happened."

Tears filled Willie's eyes as Karl continued. "Three weeks ago, I heard that my sister and her husband were also killed in one of the camps. We had been almost expecting it, but still the news reopened all the wounds. Now I'm waiting to hear whether any relatives survived: my cousins, my Uncle Ernst, other uncles, aunts. As yet I've heard nothing." Karl had finished. "And what about you?"

Willie replied in a flat voice. "My parents, my two older brothers, my grandparents. Everyone, it seems."

There was silence for a few minutes. "What are you doing with yourself?" Karl asked.

"I'm still working as a clerk at the same firm, but I don't enjoy it. In fact, I feel very unsettled. The Millsons have been good to me, but this is not my home. I don't feel I really belong. I have nowhere else to go, though."

"I know what you mean."

"How about you? Have you made any plans?"

"No, nothing. For so long, things have been uncertain and

it's been impossible to know what will happen tomorrow, let alone next week. And the truth is, I haven't felt up to much until now. I've been feeling very low, and the truth is that I've been feeling...well, almost guilty in a way, for surviving when my parents did not."

Willie nodded. "I know. So have I."

"And I find I'm also filled with great anger — if people had known about the concentration camps since 1943, even if they hadn't known *how* bad they were, why didn't they do something? Perhaps if they'd tried harder, my parents — your parents — might have been saved. I know I shouldn't keep thinking 'if only,' but I can't help it, Willie." Then his tone lightened. "Had you or Rabbi Lurmann been around, you probably would have told me to stop it and pull myself together!"

"Listen, Karl, we're only human. Of course you have these feelings — so do I and so do lots of us. I think it's inevitable." Willie sighed. "I too miss Rabbi Lurmann. I wonder what happened to him."

"I wrote to him several times while we were at Hay, but I never received a reply. I think I'd like to try and find him when I'm demobilized from the army. He was such a good man. When I first came to Huyton I was quite depressed, but he brought me out of it. In the end I gained a great deal from my short stay there. I went to his *shiurim* and other lessons at the Huyton 'university,' but it didn't last long. Since the age of fifteen my education has been constantly interrupted. I haven't been able to finish anything properly."

"My story exactly."

"Willie—" Karl sat up straighter and looked at his friend intently. "Do you know what I'd *really* like to do after I'm released from the army?"

"What?"

"Listen — when I was in North Africa, I got a few days' leave in Palestine. It was such a special experience, such an amazing few days. It was so hard to leave after a week and rejoin my unit. It felt like home, Willie. It's hard to explain, but I just wanted to stay there. Now I'm thinking of going back and settling there, and spending some time studying in a yeshiva, catching up on those years of learning I missed. And Otto could continue his schooling there. I would never go back to Germany, and I don't want to stay here either. This would be a fresh start.''

"That sounds like a wonderful idea,'' Willie said wistfully. "Eretz Yisrael...''

"Why don't you come with us then? You said yourself you're not really happy here.''

Willie suddenly felt the first ray of hope. "I would like that,'' he said fervently. They clasped each other's hands. At last they had something to look forward to.

Otto and Erich strolled through their neighborhood, which still bore the scars of the German bombings. Since Erich had learned of his parents' fate, he had not shown signs of being able to come to terms with it. He had become a virtual recluse in his room and this was the first time that Otto had managed to persuade him to leave the house and go for a walk. He was turning in on himself and his grief worried all of them.

After they had been out for a while, Otto decided to broach the subject. "Erich, you can't keep on like this. You have to face reality and start getting on with your life again.''

"I can't help it,'' Erich replied flatly. "I'm not interested in anything. I can't imagine I will ever be happy.''

"I also felt like that at the beginning.''

"Did you? But how...how did you come out of it?''

"By realizing that I had to carry on, because...well, because Hashem spared my life. I asked myself, How can I be ungrateful for such a gift? Oh, there are still times when I feel down but it gets easier as time goes on. I don't think the pain will ever leave completely, but it does get weaker, believe me. Karl has also been very good to me.''

"At least you have him. Who do I have? The Firestones are wonderful, but...I'm worried, Otto.''

"What are you worried about?"

"They've been so kind to me, and I really do feel at home with them. The atmosphere on Shabbos feels like home. They are the closest thing I have to a family. In fact I'd love to just keep on staying with them. But what if they don't feel the same way? They might not want me around for that much longer, and...and I have nowhere else to go."

"I don't think the Firestones would ever do that to you. But really, don't worry. You always have Karl and me and you're welcome to come with us to Palestine."

"Thank you, Otto."

"Things will work out in the end, you'll see."

Mr. and Mrs. Firestone were sitting in the living room. "Erich, could we speak to you for a few minutes?"

Erich sat down opposite them, noting with concern that they seemed nervous and very serious.

Mr. Firestone cleared his throat. "Erich, over the years we have come to care about you very much," he began, "and you could say that we have come to regard you as a son...you see, we prayed to Hashem for so many years to send us a son..." He cleared his throat suddenly and looked down. "Now, believe me, we know we could never take the place of your parents and would not try to, but we...well, we would very much like to adopt you if you would agree to it."

"Obviously, it is a major decision," Mr. Firestone went on, "and we don't expect you to make it immediately. Take as long as you like, and let us know in your own good time."

"I don't need to take any time!" Erich blurted out. "I know what my decision is already."

Mr. and Mrs. Firestone leaned forward with great anxiety to hear his answer.

"Yes!"

29

"WHY WON'T YOU tell me where we're going, Willie?" Karl laughed. "What's the big mystery about?"

Willie smiled conspiratorially. "Wait and see. There's someone who will be very happy to see you."

"Tell me!"

"Wait and see," Willie repeated.

Karl had anticipated spending the afternoon with Willie and making plans for the future, now that he was finally demobilized. Instead, Willie had insisted on taking him for a walk. They had reached an unfamiliar neighborhood, where the houses that had withstood the bombings and remained standing were rather shabby.

Willie turned up the walk of one of the houses. The house was divided into two apartments and Willie pressed the first bell. The door was opened almost immediately. Karl stood open-mouthed as he gazed at the elderly, white-haired gentleman with sad eyes. Then he gasped, "Rabbi Lurmann!"

The Rabbi smiled, but the sorrow in his eyes remained. "Karl, my dear boy," he murmured.

Rabbi Lurmann led them into his small, sparsely furnished living room, where the three sat down. "Willie, how did you find him?" Karl asked in amazement.

"Oh, a little detective work," he replied. "I wrote around to every relief organization, as well as the formal authorities, until someone was able to give me Rabbi Lurmann's address.''

"It was quite a wonderful surprise for me as well," Rabbi Lurmann said, turning to Karl. "One evening, this young man appeared at my door. He explained that he was a friend of Karl Alexander's. I was taken aback, for I'd never heard what became of you and assumed that you'd drowned on the *Arandora Star*, God forbid! I cannot begin to tell you how overjoyed I was. You see, I thought I had lost everyone except the one son who survived and managed to get to Palestine. And then, out of the blue, I suddenly hear that you are alive and well! I can't describe how I felt at that moment.''

"But didn't you get any of the letters I sent you from Australia?''

Rabbi Lurmann shook his head. "I was sent to the Isle of Man shortly after you left, and you know how poor the organization of these things was. They never passed on letters to us. So I had simply accepted the 'fact' that I would never see you again, Karl — God forbid — until your friend Willie appeared and told me otherwise. He has told me all about your years in Australia, and then in North Africa and Rome...'' He stopped short there. "And all about your medal. I am very proud of you, Karl.''

Karl blushed. He had told very few about the medal he had been awarded for his bravery in North Africa.

"And what happened to you in the meantime, Rabbi Lurmann?''

"At the end of 1943 I was released from the internment camp. A relief agency helped me acquire this apartment and I have had to try and carry on.''

"Why don't you join your son in Palestine? Has Willie told you that we're going there shortly? You could come with us!''

"Karl, of course I would love to. Naturally I applied for a visa, but the British are simply not letting anyone in. Those who try to get in illegally and are caught are sent back to a displaced persons' camp in Cyprus. I don't want to dash your hopes, but I think you will find it impossible to get into the country.''

Willie's face fell, but Karl remained as determined as ever.

"But if it were possible," he said urgently, "would you come with us?"

"I would dearly love to go, more than anything in the world."

"Good, because I think I know of a way."

"Karl! What brings you here? This is a surprise!" The two men shook hands warmly and Karl took a seat on the opposite side of Commander Sadwell's desk. "By the way, congratulations on receiving your medal," he added.

"I have *you* to thank for that."

"No, no — the credit is all yours. You were very courageous that day in the Western Desert. It already seems like a lifetime ago." He sighed. "What are your plans now that you've been demobbed?"

"Well, that's exactly what I wanted to talk to you about, Commander Sadwell." Karl leaned forward.

"Certainly. Is there anything I can do to help you?"

"I hope so. I would very much like to go and settle in Palestine, but I understand that it is very difficult to get into the country."

"Yes, that's right," the Commander said nodding. "The Foreign Office has cut the flow of immigration drastically."

"I was wondering whether you would be able to..."

"How many visas do you need?"

"Four. For my brother, my best friend, my rabbi, and myself."

"I will have it arranged immediately."

"Thank you so much." Karl's face was flooded with emotion.

"Don't mention it. It's my pleasure."

"We're going to miss you," Miles said.

"Things won't be quite the same without you," Joshua added.

Otto looked from one to the other. "We've been through a lot together, haven't we?"

"We certainly have," Kurt murmured.

"I hope we never lose touch with each other," Erich said

softly, looking around shyly at his friends.

"Never!" Otto replied. "Our friendship is too strong for that. We may be far away, but you will never leave our thoughts."

"What about you, Kurt? What are you planning to do now?" Karl asked, turning to the serious boy. Kurt had still learned nothing of what had become of his parents. Had their visas gotten them to America? There did not seem to be a record of them anywhere, as being alive or having died. It was as if they had disappeared off the face of the earth.

"I've been thinking about it a great deal, Karl. I have decided to go back to Vienna for a while. Perhaps I will be able to find out something more there."

His gaze left Karl's face and strayed to the window. "I don't really hold out much hope of their still being alive, but I want to *know*. At the moment I feel like I'm caught in limbo."

Karl nodded quietly. "I really hope things work out for you," Otto interjected, "but in the event they don't, you know you are always welcome to come and live with us in Palestine."

"Thank you, Otto. I too have thought of Palestine. I'll keep it in mind."

Early the next morning, Karl, Otto, Rabbi Lurmann, and Willie set off in a taxi to Waterloo Station to take the train to Southhampton where they would board the ship bound for the Mediterranean and their new home, in Eretz Yisrael.

30

KURT WAVED FURIOUSLY at the little crowd who had come to see him off at the station. Miles, his parents, Joshua, Erich, and the Firestones waved back. Nobody had quite known what to wish him before he left, and he himself did not know what he would find. But he had to do this, if only to set his mind at rest.

After a Channel crossing to Calais in France and an overland journey by train, he finally arrived in Vienna. He stepped off the train and looked around. How strange it felt to be back after such a long time. It was hard to believe that Vienna was still here as usual.

He wondered whether he would still be able to recognize anything, or remember how to get around, but he did. It all looked very much like it had five years ago, he noted as he made his way through the streets. He felt strongly devoid of feeling. But there had been some changes, he nodded wryly. He was now able to board the tram without any problem and as they rode through the city, Kurt saw that the Nazis were really gone. He wondered if part of their ideology yet remained.

He got off at the Second District, which had once been his home. Here he could see the differences. Now his heart began to pound. The Jewish shops were gone. They had new owners and new names. What did you expect? he asked himself. As he wandered down the street he came to the park. How much smaller it looked than what he remembered! He paused at the entrance, and decided to go in. He walked through the fallen leaves, and the late September sunshine felt familiar. How many Septembers had he waded through the crunchy leaves with his friends! Where were they today? Now a new generation of children were playing here the same way that he and his friends had. They would never know of the boys who had spent many happy hours here, sharing their secrets and talking about what they would do when they grew up. For most had not had the chance to grow up.

Kurt sat on a bench with a faraway look in his eyes. In his mind he could see the smiling, freckled face of his friend Hans. Which of these children's fathers had seen Hans being led away to his certain death and had done nothing to prevent it? Had it been one of their fathers who had led him and his family away? Kurt rested his head on his clenched fist, his eyes tightly shut against the tears which threatened. All those he had known and loved were gone, gone. Only their memories remained.

Kurt left the park and continued on his way.

There it was! Just as it was when he had left it for good that night and gone into hiding. Kurt hesitantly approached the door and knocked. After several endless minutes had elapsed, a young man, who looked only a few years older than Kurt, opened it. There was something mildly familiar about him. Kurt had seen those deep blue eyes before, but he could not remember when or where. "Can I help you?" the boy asked politely.

"Yes. I...I've come from England, to make some inquiries regarding my parents, who disappeared during the war. I was wondering if I could ask you a few questions," Kurt said quietly in German.

"Of course. Please come in." He was led through the hallway — his hallway — past his bedroom, and into the living room, where he stared in shock: all the furniture was his. Nothing had changed.

"Where did you learn to speak such good German?" the boy asked.

"Actually, I am originally from Vienna. In fact," Kurt added, swallowing hard, "this used to be our apartment."

"Oh?" Kurt thought he saw a flicker of recognition in the boy's face.

"Tell me, have I ever met you before?" Kurt asked. The boy closed his eyes and nodded. Kurt peered closely at him. His face was a little older than it had been, but suddenly, he could see it all again. *The boy in the Hitler Youth uniform placed his fingers to his lips; the dark night, the dead-end alley.*

"We are looking for a boy. A Jew actually, who attacked our friend here in public earlier this afternoon. Have you seen him?"

"No, I can't say I have. You must be mistaken. A Jew would have to be mad to come around these parts alone after nightfall," the youth replied casually.

"You were the boy who saved my life that night!" Kurt whispered.

They heard a key turn in the lock. "Joachim, I'm home!" a woman's voice called out.

"That's my mother."

"I'll put the shopping away and then you can make me a nice cup of coffee," she said warmly as she entered the living room.

Kurt recognized her immediately. "Helga!"

"Do I know you?" the woman asked, puzzled.

"Yes, you do! My name is Kurt Eisig."

Helga's mouth flew open but then she regained her composure. "I'm sorry, I don't think I know anyone by that name."

Kurt rose from his seat. The words seemed to rush out in a flood. "Yes, you do, Helga. You used to be our maid."

"Pardon? I have never been your or anyone else's maid."

"Helga, don't you remember? I used to live in this apartment with my parents and my little sister Ilse." His voice cracked.

"You must be mistaken," she said firmly. "I have lived in this apartment for over twenty years."

"You were our maid, Helga! You were practically part of the family. This was *our* house, Helga!"

"How dare you come here making false accusations and laying claims to my apartment!" she replied angrily. "Now, if you have nothing more to say, you may leave. You have obviously confused me with someone else.''

"This was my home," Kurt repeated in a monotone. Helga ushered him out the door and closed it behind him, turning the key firmly in the lock.

Kurt walked aimlessly away from the house. Even the survivors were being eradicated from this city, he thought to himself. He slowly made his way down the street, dragging his heels, so filled with anger, hurt, shock, and helplessness, that he did not hear the running footsteps behind him.

"Kurt!" someone shouted breathlessly. "Kurt! Please wait!" Kurt turned around to see Joachim, panting and offering his hand. "I apologize for my mother," he said. "You are right. You *did* used to live there. My mother *was* your maid. A week after you moved out, my mother and I moved in. I must tell you, as for your parents, they were here. I saw them.''

"You saw my parents? When?"

"Some months ago.''

Kurt could hardly speak. "Months ago? After the war? Alive? Here?''

"Yes, yes.''

"Do you know where they are? Where they went?''

"No, I don't, I'm sorry.''

"Are you sure it was my parents that you saw?''

"Positive.''

"Thank you," Kurt breathed. "Oh, thank you.''

The couple in shabby (but once elegant) clothes mounted the rickety stairs, their two small children gripping the iron railing. The woman looked around in dismay. Her already pallid face paled even more. Is this where he had spent the war? The man, his lined careworn face and white hair belying his age, rapped on the door.

"What d'ya want?''

A coarse woman in a dirty, garish dress and a stained apron stood at the door glaring at them.

"I think we must have the wrong address," the man said politely in accented English. "We are looking for the Kilern family."

"I'm Mrs. Kilern."

"You are?" The man's face brightened. "We are looking for a boy named Kurt Eisig. Does he live here?"

"He used to," she replied disinterestedly.

"We are his parents," the woman informed her in a shaky voice. "Could you tell us where he is now, please?"

"Oh, 'e's dead. Killed in an air raid four years ago."

Mrs. Eisig's face went even whiter and she grasped her husband's arm. Mrs. Kilern did not wait for a reply and shut the door in their faces.

The Eisig children began to whimper and their parents held them tightly, tears streaming down their cheeks. "After all this time," Mrs. Eisig cried.

"Our Kurt, our Kurt," mumbled her husband.

Kurt looked up every Jewish neighbor he could think of and who might have still been living there. Few had returned, and those that had, told him either that they had not seen his parents since before the war, or confirmed what Joachim had said: They had seen them recently but did not know where they had gone.

"Mr. and Mrs. Eisig?"

"Yes," Mr. Eisig replied.

"Please come in." The woman motioned for them to sit down, and took her own place behind the desk. "How may I help you?"

"We understand that our son Kurt Eisig, who came to England in July 1939 on a transport arranged by your organization, was...was killed in an air raid in 1941. We would just like to know if you could tell us where he..." Mr. Eisig choked up suddenly "...where he is buried, so that we could visit his grave."

"I'll just go and fetch his file." She left the room and returned a few minutes later with it. She placed it on the desk and flipped through the few pages. "You must be mistaken," she said. "I have no record here. All it says is that when one of our workers went to visit Kurt about a week after his arrival, she was told by the Kilerns that his parents had come to fetch him."

"But that's impossible!" Mr. Eisig cried.

"Does that mean he could still be alive?" Mrs. Eisig gasped.

"It certainly looks like it."

"Thank you," the Eisigs said, rising hurriedly.

Their search had come to a dead end and they could find out nothing further about their son's whereabouts. "I think we should return to Vienna," Mr. Eisig said.

"And Kurt?"

"We have tried everything, Eva. What else can we do? He might not even be in the country anymore. Who knows what became of him. Maybe he really did return to Vienna, and..." His voice trailed off.

"I want my son." Mrs. Eisig's face crumpled. "I just want my son."

Kurt had looked through every official document he could obtain. He even went through the telephone directories but there was no trace of his parents anywhere. It was pointless to remain any longer and besides, he was beginning to run out of money. He went to the station and booked his return ticket for the following afternoon.

He spent his last few hours wandering around and seeing the familiar sights of what had once been his city. He felt like a stranger there now and realized that, to him, it would never be home again.

Kurt glanced at his watch. He had lost track of time. His train was due to leave in fifteen minutes! He hailed a taxi. "West-bahnhoff!" he instructed the driver.

The train drew into the Wein Westbahnhoff and the Eisigs

slowly removed their few bags from the overhead luggage rack.
"Perhaps we could get in touch with a missing persons bureau.
Maybe they could trace him," Mr. Eisig said encouragingly.

"I hope so," Mrs. Eisig forlornly replied.

Kurt hurriedly paid the driver and jumped out of the taxi. He
stuffed his wallet into his pocket and, clutching his ticket in his
right hand, dashed into the station. The train was due to leave
any minute.

The Eisigs walked down the platform and showed their tickets
at the barrier.

Kurt dodged between crowds of people milling about. Accidentally, he bumped into a man who was shuffling along with
his wife and children. "*Enschuldig*," he apologized and ran to
the barrier where he showed his ticket and boarded the train.

Mr. Eisig stooped to pick up the object which had been
dropped by the boy who had bumped into him in such a hurry.
It was a wallet. He opened it to see if he could find some kind of
identification, and let out a cry when he saw the name written
in it: *Kurt Eisig.*

Without a moment to lose he ran up to the guard. "Please
let me through," he begged. "My son is on that train!" The
whistle blew and the train started up.

"You had better hurry then," the guard warned him. "It's
already pulling out."

"Kurt!" Mr. Eisig shouted. "Kurt!"

Kurt leaned out of the window to catch his last glimpse of
Vienna. Was it his imagination, or did he hear someone calling
his name? His eyes searched the platform and he noticed the
white-haired man with whom he had collided when running for
the train. He stared at him and his heart started pounding. The
color drained from his face. "Papa?" he whispered. Kurt

grabbed his bag and sprung out of the train door moments before it sped away.

He ran down the platform to where his father stood and behind him, his mother, with two children: Ilse, who was now eight, and a four-year-old brother, Aaron, whom he had never met. He fell into their arms.

Later he would learn of how they had escaped from Austria, only to be caught in Holland trying to reach England. They were taken to the Sobibor concentration camp where his grandmother had perished. In October 1943, his parents had taken part in the prisoners' revolt and had remained with the partisans in the forest until the end of the war when they returned to Holland to fetch Ilse and Aaron. They had been sheltered in hiding by a kind Dutch family.

In time, his parents would learn of his wartime experiences in England.

But all that mattered now was that they were together again.

GLOSSARY

The following glossary provides a partial explanation of some of the Hebrew, Yiddish (Y.), German (G.), and Aramaic (A.) words and phrases used in this book. The spellings and explanations reflect the way the specific word is used herein. Often, there are alternate spellings and meanings for the words.

AVERAH: sin.

BARUCH HASHEM: "Thank God!"

BERACHAH (BERACHOS): blessing(s).

B'EZRAS HASHEM: "With the help of God."

BITACHON: trust in God.

BRIS: the ritual of circumcision.

CHAS V'SHALOM: "God forbid."

CHAVRUSA: (A.) a partner in Torah study.

DAVEN: (Y.) to pray.

DVAR (DIVREI) TORAH: brief Torah discourse(s).

ENSCHULDIGEN: (G.) "Excuse me."

GAM ZO L'TOVAH: "This too is for the best."

GUT SHABBOS: (Y.) "Have a good Sabbath."

KABBALAS SHABBOS: the Friday night prayer service.

KASHRUS: the Jewish dietary laws.

KIDDUSH: sanctification of the Sabbath and Festivals, usually recited over wine.

KRISTALLNACHT: (G.) "The Night of Broken Glass"; the Nov. 9, 1938 Nazi riot during which shuls, Jewish shops and homes throughout Germany were burned, destroyed and looted.

MA'ARIV: the evening prayer service.

MINCHAH: the afternoon prayer service.

MISHLO'ACH MANOS: gift packages of food traditionally sent on Purim.

MODEH ANI: "I thank," the opening words of the prayer recited upon arising.

OMAMA: (G.) grandmother.

ROSH HASHANAH: the Jewish New Year.

238

SECHACH: the leaves and branches, or woven matting, that comprise the roof of a SUKKAH.

SEFER (SEFARIM): book(s); holy book(s).

SEFER (SIFREI) TORAH: Torah scroll(s).

SHALOM ALEICHEM: "Peace be with you," a traditional greeting; the opening words of the song sung upon returning from the synagogue on Friday night.

SHEMA: lit., "Hear [O Israel]," the opening word of the fundamental prayer which proclaims the unity of God.

SHIUR(IM): Torah lesson(s).

SHIVAH: the seven-day period of mourning.

SIDDUR: the prayer book.

SIE BITTE: (G.) "If you please."

SIMCHAS TORAH: the Festival of rejoicing with the Torah, on the final day of Sukkos, when the Torah-reading cycle is completed and begun again.

SUKKAH: a temporary structure which Jews erect and live in during the Festival of Sukkos.

TEFILLAH: prayer.

TEFILLIN: two black leather boxes containing Torah verses, which adult males bind to their head and arm during morning prayers.

TEHILLIM: (the Book of) Psalms.

TREIF: (Y.) non-kosher.

U'NESANEH TOKEF: a passage describing Divine judgment, from the Rosh Hashanah and Yom Kippur prayer service.

UNTERMENSCHEN: (G.) base, immoral people.

USHPIZIN: (A.) lit., guests; the spirits of the Patriarchs and other Jewish leaders who are welcomed as guests in the SUKKAH.

YOM TOV: a Festival.

ZEMIROS: songs of praise sung at mealtimes on the Sabbath and Festivals.